HOLD ME DOWN

Hold Me Down

Clea Simon

Copyright © 2021 by Clea Simon
Cover and jacket design by Mimi Bark

ISBN 978-1-951709-51-8
eISBN: 978-1-951709-27-3
Library of Congress Control Number: tk

First hardcover edition October 2021
by Polis Books, LLC
44 Brookview Lane
Aberdeen, NJ
www.PolisBooks.com

POLIS BOOKS

For Jon

Chapter 1

Ten songs in and she stumbles, her tongue tangled in a lyric she should have down by heart. So much for hubris, Gal tells herself, struggling to get back in sync. To get back on the beat, fingers moving one-two one-two over the thick bass strings. So much for aging.

Lina, her guitarist, looks over, the slight rise of her eyebrows as eloquent as the fill she plays to cover. She's fast—all metal and speed, still—and she hangs on the last barbed note, stretching it out as she waits for the high sign, the cue from Gal. A stadium move, but it has the crowd cheering.

It's been years since Lina's had to do that, Gal realizes, chagrined. It's been years, period. In response, Gal grabs the mic stand, pulling it closer with her left hand while her right keeps the rhythm, thrumming away on the open E. The move centers her. She stands a little straighter, and then she's back. Belting out the chorus she knows as well as the tattoo on her wrist—an F clef, faded blue—as the song pours out of her, the words coming easily now. Winding up to the hook. The line with the hiccup. One extra beat that makes the rhyme different. Makes it stand out.

She sees that now. Feels the crowd inhale in anticipation as

7

she rounds into the chorus for the reprise, once again in time with Lina and Bobbi Jo. She's learned a lot about songwriting in the last twenty years. Knows the tricks that turn a pop progression into an earworm. Wields them at will when she sits down at the piano. Or tries to, anyway. She hasn't had a hit like this one, written by instinct, since then, but she's done all right. And tonight, well, tonight is all about revisiting the past.

A brief pause between numbers. Lina's changing guitars; Barry acting as her tech as he runs out with the Strat. Gal takes a moment to eye the crowd, really check them out, before Bobbi Jo counts off the beat. She doesn't need the set list. None of them do. They're not doing anything new tonight, and the progression is obvious—one song to the next. She hears the tick-tick-tick of Bobbi's sticks and the feedback begins to growl. Breathing deep, from the belly, she steps back up to the mic stand and once more begins to sing.

It shouldn't be automatic. Not tonight, and certainly not after that memory slip. Still, Gal can't help drifting. Maybe it's the crowd. Too many familiar faces missing; too many gone for good. Maybe it's the venue. After years of smaller clubs—coffeehouses, mostly— she's forgotten how far back the Ballroom goes, its rear corners shrouded in darkness. The houselights are down, and she can guess how she looks—how the band looks—from out there, so bold and so bright. Older, sure, but tough with it. Initiates. Blooded, in ways they can only imagine.

What those upturned faces don't suspect is how much is visible from up here. She can see almost everything from the stage, back into those dark corners, and in the touring years, she did. Fucking, fighting. The crowd as oblivious of her gaze as they are connected to her, as if she were, in fact, some kind of dispassionate god. The way they want her, up here, high above them. The power of it. Pure sex, drawing them to her still. The control.

She closes her eyes then. Tells herself she wants to concentrate. To be in the moment, for this number and the one that comes after. The big climax, Aimee's song, the reason they're all here tonight. Bobbi Jo plays the opening roll. Not Aimee—who is?—but steady, with the hi-hat offsetting the big bass beat. And then it's time.

Gal waits for the surge of emotion that comes when she sings her old friend's lyrics. "*A different kind of love, but it's got me.*" It always takes her hard, leaving her wired and jagged after. "*Different, sure, but right.*"

Memories of touring, of doing these songs night after night. Of Aimee, a monster on the set, her shoulders mounded with muscle. Lina to her right. The women who came before, who came after. Musicians and mates, all blending together now. That must be why her mind is playing tricks on her. Why she would forget the words to "Hold Me Down," her own breakthrough song, the one that made the band. Why she would think, for a moment, that she saw a face— his face—shining up, pale and sweat-slick, from the middle of the heaving crowd.

CHAPTER 2

She takes her time, once the set is done. The obligatory encore, the cheers. Not so eager to jump from the stage to the after-party anymore. And it is a party. A celebration, they called it, which sounded better than a wake. Remembering Aimee, the invites had read—the implication that if you had to ask, you probably shouldn't come.

No, she's being harsh. As Gal wipes down her bass, she laughs at her own pretensions. The stage magic has dissipated. They're not stars anymore. There's no reason to be exclusive. She flips the instrument over, making sure to dry the spots where the varnish has worn off. The wear and tear of the road. Her history is in that blonde and battered wood, and she's not going to set it aside again. She places the heavy solid body carefully in its case, with its threadbare velvet and stickers from clubs long closed. Watches to make sure that one clasp, the broken one, catches before she props it against the wall beside Lina's guitar.

Lina's out at the reception already. Gal can hear her raucous laughter from the adjoining room. It brings her back, and she lets herself remember the girls they were. Lina, so young and wild. Fierce still, she tells herself, despite her shock at seeing her bandmate grown plump, her coal-black spikes now a mellow brown. She hid it, at least she hopes she did. Much as she worked to cloak her surprise when Aimee first brought her around—a tiny slip of a thing who plugged into a borrowed amp one night and blew them all away.

Lina wasn't their first guitarist, hers and Aimee's. But she was the one who stuck, whose speed metal attack played so well against her own caustic vocals. And it was the label that had brought in Mimi when the suits had insisted on another bassist. To free Gal up to focus on her singing, they said. To be the front woman they wanted, the star.

She'd played some of Mimi's bass lines tonight. Poor Mimi, gone too soon, her and Britta, the drummer on their later tours. An OD and a heart attack, both victims of the road, the drugs, the drink. Not Aimee, though. She got out. She had a life. Gal turns to look at the drum kit, broken down now and ready to go. Bobbi Jo did her homework. She must have listened to those old records a dozen times, the way she replicated every solo, every fill. She should go find Bobbi Jo, Gal tells herself. Making herself turn toward the door. Should tell Bobbi Jo how grateful everyone is.

Gal leaves the band room—the backstage of the old theater— and takes a breath before heading to the lobby, the sounds of the party in progress coming through bright and loud. If she's going to be honest with herself, and she tries to be these days, she's reluctant to leave the cramped and quiet space for the crowd out front. Some of it, she knows, is the drinking, or rather, the *not* drinking. Not drinking is an active choice on her part. An effort, rather than an absence, especially in situations like this.

It's not like she wants to drink, not really. She's no longer the rocker on tour, getting high, getting crazy, just for the hell of it, and she's old enough to know she probably sounds better sober, at least at this point in the game. But holding a beer would feel natural.

Walking to the bar would give her a trajectory. An excuse to cruise through the room, all the while looking for…what? A ghost?

Crazy. She shakes it off. The memories. She's lingered here too long. She heads into the long hallway that runs all the way to the front of the house. As she passes the big double doors—the load-in—she's tempted. Not for the old back alley antics, not anymore, but to duck out and escape. No, not tonight. She keeps going. Toward that braying laugh and Lina. She sees her as soon as she enters the room, short as she is, through a gap in the crowd, standing with her wide-legged stance as if she were still playing, and it takes Gal a moment to adjust to the sight of the dowdy, middle-aged mom before her. On stage, she almost forgot. And that laughter. Forcing a smile, Gal approaches, wending her way through the crowd. She'll find Bobbi Jo in a moment, once she's acclimated again. Find Walter. He'll know who else has shown up tonight. She looks around, suddenly anxious to locate him. She'd spotted him in the crowd, staring straight at the band even as the crowd surged around him. But now the stout, balding man—Aimee's ex-husband—is nowhere to be seen.

"Gal!" Lina's voice breaks into her thoughts, and Gal looks over to see the guitarist's full moon face beaming. She beckons her over to where she's standing with the kind of woman they'd have labelled "a suit," back in the day. Grey hair, a tailored jacket. Catching Gal's eyes in the mirrored wall—the old lobby's been sort of restored—she turns, her face somehow familiar. "Come on over," Lina calls.

"Hey." Gal does, grateful for the respite. "You see Walter?"

Lina cranes around, the spiked hair already settling back into her soccer mom bob. "He's here somewhere." Her voice sinks lower. "Probably back at the bar."

Gal nods, withholding comment—the man has lost his wife, ex or not—and studies her own face in the cobwebbed reflection. The lines, the dark and hooded eyes. More Keith than Mick, she always

12

said. These days more than ever, even if her newly chestnut mop—a splurge to salve her nerves—softens the harder edges.

"You sounded good," the suit says, her voice low and warm.

"Thanks." Gal takes in the tall, tailored figure who has just complimented her. Grey hair, worn short, but stylish. An expensive cut that fits with the raw silk jacket on her lean frame. They're at odds with the voice, the face, making it harder for Gal to place her. "I'm sorry…" She holds out her hand, hoping for a clue.

"Shira." The woman smiles as she takes it, and Gal gasps, eliciting more of that whooping laughter from Lina.

"Shira! It's good to see you." Gal recovers fast. Their eyes meet and Gal feels the years roll away, as if a peek at the mirror might reveal the slender, nervous woman who first played guitar for the band. Never as comfortable on stage as Lina, never as good, truth be told, she's clearly found herself in the intervening decades. "Are you still in town?"

"My firm's downtown." The Shira of old was never so relaxed or confident. "I'm a partner at Holk and LaCost, but I'm living in Newton. Tim and I have two boys now."

"Of course." She knew about the sons, the marriage. Law school. Boston was—maybe still is—a small town at heart. And clearly Shira found her own way, once the rock and roll was out of her system.

"Have they heard the stories? That their mom was a kick-ass guitarist?" She's more comfortable now. Besides, it's a compliment. But for a moment, a split second of worry, she thinks she's gone too far. Shira's face has frozen, her eyebrows raised ever so slightly, before she responds with a gentle smile.

"I've shared some memories," she says. That's vague enough to cover a multitude of sins. "But you, Gal, you look good. You look like you got out okay."

"Gal's never really gotten out," Lina cuts in, the pride in her voice rubbing Gal the wrong way. "She's still playing. Aren't you?"

Now it's Gal's turn to smile, to be a bit enigmatic. Funny to think that these fault lines remain raw after so many years. Or maybe it's just her, feeling ill at ease. Missing her best friend here, in their old stomping grounds, more than ever.

"I play a little." She looks over at the bar. No Walter, and so she turns back to Shira, trying to make out the expression on her face. Puzzlement or skepticism? Well, the woman has the right. "I live upstate and some of the local coffee houses are kind enough to humor an old lady." She says it as a joke, one she's often used. Only tonight, right now, it sticks in her throat a bit. Are they humoring her? Is she an old lady? Shira, grey as a ghost. "I don't record or tour anymore." She puts that part of the equation to rest.

Shira nods, like she understands something. But it's Lina who picks up the conversation. "You said you were writing, though. Working on some new tunes."

"Yeah," Gal concedes. "I don't know though. I'm not coming up with anything I'm happy with. Nothing I really want anybody to hear, you know?"

"I think I might." It's Shira, to her surprise, who responds. "I gather you've been through a lot."

Gal pauses, the ready answer stuck in her throat. Maybe it's the way Shira is looking at her—a steady, appraising gaze. She takes a breath, about to speak, when a male voice breaks in.

"There you are." Balding, pink-faced. Not Walter, the newcomer reaches out for Shira's arm. She turns his way. "We should get going, hon," he says. "The sitter."

"Of course." She returns his smile, and this time it reaches her eyes. She's still smiling when she turns back to Lina.

"I guess I'd better run," she says. And it could be her imagination, but Gal thinks the neatly coiffed woman is taking a deeper breath.

That she's bracing her shoulders as she turns toward Gal.

"Gal." She fumbles with her bag, and in a moment, she has pressed a card into Gal's hand. "Please," she says. "If you want to talk."

"Sure." Gal's mouth is dry, and the word is barely audible. Shira smiles again and dips her head as if in benediction, before turning and walking off.

"What was that about?" Lina's noticed it too, but Gal can only shake her head.

"She can't still be angry," Gal says, more to herself than to the other woman. "Can she?"

Chapter 3

"She's good, isn't she?" Walter, the next day, wincing a little. Wringing his big, scarred hands. Hungover, Gal figures. Making conversation despite it all. "Bobbi Jo, I mean."

"She's no Aimee." The words are out before Gal can stop them, and she turns from the linens she's folding to gauge her old friend's reaction. But Walter is smiling, a shy, private smile. Catching her eye, he shakes his head.

"No, she's not," he says, his voice so soft she wonders if it hurts. "But she's good."

Gal only nods this time. The lesson learned: things not to say to a widower, not when you're helping him pack up his late wife's belongings, anyway. Late ex-wife, she corrects herself, though she doesn't know if they ever finalized the split. Not that she's going to ask. She's stuck thinking about the after-party, about Shira and that strange, intense look.

"She talked about you a lot." If Walter notices her silence, he's too kind to comment on it. That's Walter, strong and long-suffering. He really was the perfect roadie, though from the lines around his mouth and the sunken darkness of his eyes, the suffering part has taken its toll. Those eyes are turned downward now, but he's no longer staring at his knuckles. He's looking through papers. Clippings, she sees, the newsprint yellow with age and from having been stored badly, loose in a box in the bottom of the closet. Stories about the band, most likely, but she can't tell from his face.

"Those last weeks," he says, as if he's reading. "Toward the end."

"Come on," says Gal, the guilt putting an edge on her voice. She wasn't there. Hadn't visited in months. She also hasn't slept well. The show, and all those memories, kept her up. Seeing Shira, what she said. Her dreams were weird and amorphous. In one, she was drowning. "That was a lifetime ago."

"Yeah, but that was her youth." A falling tone. Fatigue, Gal thinks. The finality of it all catching up to him. "After that, she lost something…"

Gal swallows the urge to argue. To talk about the fickle nature of the audience. About how the fans always ask for a little more, a little extra on top of what you want to give. She knows better than Walter does about the other side: the crowd feeds the performer, too. There's a charge from being on stage, something mutual. Maybe Aimee did miss that. Maybe, she thinks, that's what she's missing these days. That rush.

"We got old," she says. "Older, anyway. And you and Aimee, you settled down." Got straight, she means. It would take Gal years to give up that kind of partying.

"And you went on to fame and fortune." He picks up another clipping, this one brown at the edges. A sigh and he rubs his bald spot, his arm ropey with muscle. "She knew you loved her. She knew you came when you could."

She's listening, she realizes, for an off note. An attack. But all he sounds is tired.

"She just wanted to talk about the old days," he says, his soft voice fading again, inexpressibly sad. "The glory days."

"Glory days." She laughs, more an exhalation than anything else. As if she'd been holding her breath. At any rate, she's filled the box and reaches for a marker. Sheets and pillowcases, she writes. Hospital bed. "Well, we were young."

The squeak of the marker, or maybe it's the smell of the ink, brings back her memory slip. The odd off moment from the night before.

"Walter?" She turns and places the box with the others. Waits for him to turn, too. "Last night, did you see someone—one of the guys from the old days—out on the floor?" As soon as she says it, she realizes how stupid she sounds. "I'm sorry, I was going to ask you last night, but I couldn't find you."

She sees his face tighten, the brow come down. A feeling she remembers. "I'm sorry." She repeats herself, but he waves her off. "It's just, I thought maybe you were talking to someone. I can't remember his name."

"You probably did." That smile again. More a rictus, she realizes. She shouldn't be pushing him. "I was—I kind of overdid it last night." A shamefaced glance. He knows she can see it on him. "I think everyone who could came out last night. Aimee would've been proud."

"Aimee was the heart of the band. Its beat, anyway." She means it, but her thoughts are elsewhere. That face. But before she can try to pin it down, the sound of the door and young voices interrupt.

"Dad." It's Camille, Aimee's daughter, and she's brought a friend. "Hi, Gal." Her smile so like her mother's, Gal can barely catch her breath. "This is my roommate Linda."

"You were great last night." Blue eyes enormous in a pale round face.

"For old biddies." She smiles to take the sting out of it, proud of herself for not asking the girl's age. Camille must be, what, twenty?

18

Twenty-one? Her friend is shorter, stouter. A fair-haired satellite to the willowy Camille. "We were missing Camille's mom, though."

"Nah, you were great." With her dark eyes, her hair its natural reddish-brown, Camille may look more like her mother, but that urge to cover up—to make nice—that must be her father. "Dad, you want me to take these?"

His hands tighten on the page, but his daughter is pointing to the boxes Gal has already taped and labeled: Clothing. Towels and bedding. Six of them, large but light, stacked in front of Aimee's old upright, one life eclipsing another.

"Thanks, sweetie."

The slight young woman grabs a box and, realizing its lightness, hefts another on top. Rises from her knees—Walter's taught her well. Her friend pauses, and Gal thinks she'll speak again. Say something about the band.

"My church is really grateful, Mr. Lanell," she says instead. He dips his head, and she turns, squatting, as if expecting the remaining box to be heavy as lead or maybe just following Camille's lead. Gal glances over at her old friend, but she holds her tongue.

He's seen the look, however.

"Church?" she asks once the two have left the room. They both know how Aimee felt. How Walter did too, at one point.

"Makes her happy." He doesn't meet her eyes. "I almost lost her when Aimee and I split up."

"Nonsense." Gal's response is automatic. She may not know parenting, but she knows this man. "You're her father."

He snorts. In this, at least, like her own old man, long gone and not much missed. "Aimee wouldn't want me tossing that stuff, or I'd have burned the lot two months ago. The piano too, to be honest."

Gal nods, accepting the non-answer. The history. Walter moved back in when Aimee was in hospice. Six long weeks of drugs and waiting, the condo turned into a hospital room. Talk about heavy lifting. He hasn't recovered, she can see that now as he stares after the girls. Sees the strain in his face, hears it in his voice. He's fought hard for his equilibrium, but it's fraying. No wonder he went on a bender last night.

"Hey, Walter, you okay?" Maybe he's just hungover. She's not one to talk.

"Yeah, I just overdid it." He looks at the floor, which refuses to open for him.

"It was a big night."

Another grunt. "Camille was there. Her friend, too."

"They're good kids," she says, at a loss for what else to say. Understanding, at last, the shame.

"She's my life now," he responds without turning. "She's all I've got left."

He licks his lips, and she sees how dry they are. How chapped. How much did he drink? Not that she's surprised. The night, the benefit, was a big deal. The culmination of her old friend's dying wish that the band would get together one more time. That it also offset some of the bills was a bonus. Gal hasn't looked at the accounts yet. Nobody's had time to catch their breath. But the room was nearly full.

Maybe it was too much, though, even this long after. Or maybe it's just the end of a particular phase of mourning that has drained Walter so. He's got to go on, after all. Back to his own apartment, to a life without Aimee, without even the possibility. She can escape the whole scene in a couple of days. Pretend nothing has changed.

"Maybe I should go," she says. She's tired too, deep in her bones. "Let you get some rest." The linens and towels were the last of the household items. Now it's only keepsakes. Aimee's books and records, and those clippings. "I'll come by tomorrow and try to make sense of the books."

He nods. "Thanks, Gal. She really did love you, you know."

"I loved her too, Walter." She steps closer, as if to embrace him. But he's holding tight to that one yellowed sheet. His eyes on some faraway memory as the brittle edge breaks off and falls to the floor.

CHAPTER 4

She can still remember the night she met Aimee, as clear as if it were the week before. Taji's, a Friday, but early, maybe 10 p.m., before the first band started. Hot too, the club's AC no match for the August night.

"Can I help you?" The bartender leaning forward on his ink-covered arms, looking tired already, drained by the heat.

"Bud Light, please?" She wasn't going to drink it, but it would give her something to hold. For an answer, he reached into the cooler, popped open the bottle and then moved on. Gal, in those days, wasn't putting out anything but mousiness. A plain girl with a nose.

"Frankie!" Aimee was another story. Bright blonde, back then, her hair spiked stiff with the home bleaching, she almost climbed onto the bar, slapping it twice to get the tired man's attention, her arms bare and muscular in the cut-off tee. "Help me out here!"

To Gal's surprise, he seemed amused rather than bothered, a lazy grin wrinkling up those large, dark eyes as he poured her a shot of something brown. "Here you go, Aimee."

The blonde—Aimee—must have seen Gal watching, because she raised that shot in a toast. Gal caught sight of her unshaven armpit. The edge of a Celtic knot tattoo just below the dark tangle of hair.

"You here for the Grants?" The room was deserted, maybe three other people in a space for two hundred. But the question gave Gal a charge, like maybe she wasn't stupid to come out so early.

"Uh-huh." She nodded and raised her beer in return, the sweating bottle cold in her hand. Condensation dripped down her arm, and she was suddenly aware of her belly, the way her t-shirt stretched over her breasts. Feeling awkward, bottle warming in her hand, she crossed her arms as if to hide herself.

"'Super Surf'?" The other woman's eyes were on her. Watching her face, Gal realized. Some kind of a test.

"'Tagalong.' The B-side." Gal had bought the single when she heard it on the local college station, but flipping it over was the real revelation. Distracted, she stood up straighter. "The way the key keeps changing—up, up, up—and that solo?"

The blonde leaned in. "Yeah. Radio should be all over that. Crazy." Then she tilted her head and frowned. "You play?"

A nod. Gal almost afraid to admit it. "Some," she said at last. "Piano, and, well, bass. And you?"

"Drums!" An open-palm tattoo on the bar: rat-tat-tat. "We should form a band." Surprised, Gal let loose with a wide smile, and the blonde grinned right back. "Frankie," she called, turning from Gal with a wink. "Help us out here!"

They didn't talk again that night, not about the band idea anyway. Aimee seemed to know everyone who came in, not that there were many of them, greeting each with a shout or a slug as Gal looked on, mesmerized. But as the Grants took the stage, she caught Gal's eye and they both moved up front, Aimee beating out a rhythm on the chest-high stage while Gal danced in place. When she saw bleached spikes up front again the next night—at the Cellar, this time—she worked her way through the crowd to stand beside her. Afterward, at the bar, they took apart the headliner. The new drummer, that last song.

"This is whack. Let's go to Jag's." Aimee, always wanting more. "The Visibles are playing."

Gal's face fell. The ten dollars in her wallet had to last till Friday.

"Come on," Aimee urged, tugging at her arm. "Reggie's on the door. He knows me."

There was no saying no. Still, she hung back, on the sidewalk, while Aimee went inside. Unsure. Abandoned.

Only not, as Aimee popped back out minutes later, laughing. "Lick your wrist," she commanded.

"What?"

But the muscular blonde had already grabbed her hand and turned it, her tongue warm and thick against the tender skin, and then she was pressing their arms together, holding her tight.

"There," she said, and Gal look down, the stamp blurred but dark enough.

"You go in first." Aimee gave her a push.

Two nights later, out again. Aimee waiting, a beer beside her shot at the bar.

"I knew you'd be here." She handed Gal the bottle, and they clinked. "So, listen, the Gotcha are looking for someone to share their practice space. We'd get two nights a week for a hundred fifty a month." Gal opened her mouth to complain—she was barely covering her rent—but Aimee held up a hand to stop her. "Four ways, that's, what? Like, thirty bucks? Besides, I think we should pay less. I'll offer them one twenty."

"Four ways?" She was intrigued, and Aimee's grin showed Gal

her new friend knew it. Everything came together quickly after that. Shira worked with Gal at Raspberries, and Aimee thought the leggy guitarist had a good look, what with her height and that shock of black hair. It was Shira who brought in Dru to play rhythm. The waifish guitarist seemed half out of it—Aimee thought drugs, Gal stage fright—still, it was easier and cheaper than placing an ad.

"What are we going to say? Girl group, into Stooges, Stones, and Pistols?" Aimee had offered that up, just the two of them left in the dank basement space. The newcomers had left. "I don't want to know what we'll get."

"We might get someone really good." Gal wasn't sure about the second guitarist. Something about the way she shied away from eye contact made her uneasy. "Someone who could set us apart."

"On rhythm?" Aimee's dark brows rose nearly to her straw-colored bangs. "Be real. Besides, why would anyone who was already any good want to play with us?"

It wasn't a question Gal could answer, and besides, they were running late. Aimee had already broken down her drum kit, as much as she ever had, and shoved it back against the wall where the Gotcha were less likely to spill beer on it. Gal's bass and cords were packed up, her amp tucked back as far as it would go.

Looking back, she can't remember if they went out that night or where. Probably, she thinks now. It seemed like they always did. In her memory, those early days were steeped in the funk of the practice room and the smoke of the clubs. She must have slept and worked, even gone outside at some point for air. She managed to pay rent, but she has no memories of that either. She and Aimee were creating something. Building a band, and a musical legacy that would live on even after her friend was gone in a handful of clippings and two great songs.

CHAPTER 5

"You take your time." Russ, on the phone, sounds so warm Gal nearly tears up. "Take all the time you need."

"Thanks." She blinks and makes herself sit up, wiping her boot marks from the desk's veneer. The motel isn't bad, for the price. Walking distance to the T, if she doesn't want to drive, with a queen bed all to herself. Right now, after the day with Walter, after all the memories, she could fall asleep anywhere, even reclining in the knockoff ergonomic desk chair, plastic webbing where the nylon should be. But she knows better than to give in to Russ's gentle entreaty. Knows the consequences, and so she stands and begins to pace. The better to get this conversation over with. This is Russ, not Aimee. Nobody will ever be again. "I appreciate you looking after Honey."

"Honey's a great cat." The man on the other end is smiling. She can hear it in his voice. "She's happy at my place, but she misses you."

"Yeah, well." She cuts him off before he can say more. "It'll just be a few more days. I need to follow up on the money. I don't want Walter to have to deal with that."

"That's fine." She hears him moving. Cleaning up after a job.

Maybe reaching for a beer, since she's not there. "That'll give me time to finish."

She stops short. "Russ?"

"Your bathroom," he says. The clunk of metal. Tools, then. "I'm not doing anything we haven't talked about."

She makes herself inhale and hold it as she counts to five. As she exhales, he begins to talk again.

"I fixed the leak—the faucet only needed a washer. But then I was thinking about how cold it gets in there in winter, and I thought it wouldn't be a big deal to add some insulation. Re-caulk that window. And now's the time to do it, before the weather turns."

"And because you've got so much free time." Summer is his busy season. She couldn't afford what he charges through Labor Day. All she asked is that he drop by. Feed the cat. They're neighbors, after all. Separated by only a half acre of scraggly woods and weeds neither wants to deal with.

"Hey, call it selfish." He might have been reading her mind. "I don't want to freeze come November. Assuming, that is, I'm still invited."

She sighs and closes her eyes. She can picture his crooked grin, the wiry hair that's now going grey at the temples and over the neckline of his work tee. Can imagine the smooth places where his hands are callused, too, and knows she's not ready to cut him loose. Not yet, although at times like this, she thinks she should. If only he would quit pushing.

"Well, thanks." She avoids the implied question, countering with one of her own. "You need anything from the city?"

The moment the words are out of her mouth, she regrets them. If he says "you," she'll lose it. If he says anything…

"Nah, I'm fine." Either he's oblivious or smarter than she gives him credit for. Either works.

"Great," she says, more than ready to end the call. "I'll touch base when I know more."

Once she's off the phone, the bed doesn't look so inviting. The family next door—two youngsters accusing each other of cheating—doesn't help. Thank God she's got earplugs, even if her audiologist didn't intend them for sleeping. But Gal's learned the hard way that staring at the ceiling when you're not tired doesn't make sleep come any faster. Better she should get something to eat, she tells herself. Get some air, out, by herself.

It's habit that has her driving back toward the Ballroom, toward the scene of last night's triumph. At least, that's what she tells herself as she takes the old shortcut down Water Street, the one that should dead end on Boylston. Habit and curiosity, it's been so long. The Ballroom was the obvious venue for the gig last night. It may no longer be the premiere club in town—things like that don't last—but it was the place to play back in the day, the club they finally got booked into once her song hit the charts.

Gal thought back. Counted it out. Two-plus years after their first tentative rehearsals; eons in band time. They'd been touring that summer, another hot one but at least they'd been on the northern circuit that time. Cleveland, or maybe Madison, when they'd heard the news. Their second tour, but the first with the label. The first real tour, as she thinks of it, covering the country with a crew and a bus, which made the long hauls—Nebraska, Montana, twelve-plus hours between gigs—work. With their own equipment by that point, too, and microphones that didn't smell like vomit, not even after three months playing every college town from Boston to Olympia. When Gus called with news of the gig, the rest of the band—a trio by that point—had been thrilled.

"Headlining?" Aimee hadn't believed it. Shot straight up, her dark eyes open wide with glee. They had been in a motel room like the one Gal had just left, and Aimee, as usual, had hogged the bed. "Not opening?"

"We've paid our dues." Gal wasn't a newbie anymore, nursing a beer, her feet up on the bureau. "And it's been a while since we've played in town—since, what, June?"

"May." Lina, their guitarist by that point, changing a string. She'd replaced Shira before the first tour. Dru hadn't even made it that long. "It's a step up, though." She paused, looking around. "Last time it was Taji's when we got home. Man, that was wild."

"Soundcheck's at seven." Gal had no time for reminiscing and arced the can into the trash as she stood to go. "We should get moving."

"But we're going to do it, right?" Aimee scrambled to her feet, clumsy despite her muscle. Buzzed already, Gal thought. She'd learned, since Dru. She saw the signs as her drummer leaned into the mirror, mugging and fluffing her hair. Not that it ever affected Aimee's playing. "I mean, the Ballroom?"

"Let me think about it." Gal was already at the door, ready to head out. No band is a democracy, not really, and she'd emerged as the driving force.

"We'll get a guarantee." Lina grabbed her gig bag. Despite the heat, she hadn't even bothered to shed her leather jacket. "And we're bigger now, maybe even charting with all the airplay."

"So maybe we should make them work for it." Gal kept her voice smooth. Impassive. A little buzzed herself, just enough to take off the edge. "Make them work for us. Hey, Aimee, we've got to go."

The scene comes back like a video as Gal drives. Funny, how long since she's thought about it. About that tour, that homecoming. The Ballroom and the party after, so different from the one last night.

29

The light changes and she realizes she's come up the back way, as if she were loading in. The club, an old vaudeville house, a brick monolith looming up on the right. Only as she draws closer, she sees the ambulance blocking the street. The police cruiser pulled up on the sidewalk by the alley to the stage door.

Not my problem, she reassures herself as she slows. Too late to turn, she'd back out, only the cop standing there is staring, and she's not sure of the law. Can't quite dismiss the mental checklist—no drugs, no drinks—even after all these years. The ambulance has to pull out soon, she tells herself, and sure enough she sees some movement. Two men in blue jumpers come out of the alley, rolling a stretcher between them. She stares without wanting to, the way you do, as they open the ambulance doors and lift it in. There's no siren on the truck, no lights flashing, but that doesn't surprise her. The body on the stretcher is covered, head to toe. And in one awful, breathtaking moment, she knows who is lying there.

CHAPTER 6

"Did you hear anything about an accident last night?" She can't be right, she tells herself. She's not psychic. Not…involved.

But Gal's not sure who to ask, so she calls Lina when she gets back to the motel. After seeing the ambulance, she no longer felt up to driving around. She'd been out of the city too long, grown too used to the slower pace of her upstate home. Bearsville still feels rural after dark. "Maybe something with drugs?"

"At the show? No." Lina's at home. She lives in the suburbs with her wife and kids. She'd offered Gal the guest room, but after all this time, Gal values her privacy. "I don't think our crowd is what you'd call the heavy partiers. I mean, not anymore. Besides, we'd have heard."

"Yeah, I guess you're right." She's pacing again, but not to keep awake. The sight unsettled her—she really has grown unaccustomed to the urban jungle. "It was probably some poor homeless guy."

She waits for the question. Realizes she's doling out information like chum. That she wants her old friend to ask, so they can speculate. So she can share. But Lina's a mom now, and it's late by her standards. Gal hears young voices, high and bird-like.

"Probably," is all she says. "Talk tomorrow?"

"Yeah," says Gal, suddenly wishing she'd taken her old bandmate up on her offer. The comfort of people, a memory of companionship, lounging on the bed. "Tomorrow."

Maybe it's being back in the city, but she can't sleep. Can't get comfortable. The room's not noisy, not really. But they're the wrong noises. The muffled hubbub of the street outside. The beep-beep-beep of a truck backing up. And when she does drop off, she dozes lightly. A voice—or maybe it was a dream—wakes her, and she throws the covers off in alarm. Her heart is racing. A dream, then. The world outside is quiet by that point, the hum of the ventilation system a low and steady purr.

It's too quiet, that's what it is. The sounds all wrong somehow. Russ would have a laugh.

She hadn't realized what a restless sleeper she was until he started spending the night. He'd scared her, that first time, shaking her awake before dawn.

"What the fuck?" She'd pushed him off, freaked to find him looming over her. Fear turning quickly to annoyance.

"You were having a nightmare." He'd pulled back, concern apparent even in the half light of her room. "It was like you were trying to scream, so I thought I'd better wake you."

"I was?" Nightmare? She didn't even remember. "I'm not usually a heavy sleeper."

"Well, yeah." He nodded toward the hall light, which she'd left on, and the glow of her phone recharging. "Too much light."

"I'm used to it." She didn't know why she felt embarrassed, but she made sure she'd taken her pills after that. If she had any more dreams, she didn't remember them.

Now she finds herself lying on her back. Staring at the ceiling and listening to her own pulse. The pills no longer work the way they should. Her doctor won't give her anything stronger. But the beat in her ears, that she feels in her throat, is her cue. She needs music. Something loud. She's always been this way.

Earbuds in, she spins through the choices. Something old, yeah. Something she knows. She finds Aimee's song and clicks on it to repeat. Lies back and lets the music wash over her. Through her, just like it did back then.

She wakes with a start, as sudden as a kick drum. Tosses the covers back and sits up. She's lost the earbuds overnight. Lost her phone too, but she finds that, underneath the cheap motel pillow. The earpiece isn't far away, though it seems she pulled it off in her sleep. Another habit Russ doesn't understand.

"It's being on the road," she'd tried to explain. "Things are never quiet, and you're always listening to music. Now it's the only way I can relax."

He'd shrugged and smiled, like he did with most things. Probably the only reason they were still seeing each other, if that's what it is, all these years later. Gal knows she's demanding. Set in her ways and stubborn. All that time on the road, she's not used to catering to a lover. She's not going to start now.

"*A different kind of love…*" She sings in the shower, the morning hoarseness dissolving in the steam. These days, the roughness is from age, a certain tightness that gives more heft to her lower range but makes it harder to get started. It's not like the old days, when the clubs were full of smoke. Then she'd wake, her mouth dry and ashy, no matter what she'd drunk—how much—the night before. She'd stopped smelling it, after a while, but then she'd pick up a shirt, a pair of jeans, after a week or two at home and it would hit her. Life on the road was different, that's for sure.

"*Different but it's got me.*" She's still humming as she dresses. She's sung it often enough. Made it her own after Aimee left the band. A parting gift, in its way, Gal had always thought. *"Different but it's good..."*

For the first time in ages, she wonders if Aimee missed it: the band. The life. For all the craziness, there was a particular freedom to being on the road, almost as if one didn't have flesh. Have skin. The sensation comes back to her now as she closes the door with a soft click behind her. Maybe she needs to travel more.

It's hard to remember why it all went bad. Exhaustion, they called it. The catch-all for the press and the fans, but there was something to it. That feeling of emptiness, that there was nothing left to draw on. She remembers it vaguely, but it's so distant now, it seems unreal, like someone else's memory. Was she drinking too much? Sure, they all were. Those who had remained, at any rate.

Aimee was long gone by then, having given up the band for Walter and her kid. A half life, Gal had thought. Somehow faded or indistinct. But who knows? She sighs. She certainly has never found anything like Aimee and Walter had, though she's honest enough to admit she hasn't really tried.

"Different kind of love..." Well, it was certainly that. And maybe it was just a choice—excitement over something steady. Thrills, rather than comfort.

Her phone rings as she's walking out of the lobby. The place offers coffee, but she's seen the Starbucks on the corner and she's feeling like a treat. She answers, not bothering to see who's calling. Not that many people have her number these days. Not that many care.

"So I made some calls." Lina, a note of stress in her voice. The kids, Gal thinks. Another choice she doesn't regret.

"Good morning." Gal tries to laugh it off. Lina always was all business, even before she went cold turkey, as serious about her family as she ever was about the band. She pictures her tuning, listening for play in the strings that would never be heard from the floor.

"You said 'accident,' and I was worried." The laughter dies in Gal's throat. There's a tension in Lina's voice that sets off a warning—like a high-pitched whine almost out of range. "You said something happened after the show."

"Yeah?" That anxiety is contagious.

"It was Tom—Tom Kennedy—from the old days." She pauses, and Gal shakes her head, confused. "You know, T.K.," her friend says, almost as if she can see. "I don't know the details—some kind of fight or a mugging, someone said. Or maybe he fell, hit his head. But it was T.K., Gal. And he's dead."

T.K. Gal can barely swallow, much less speak. Somehow she chokes out her thanks to the friend who has done the work and then she gets off the phone. Starts walking, and then stops again, unsure of where she's going or why. Unsure of what to do. T.K., she thinks. And he's dead.

"Damn it, T.K." She says the words aloud, and the sound of her voice is strange to her, as if it came from far away. A frisson of fear sending a shiver down her back. And just like that, another thought springs up, the words forming before she can question why.

"It should have been me," she says.

CHAPTER 7

Fearless. That's what they called her, back in the day. The critics. The fans. Her bandmates, too, though their praise could be mixed at times, even when the band was at the height of its fame.

Gal had only laughed. "What's the point of fear?" she remembers telling some writer. Not a zine this time, but a young guy from a big daily. Chicago? "We're all going to die anyway."

It must have been Chicago. By then they had the rider and she was drinking bourbon, top shelf, just enough to take the edge off before they hit the stage. The show was sold out, first time for a big venue on the tour, and she remembers the jolt when she'd found out. As high from the energy as the booze.

"The way you move out there. Your attack. Everything so…" He'd tilted his head, leaving his sentence open for her to finish, and she'd laughed again. He was smart enough to know he was cute. To know that his whole bookish look—the hair a little too long, the Oxford shirt—was like catnip after a steady diet of greasy denim and leather.

"Life is there for the taking." She'd been purring, making no bones about her lust. "Why should I miss a thing?"

Had she fucked him? She didn't think so, not then. She was too

36

excited about the gig. All her energies geared toward the stage. Even soundcheck had been great. She could hear herself. Hear everything, and the final run through, "Hold Me Down," had whet her appetite for the night. Even as she toyed with him, her cute little mouse, she'd been listening. Voices, some shouting, as the opener loaded in, the volume amping up as the room began to fill.

"'Scuse me." The stage manager, his head poking through the opened door and pulling back just as fast. Funny how careful he was with her—with all of them—as if privacy were possible on the road.

"But the way you push the envelope." The pretty boy wasn't letting go, and she remembers pausing. Really looking at his Ivy League face, the half smile that lingered on his lips. "The songs, sure. That's your art, and you deliver. Raw, visceral. Like Iggy, only..."

"Female?" She should have known. College boy. Couldn't deal with a woman like her.

"Only more vulnerable somehow." His words snapped down and she had the urge to smack him. Wipe that smirk off his face.

"Vulnerable?" Angry or not, the laughter bubbled up like lava. Like vomit, bitter in her mouth. "I could eat you for breakfast." Did she say that? Maybe she did. Did she fuck him, after all that? Up against a wall covered in graffiti and gum? She doesn't remember. If she did, it was to adjust his attitude, as much as to put his spine out of place. This was her world. He'd play by her rules or not at all.

The gig, that was the point. She'd been on fire. The bourbon only helping her focus, helping her keep it all together. She'd found her voice by then, a raw growl that some wag had dubbed feral. She'd still been playing then, as well as singing, if that's what you could call it. Wearing her bass low on her pelvis. Solid and thick against her hip bones, an extension of herself. She'd never felt bound by it, never held back, and she loved the added power. The volume, the distraction. Feedback when you stepped too close, and a shock when you turned away, but she couldn't keep still.

A panther. That's what she was, pacing. Juiced as her amp, and twice as loud. *Vulnerable, my ass.* She'd been so strong then, the bass weighed nothing. Two years of humping her own amp, of no sleep, had honed her body, ridding her of that girly softness. Those weights of Aimee's that she'd picked up, doing curls for the fun of it. For the definition of her arms.

She was sweating by the time they got to "Get Off," some eight songs in, when she'd hit the sweet spot. The moment when everything seemed to slow. Some of that was the bourbon—the buzz had mellowed and the air tasted sweet as she inhaled. The lights were crazy—this was a theater, with a proper setup. Man, those spots were bright. She'd turned to Lina, laughing. Nothing to say, really, and her bandmate as wide-eyed and eager as she felt. Mouth open, glistening. She could do anything up there. They all could, and in that moment of syrup-slow time that could have lasted forever, she shook her head, sweat flying off in droplets. And then she heard it—Aimee's count. Her sticks beating off the one-two-three-four and there was only time enough to breathe and life came back in a rush. In a roar.

She really tore into "Get Off" that night, loving the sound. Loving how the fans up front pressed hard against the stage, the wild, wet need in their eyes. "Get Off" had led into "Hold Me Down," their usual closer, but Gal wasn't ready to go. The crowd was hot and loud as she began the four-note tattoo that signaled "Rot Gut." This wasn't on the set list. She didn't care. She knew the band would be behind her, and, sure enough, within a measure, Lina had caught on. Aimee rolling in as if that was the plan from the start. They were watching her then, taking her cues. "Boyfriend," an oldie, the lyrics half forgotten. Not that it mattered, with that volume, with that crowd. And then "Dog," for Iggy. Iggy and that pissant journalist, the one who'd called her weak. They'd turned on the house lights by then. Pulled the power before the end, the house sound giving out until it was just the amps on stage. Gal screaming out the lyrics, her voice shot to shit. Her girls with her at every step. She can barely remember stumbling off stage, Aimee holding her up. Someone handing her a flask. Southern Comfort or something sweet. Still, it burned, her throat so raw.

The bar had closed by then. By the time they had finally unplugged, Aimee breaking down her set. They had a roadie—not T.K. anymore, but some poor slob, a lackey from Gus's crew, packing up. Lugging her stage amp out the back door to the bus. She had her bass, though. Kept it by her. Heavy now, like a body, when she leaned it on the bar. He had to have been watching. He had to know, but the bar man wouldn't meet her eyes. Pretended not to hear. Well, it was his license, and besides, someone had a six-pack. A case. Someone always had a bottle for after, for when she was so thirsty. So hot she was burning up. The club was closed. The bouncer moving them out, but someone knew about a party. You needed to unwind.

Was she still drunk, the next day, by the time they hit the road? She can't remember. Just that they got there, another gig. Another night of excess. Another ferocious show.

Yeah, she was fearless. Fearless as fuck. There wasn't a boundary she didn't push, a line she didn't cross. And, hey, she survived, didn't she?

CHAPTER 8

"It's the mess, isn't it?" Russ sounds amused when she tells him. "'Cause I know it's not the noise."

"You're so full of it." She could laugh. They have that kind of connection. "Like I haven't lived with a crappy bathroom for nearly twenty years now. Like you aren't neater than I am."

She'd had to call, finally. Call him off, actually. It wasn't fair not to when he might be taking other jobs—paying gigs—rather than working on her house. She wouldn't be driving back tomorrow or the day after, likely. His response—casual, accepting—is a relief, coming after a pause that made her wish she'd simply texted.

It's Walter, she tells him. Yeah, she should have seen it coming. Should've guessed. It must be hard letting go, and finishing up here—with the concert over, with the packing up almost done— puts him one step closer to moving on. Still, Gal had been taken aback that morning when he'd asked her to take over.

The concert had been a success, at least by the terms they'd set. The room hadn't been sold out; nobody had really expected that. But most of the tickets had gone, and a lot of people had been in touch about donating after the fact. That's what she was dealing with now, largely. Taking their money was fine. It was listening to

40

the excuses that tired her out.

Some of them had obligations. She got that. Kids, jobs, whatever. They all made claims on people's time. Then there were the folks who'd moved away or had tickets for something else that night. But as she read through the messages on the benefit page, as she started returning calls, she had a hard time holding her tongue. Couldn't make it? Really? Couldn't be bothered to get their fat asses off the couch, more likely. It was the kind of crack she'd make to Aimee back in the day. It wasn't like they wouldn't have gotten something in return. The band had sounded great. She wished she could just tell them off, but no, it was a benefit and money was money. Well, maybe there was a reason Walter didn't want to deal.

Needing a break, she'd started on the receipts. Even as bare bones as they'd done it, there were expenses—the hall had cut them a deal, the sound guy worked for free, but she needed to make sure the house staff got paid. If Gal had learned anything over the years, it was that you should always tip your bartenders. But after an hour of that, she'd had enough.

"Hey, Walter." She stood and stretched. Stared down at the dining room table, covered with papers still mostly unread. With a sigh, she turned away. Yelled over to the small office where Walter'd been closeted since she came in. His office once, then Aimee's, now his again, as it had been since she started hospice. "Want to get something to eat?"

"I need to wait for Camille." His voice was flat. Tired, probably, but she rolled her eyes. Camille was in college, she wasn't some latchkey kid. And then it hit her. It wasn't that Walter was worried about his daughter. He simply missed her. Wanted her company before she took off again, no matter how he put it.

"'Kay, then." She didn't need to ask permission. He'd even given her a key. "I'll be back in a bit."

41

When she'd stepped outside, the enormity of it all nearly knocked her back. Here she was, standing on a side street in Brighton. It was almost like she never left, only, well, everything was different, wasn't it? And there was just too much to do.

That's when she called Russ. It was only fair.

"Anyway, Walter's not dealing," she says again, by way of an explanation. "I don't know what he's doing in his office all day. Besides waiting for his daughter, that is."

"Sounds like that's what he needs to do." Russ could be a zen master. That's why she keeps seeing him, she realizes in a moment of clarity made possible by distance. Made possible by her affinity for the man in mourning two flights up.

"Yeah, I guess." She feels petty now for grumbling. What's a little paperwork? A few phone calls? "I figure it should all be cleared up in a day or two."

"Sounds good." Sounds noncommittal, she realizes. But that's the way they are, her and Russ. Neither of them is the type to want strings, to want the mess. She hangs up, then. There's nothing more to say. Besides, she called him. To wait for any other response would be to threaten the balance. What they have is good, for what it is. While it lasts. And she really wants something to eat.

Brighton has changed, but not that much. The Greek place on the corner now has a different name, and the prices are a surprise. She orders a melt and takes a seat.

"We'll call you, Gail." The server, some young dude with a man bun, smiles even as he mispronounces her name. She smiles back, showing her teeth in a joyless sneer. This latest trend in marketing—she couldn't call it customer service—annoys her, and she relishes his mistake.

Maybe she's bitter. Maybe she's just old. The sandwich, when it comes, is tasty, and she realizes how hungry she is. Grateful for the side of chips that crunch like they've been fried recently, somewhere in the back. As she licks the salt from her fingers, she grows aware of eyes on her. Someone watching. Yes, an older man in the corner, dark eyes set deep in a weathered face. She sucks one finger, staring back, the eye contact a dare rather than flirtation. She still looks good. She knows that. She eats what she wants, pretty much. Not as skinny as she was in her partying days, but lean. None of that girly softness that used to plague her so. Those long walks she takes instead of drinking probably play a part.

When he stands and nods her way, she feels a little charge. She still has it. This is why she keeps Russ at arm's length. Options. When he passes by her on his way out, eyes ahead and silent, she makes herself laugh. Yeah, well, the sandwich was good anyway.

"Hey, Walter." Not so good that she doesn't feel her mouth water when she lets herself in. The smell of onions browning. Meat and spices. "I got you a roast beef."

"Hi, Gal." Camille, in the kitchen, a wooden spoon in her hand. "I'm making chili. Do you want to stay?"

"Just ate." She raises the bag as evidence. "I'm glad you're here, though."

"Gal." Walter wanders in. He looks old. Tired and worn, and for a moment, Gal is speechless. "Thanks for everything you're doing. I was just telling Camille."

It's a dismissal, although a kind one, and as he walks over to his daughter, wrapping an arm around her, Gal actually takes a step back. "I can finish up tomorrow," she says. "Thanks, anyway."

Neither makes an effort to dissuade her. Neither walks her back to the door. They've got each other, and their pain. She'll take the roast beef, she figures, as she heads back to her rented room. She's spent enough nights by herself that she hardly even wants to drink anymore. Maybe she'll fool around with her bass, the quiet buzz of the unamplified strings familiar company. See if something comes as she rambles over the notes. She hasn't been writing much lately. Nothing worth the name. But being back here—Brighton, with Walter, with everyone—makes her wonder if there's something stirring. A tune, a lyric, or both.

"Something in the water," she says to the empty street. "Something I drank last night." It's not a good line, but at least she's thinking that way. Letting the words just flow.

CHAPTER 9

The phone wakes her, and she grabs for it, fumbling in the dark. The voice—crying, breathless. It's Aimee. She's hysterical, sobbing so hard she can't talk.

Gal's own throat is dry, and she gasps for air, for sound, as she sits up to answer.

It's not Aimee, of course. Aimee's dead, but she'd been dreaming of her friend, her bandmate. A hazy nightmare of Aimee drunk and crazy. Heaving in an alley, as Gal held her hair back, as she wiped her friend's sweaty brow with her bare palm.

In the dream, Aimee is babbling. Words choked out between spasms, making her cough so much, Gal just wants her to be quiet. To calm down. That drunk, you can aspirate. Give yourself pneumonia, or so she's heard. But dream Aimee is desperate to get the words out. The words as important as the sick that spews once again to splash at their feet. Something about control, about an attack, that even as she was sleeping struck Gal as familiar, as important in that horrible nightmare way. Clinging to her, like the stench of vomit, even as she wakes fully and realizes that it's morning, and that it's not Aimee on the phone. It's Camille.

"It's Dad." The younger woman is sobbing in earnest now. Her

45

voice so tight and scared that Gal has a moment of panic herself. Thinks suicide or his heart. They're not that young anymore. The lives they've led. "You've got to help."

"Call 9-1-1." She finds her voice, but Camille is talking over her.

"No—I—they took him. He's—it was the police. I think he's been arrested," she says. And Gal is fully awake.

"Arrested?" The word doesn't make sense. "For what?"

"I don't know." The question cuts through Camille's agitation. Calms her. Now she just sounds miserable. "They asked him to go with them. They took him away in a police car. I don't think—I don't know—but I don't think he was surprised."

A dozen thoughts crowd through Gal's head. A hundred memories. Drugs, sure. Some petty vandalism. That time they saw a sign for Dick Street and simply couldn't resist. "Where'd they take him?"

"Brighton, they told me. I think, anyway. It all happened so fast."

"I'm coming over." She doesn't have much, but she'll figure it out. Bail. The benefit proceeds.

"No, I'm going over to the police station. I just…I didn't know who else to call."

"You did the right thing." Phone tucked against her shoulder, she's already pulling her jeans on. Looking around for her shirt. "I'll meet you there."

She hasn't showered. She's only finger combed her hair, and the looks that greet her let her know they've noticed. Three cops, all male, and the temptation to tell them off is so strong she has to bite her tongue. This isn't about her. Not about those strait-laced sexists either. She marches up to the fat one, ready to take him on.

"Gal!" At the sound of her name, she turns. Camille, wild-eyed and tearful, is running toward her. Gal reaches out to embrace her, but the slender brunette only takes her hands in her own and pulls her away from the cops.

"I can't find out anything." Her brows, so like Aimee's, bunch up. "They won't tell me anything. Only that he's being held for arraignment."

Gal feels her jaw clench. Cops. "What are the charges?"

"I'm not sure." Camille looks back over her shoulder at the uniformed men, all three busy pretending they're not listening. "Something about a fight? After the show?"

T.K. A chill runs over Gal and she swallows hard, her mouth gone suddenly dry. The panic of a trapped animal. "Bail," she manages the word, and her brain begins to work again. "There must be—does he have a lawyer?"

Camille shakes her head. "I don't know. I don't know anything." Her voice rising and getting tighter.

"No, please, don't worry." The girl's distress centers her, and Gal manages a smile. "He must have—someone must have helped him with your mother, her estate."

A flash of pain on the young woman's face. Or, no, confusion. It's almost more than Gal can bear. "Please," she squeezes Camille's hands. "Don't worry. I'll go back to the apartment. I'm sure there's something in his files. He didn't have his phone, did he?"

Those brows again, but then the girl shakes her head. "No, I don't think so."

"Okay, if I can't find anything else, I'll just grab that and bring it back. Unless," she pauses, unsure of herself, "you don't want to go with me, do you?"

"No." More certain this time. "I want to stay here."

"'Kay, then." Gal studies her face. "I'll be back as soon as I can."

She's dying to be gone. To get away. And, in truth, Camille seems more focused now. She knows she's not alone, Gal figures. She knows that there's a plan. What that plan is, Gal isn't sure, and as she drives, more slowly this time, back to the apartment, she goes over the benefit papers in her mind. Surely there was a lawyer involved in there somewhere. Surely someone had to sign off, legally, on the whole thing.

She finds a space not two blocks away, and even as she's parking, she's thinking through the contracts. Vendors, the releases. Everything she sorted on that dining room table.

It's all been moved, she sees when she lets herself in. The piles of papers now neat stacks on the sideboard, tile trivets weighing them down. Gal looks around, disoriented for a moment, when a memory, as strong as the smell of frying onions, hits her. Of course, Camille made dinner. Father and daughter sat down to eat. And just as quickly, she remembers: Walter was in his office most of the day, even when she came back with that extra sub.

Fighting off a slight sense of trespass, she opens the door to Walter's office, the office he reclaimed. It's surprisingly tidy. Or, she realizes, chuckling, maybe not so surprising. Walter's always been neat. The one who took care of everything—the band, their gear. Taking over when they weren't on tour, when they were off the label's time clock. Back at home. A wave of grief, warm and awful all at once, takes her, and her eyes fill up with tears. Aimee. Damn, they had some fun. But this is not the time to reminisce.

She hits the light and walks up to the desk. It's as neat as the rest of the room, and for a moment, she wonders if Camille has been in here. But no, the young woman she left at the police station was too distraught to have arranged everything just so. Instead of trivets, a brass hippo holds down one tidy pile. The one beside it, a handmade ashtray, lumpy and pink. Camille's work, Gal realizes with a start, and for a moment, she flashes back. Aimee had never talked about having kids. Gal had no idea she'd want to be a mother.

Walter, though, he took to it right away. Maybe she'd never really known the man.

Pulling out the chair, she sits and looks around. Wonders which drawer to start with first. Which pile. There's no phone, nothing obvious. No Rolodex like in the old movies, where she could look up "lawyer" and find out who to call. And then she realizes what she's seeing. The stack on her left, the one with the hippo, is all insurance policies. The car, the condo. Camille's health insurance, still under Walter's name. To her right, under the ashtray, are bank statements. And on top of those, a list in the neat, block handwriting she came to know so well. Only this time, it's not a tour itinerary, the name of a venue or a city. Not even a setlist, which Walter did as often as not, especially on those crazy nights when the party had started early. No, this is a list of passwords and the accounts they open. And it hits her. Walter expected this, or at least he expected something was going to happen. While she'd been working in the dining room, Walter had been in here, putting his affairs in order.

CHAPTER 10

Her head is spinning with the implications, but there's no time to sort them out. Besides, right there, on top of the passwords, is a Post-it with a name and a number. Albert Gallegio, it says, lawyer. That as much as anything drives home Gal's initial impression, but even as she snatches it up, she begins to argue with herself. The man is settling up his ex-wife's affairs, she thinks as she locks the apartment door behind her. He's a parent. He owns property.

As she drives back to the station, she can't stop poking holes in her own argument. She owns property, too, an acre with a house big enough for a family of six. Yeah, she talked to a lawyer at some point. She remembers the closing. The endless papers she needed to sign, though that memory kind of runs together with the label contracts and the publishing. She certainly didn't keep the lawyer's number around. She'd be hard pressed to remember his name.

By the time she gets back to the cop shop, she doesn't know what to think. Only that she has the contact info for a lawyer and that Aimee's daughter needs her.

"They still won't let me see him." Her eyes as big as Aimee's, the tears and fright Gal sees there bringing back that nightmare. "Nobody's telling me anything."

"I found a name." Gal explains, pulling the sticky note out of her pocket. "Do you want me to call him?"

"No." Camille reaches for the paper, her mouth set firm now that she has something to focus on. She looks so much like her mother that Gal is almost thrown. "I'll do it. I should be the one. But thanks."

Gal hesitates, wondering what to do next. But Camille is ahead of her.

"I called Linda," she says, and Gal remembers the roommate, the one who took the sheets. "She's driving over. I really appreciate what you've done."

But you don't have to stay. Gal forces a smile. Of course the girl wants her friend. Someone she knows rather than her dead mother's old bandmate, a remnant of the past who's been absent for much of her life.

"I'm glad," she says, a little hurt. A little relieved. "And, you know, if you need anything…" She leaves it open and another thought occurs. "I'll keep on with the paperwork from the concert. Maybe I'll even have that done before your dad gets out."

The smile Camille gives her looks more natural this time, and Gal feels herself beaming back. This really is Aimee's daughter. If only she could do more.

As if for penance, she returns to Walter's place. To the stacks of paper on the sideboard. She's gotten better at this kind of thing now that she's on her own. In a way, it brings her back. Those early days, before the label took over, sending in a road crew that packaged them up and shipped them from city to city as if they were produce or a bag of traveling cats.

Maybe they were, she chuckles at the thought, pulling another pile of receipts toward her. Flipping the yellow legal pad to a blank page. The way they were fighting by the end, they certainly weren't human. Gal sighs as she remembers. Thinks of the time lost with Lina and Mimi, crazy Mimi who took over her bass lines. Rock steady, no matter how stoned, falling in line behind Britta on drums... Aimee was gone by then. She'd left the band not long after that first triumphant homecoming.

Sometimes, Gal thinks, the loss of Aimee was what pushed her over the edge. She was tight with the girls, at least at first, and partying with Mimi was a blast. But she and Aimee, they were sisters. The trouble twins, someone had named them—Walter, maybe? Back before those two hooked up, when he was just the roadie. Road manager, if they'd thought to call him that, before the tour became a way of life. Before the label took control. She and Aimee both drank too much back then, but they were younger, too. They could handle it, and they looked out for each other. Gal thinks back on her dream. A memory? Yeah, probably, though as she recalls things, it was usually Aimee taking care of her, rather than vice versa.

Gal puts her pencil down. Closes her eyes and takes a breath. It's a technique Russ has taught her. It helps with the not drinking, though he doesn't say that. Centering, he says. One of those new age-y things that makes her so certain they're not going to last.

Now, though, it works. One deep breath, and then another. Thinking about her friend who died and how they used to be.

"What's the matter?" She remembers one of those first gigs. A pub in Cambridge. A Tuesday night. She and Aimee had been playing together a few months. That was when Dru and Shira were still in the band.

"Nothing." Aimee loading out. And, because she'd already hefted her own amp into the van, Gal went to help her. Besides, she knew it wasn't nothing. Something about the set of her drummer's mouth, as tight as if Shira had run away with the tempo again.

"You just seemed so uncomfortable, you know?" Aimee handed her the cymbal bag, patched with duct tape and stickers from other bands. "Like those weren't even your songs."

"The sound sucked." Gal climbed into the van. "How could I relax when that feedback started up, like, every time I breathed?"

She was making excuses, and they both knew it.

"I just wasn't feeling it." It was easier to confess when she was looking away.

Aimee didn't say anything, and when Gal turned back, ready to take the next bag, she searched her friend's face for understanding.

"You know?" she said at last.

Aimee only shrugged. "I guess," she said. "Just…we sounded so good on Sunday."

She was right, Gal knew. The band had started to gel, even with Shira's lousy time, and they'd begun to come up with some decent originals. Yeah, they weren't *that* original—Gal knew you could hear the Nuggets tracks she'd patterned each one on—but they had them down. And Aimee knew how to play off them. Make them electric, alive, with the beat. They had potential.

Sure, they'd gotten the gig because they knew the guy handling booking. Knew him—and bought him drinks for three nights running at three different clubs. He had really liked their tape, too. Gal could tell. But the way they had just sounded? The way *she* had sounded, her singing hesitant and her bass line stuttering behind the beat? They'd be lucky to get another Tuesday.

That Thursday, back in the practice space, she'd worked them liked a demon, going over and over the set. By Sunday's practice, she thought they had it down; the tension, the uncertainty all laid to rest by the repetition. She knew their songs cold. Almost too well, she let herself worry. Any more practice and her delivery would end up being rote. But she'd wanted to be sure her fingers didn't get tangled up again, her lyrics choking in her throat. They were getting another shot. Another Tuesday, playing for the door. It wasn't like there was a lot of competition.

"Let's switch it up some," Aimee, loading in the next week, had suggested. "Just to keep it fun."

Only a guffaw from Shira had let Gal know the drummer was joking. Was, perhaps, dealing with her own butterflies before the set. There were people in the club that night. Friends of friends, mostly, the same ones who had come out the week before. But there were a few faces Gal didn't recognize. One, a rangy guy with a lopsided grin on his freckled face, offered to help as Gal reared back to raise her amp up onto the riser that served as a small stage.

"I've got it. Thanks." She'd been a bit breathless, but really, once she had it off the ground, it was easier to do it herself.

"Suit yourself." That grin. "If you want to throw your back out. Let me."

He sidled up next to her and reached around the cabinet, pulling it free. A moment later, it was up on the riser. "Here?" He had it stage left, where she liked it.

"Yeah, thanks." She followed, case in hand.

"I used to roadie for the Underdogs." He turned, wiping his hands on his jeans. "We were hanging out down the hall, in space 260. Thought we'd check you out."

The new faces—other musicians. Well, that was good.

"Thanks, again." She held out her hand. "Gal," she said.

"T.K."

"You feel like giving me a hand too?" Shira had come up behind her. She didn't use half of what that Marshall could give, but Gal knew she liked the look of it.

"A Marshall? Sure." The way he named it. Gal had a quick gut take that the freckled newcomer had sussed out Shira's weakness. Still, it didn't hurt to have someone helping—not just with the equipment, but with the prima donna guitarist, too. "Here, let me."

"What's the deal?" Aimee, who had already begun to campaign for replacing Shira, came over as the raw-boned man and the guitarist leaned in, laughing.

"He's with the Underdogs. You know, down the hall." Gal watched the two. This T.K. sure had gotten Shira's number fast. "He's a roadie."

"Well, hell." Aimee turned back to her kit. "If he wants to roadie for us, I'd give him a cut."

Gal eyed the crowd, such as it was. "We'll be lucky if we get twenty-five bucks."

"And beer." Aimee looked up as she fixed her kick drum in place. "Don't forget we drink free."

T.K. seemed to know the drill. "Here you go." Once they'd done their rudimentary soundcheck—once the sound guy had shown up—he'd gotten them a round, five plastic cups all bunched together in those big hands.

"It's warm." Gal had taken a sip and turned away. Never a huge drinker, the cheap beer tasted bitter and thin. Her mouth was dry enough without it.

"Come on." Aimee had laughed. "You need a little lubrication if you're going to get up and sing."

"I'll be fine." Gal had put her cup down. "Besides, the bartender wants us to go on."

It was an excuse. The bartender didn't seem to care if they played at all. But Gal was sick of waiting. Tired of worrying if, in fact, tonight she would be able to sing and play without that horrible brain freeze, as Aimee had dubbed it. Just the thought of how her mind had gone blank the week before was enough to get her heart racing. She knew these songs. Hell, she'd written most of them. And she'd worked for hours, on her own as well as with the band, to make sure she could play and sing without one screwing up the other. Yeah, she wrote simple bass lines. This was rock and roll. The point was, she had rehearsed them enough, she should be able to find the notes without thinking. Hit the fills, the breaks, by muscle memory. And the lyrics? They were her words. Her thoughts. There was no way she would look out from the stage and forget them all again. It wasn't like there was even anyone here. Fifteen people, four of whom she knew, including, now, that one roadie wannabe, T.K., from down the hall. Who now stood before her, holding up a shot glass.

"Drink up." He handed her the glass, filled to the brim with a caramel-colored liquid. "You look like you could use a little courage."

"I'm fine." Even as she said it, she saw him smile. So her fear was that obvious. Her reluctance. She grabbed the glass and tossed it down, doing her best to suppress the cough that followed. That made him throw his head back with a laugh, and between the laugh and the way his eyebrows had shot up, Gal knew she'd scored some points.

"Gal…" Aimee, calling her to the stage.

"Knock 'em dead," T.K. said, taking the glass from her.

The first song was the hardest. Something about hearing her own voice over the PA. Or maybe it was the way the guys from down the hall, that roadie and his friends, had looked up at her as she started to sing. But the practice paid off. Even when she couldn't think, her hands found the notes, and if she screwed up the first verse, nobody knew except her bandmates. If anything, their reaction made her better. Seeing Shira roll her eyes got her angry, and the heat seemed to melt the freezing fear. Gal almost walked off during Shira's solo, wanting the tall brunette to feel her disrespect.

T.K. was waiting beside the riser, another shot in his hand, as she turned away from Shira and her tricks. He held the short glass up to her, and she downed the liquid amber while Aimee counted down the next number. She felt looser then, the fear dissolved in the rush of warmth; the music inside her starting to glow. As she walked back to the mic, she looked out now on fans. Adoring faces, each one basking in her reflected light, and she marveled at how she could ever have been afraid.

CHAPTER 11

Another world, a lifetime ago. She opens her eyes to the papers before her: hospital bills, a few marked paid. The donation receipt for the wheelchair. A letter from the hospice, polite but routine. Gal's a writer, of a sort; she recognizes the rhythms of someone used to hitting their beats. Kind but a bit formulaic in its expression of sympathy, the conclusion a little rote, tying up two-thirds down the page, like a three-minute song designed for radio play.

Not that her own writing's much better, these days. No, she stops herself, hands flat on the desk. She's not even this good. Sobriety calls for honesty, and while she's not a twelve-stepper, she accepts the basic principles.

She can't do it, not like she used to, pulling something out of herself she didn't even know was in there. Working a line into a hook, the words fitting the music that just kept coming. Whether that was because the booze gave her something or, more likely, because the years of hard living took it away, she may never know. She can recognize a cliché, a worn set of changes designed as an earworm. But she can't even do those anymore. And the brilliance?

Another breath, a deep inhale. That's what Russ would never understand. It was magic, in its way. Being up there, on stage. Not just the crowd—though, yeah, to have them staring, wanting, at her mercy was a rush like no other. More than that it was the music itself. Like lava flowing through her. Relentless. Hot.

And out of control? Sure. Her music shaped who she was on stage and off, but to feel that power again? She'd give up a lot to get that back. All of it, maybe. If she could. She rubs her thumb over the F clef on her wrist. A reminder, faded now, of what she had. The cost. Russ has caught her, a few times, fooling around with her guitar. "Play me something," he says, if he's in the mood. The last time—last week, before she came down here—he actually lay at her feet, his legs crossed at the ankle, and his head resting on his hands.

"I don't usually play lullabies." She had done her best to growl. The man was cute, and he knew it. She needed to keep him in his place.

"Play me something new." He'd looked up at her, his voice teasing.

She's tried. He probably didn't know, but she'd been trying for weeks by then. "Blues for Aimee," she'd been thinking of calling it. Playing around with a simple melody since she'd gotten the news. The hook wasn't bad. As far as she could tell, it wasn't something she'd used before, nor cribbed from a half-remembered favorite on the radio. But it wasn't what she wanted, what she almost half heard in the back of her mind, mournful, but full of life. A tribute she could bring to the benefit. A gift for Walter and for Camille that would have her joy, but also anger. Something raw and real.

"Fuck off." She'd kicked at Russ and stood. "I've got to pack."

Aimee had walked away, just like that. Around her, in the dead woman's apartment, Gal sees the evidence of her next life, the one she chose. Photos of Camille and her parents. Camille at her high school graduation, a little chubbier than she is now. Her grin—

Aimee's grin—the same.

Gal picks up the one of Camille with Walter and Aimee and studies it, looking for traces of her old friend in her daughter. For traces of Walter. Camille takes after her mother, for sure. Walter less so. "She's lucky that way." Gal can still hear Aimee joking, ribbing her husband of, what, twenty years? It was a barbless jibe, a comfortable tease. Nobody could doubt the bond between the three of them, not then, not even after the split, no matter how much Walter might worry. Looking at the photo, Gal can only shake her head. How could so much have happened since Aimee left the band? An entire life, and not just Camille's.

Another breath, deep and calming. It wasn't like Gal hasn't done things. Aimee left just as they were on the brink. "Hold Me Down" was charting, and the label was throwing money at them. Well, kind of. It wasn't until she got out, got clean, that Gal realized how the circuit actually worked. You didn't get paid, not really. It was all their own money, everything from the per diem to the crew. They spent until they went into hock, and yet somehow they didn't have control over any of it.

Shit, she was lucky. She did get out, and thanks to her publishing rights, she had enough to buy her place. To keep from having to get a day job or join some sad oldies tour. And it wasn't like being in a band was the only way to get into debt. The pile of paperwork in front of her is proof of that.

She replaces the photo and positions it with care, enjoying the act. The image of her old friend. She's done what she can in here, and she needs to get back to the concert accounts. She tells herself that it's a way of visiting, of remembering, and it hits her. That must be why Walter had everything out, so neat and right at hand. He was going over their life together, remembering, and only her latent paranoia had made her see it as something different. Something suspicious. Russ would have a field day.

Getting his affairs in order. Well, yeah, of course. Like a responsible father does when the mother of his only child has died.

Gal stands and looks once more at the desk. At least she was able to find the attorney's name and number for Camille. A small but maybe useful task, fitting for an honorary aunt who was never around much anyway.

She's back at the dining room table, almost done with the receipts. She's making a note about the t-shirt vendor—they need to order more, in the larger sizes—when Camille bursts in, dropping her bag on the floor.

"Hey." Gal looks up. Camille, but Walter isn't with her. "Is there any news?"

Even as she asks, the doubt grows. She shouldn't be here. This isn't her home. "I'm almost done here," she says, half in apology. "Have you had anything to eat? Did Linda get here?"

If the girl wants her to leave, she'll take the vendor's info with her. She can finish this up at her motel.

Camille only shakes her head, though at which question, Gal can't tell. Her eyes are wide and her mouth slack with what could be exhaustion. Or no, Gal thinks, her own chest tightening up with fear. "Camille, what is it?"

"It's Dad." Camille leans forward and Gal rises, ready to take the girl, Aimee's daughter, in her arms. "He's acting crazy. I don't know what's going on."

Gal nods, a crisis she can understand. "He's grieving, honey. Grief comes in waves."

"No." Camille shakes her off. Picks her coat off the floor and hangs it on the hook on the second try. "It's not—I called the lawyer."

Gal waits. Gives the girl her space. Money, she thinks. Or that friend, the church-y one. Gal knows the type from rehab and how judgmental they can be.

"Dad won't talk to him." Camille's voice is soft, thick with tears. Or maybe anger, the thought hits Gal. "He could, I checked, but he won't." The lawyer, then, not the friend. "He says he told Dad what was going to happen, a hearing and then bail, and if they have to, a trial. But he says all Dad wants is some time to settle up. That he doesn't want to defend himself. That he wants to confess. To murder."

CHAPTER 12

Walter was an asshole. The kind of jerk who went around picking up empties and pointing out the time, at least by the first tour, when he'd become a regular part of the band. T.K. brought him around the first time—a sidekick, shorter and a bit pudgy, even then. They'd landed a slot at the Channel, middle set with no real soundcheck, and T.K. said he could use an extra hand.

"We only have, like, twenty minutes to set up," he'd said by way of an explanation. "This way, we'll have time for a mic check. Maybe even a run through."

Aimee had given him her look, the scary one, at that "we." T.K. was their roadie, that was it. Gal didn't let on that she'd heard him styling himself their manager. As long as he carried her amp. But T.K. didn't see it, or he wasn't fazed, not by then. "Walter's cool," he'd said. "He doesn't drink much."

Didn't talk much either, except to T.K., and regardless of his buddy's promise, he consumed as much as any of them, getting quieter as he got soused. And then, oddly neat. Gal can still picture him, stumbling as he bent to retrieve an empty bottle. Righting himself, and then ever so carefully picking up another.

"Thanks, Grandpa." Shira had given him the nickname, and it

stuck. Grandpa and T.K. became a fixture. The road crew, such as it was, though by the time they were actually touring, T.K. was gone. T.K., and Shira, too. Those first few months, though, it had been nice. Not only having the two men to do the loading and unloading, but the feeling that they had a crew. That they were legit.

Aimee had called bullshit on that from the start. "We don't need them, you know."

"Define 'need.'" Late Sunday, after practice, she and Aimee had gone back to her place with takeout Chinese and a quarter ounce. Another thing T.K. was good for. "Do you really want to hump your kit around?"

"Shira thinks T.K.'s creepy." A non-answer if ever there was one. Aimee crashed on the sofa and lit the joint.

"You just want to get rid of her." Gal took a hit, holding it for as long as she could. "Admit it." She coughed.

Aimee shrugged as she inhaled. They'd been talking about this for a while now. Aimee had even brought in her friend, Lina, to play with them. A Wednesday, early, usually not their night, but they'd heard the Gotcha weren't going to be using the space. Neither of them had called it a tryout, but that's what it was. Lina jamming with them, and then running through their usual set list with Gal and Aimee joining in. She was good, too. Aimee handed the joint back, her brows raised even as the smoke leaked from her nostrils.

"Okay," Gal said at last, responding to the question in Aimee's eyes. "I do, too."

The problem wasn't only Shira, of course. Even though Gal had relaxed and started enjoying herself, the band was still missing something. Aimee had brought it up a few weeks earlier, cornering Gal one of those nights when the two of them had sat up till dawn, shooting the shit.

"We're pretty good," said Aimee, lying on her back on the rug, her feet up on the sofa, where Gal was sprawled. "A pretty good bar band."

"Fuck you." Gal had swatted her feet. "We're great. Well, we will be great."

"We could be." Aimee lit a cigarette and watched the smoke curl. They'd finished the joint by then and hit a mellow place, both comfortable and drifting in their own thoughts. "With the right guitarist."

"Guitarist?" Gal lay back, intrigued. Relieved, too, if she let herself admit it. For a few moments there, she had thought Aimee was going to call her out as the weak link. The lingering stage fright, the songs that came out stilted, like she was still some mousy high school girl.

"Uh-huh." Aimee seemed to see something in the smoke, so Gal let her go on. Let her talk her into trying out Lina. What her old friend—they'd been in some college band together—could do.

"I want to sound raw," Gal finally broke in. She was stoned, and the words spilled out like a confession. "Direct. Like I opened a vein…"

She stopped, the words sounding overly dramatic even to her. Which was the problem. All her songs felt derivative, as if she were writing about someone else's experience. "I want to sound authentic." It was as close as she'd come yet to confessing to her friend and drummer.

"A good guitarist would help."

Aimee was right, though neither understood just how much trouble the switch would make. Shira had friends, and once they'd told her she was out, they stopped coming to the gigs, or when they did, they made trouble. At clubs like Chad's, the bouncer didn't care much if someone threw a beer.

That trouble, as much as anything, was why they booked their first tour. It helped that Lina knew people. She'd lived in D.C. for a year, and because of her they got a middle set at the Ten-Thirty that served as a launching pad.

That was still to come, though. That night, Lina, the tour, and all that came after was just smoke, looping lazily over Aimee's head. Twisting, like the problem of Shira and her complaints. Whining about the scene.

"What's Shira got against T.K.?" Gal getting up finally to clear the rice bowls, the sticky spoons. "I thought they had a thing."

A shrug as Aimee took a hit. "You ever think about what's in it for them? T.K. and Walter, I mean, lugging our shit?"

"Glamour and excitement?" Gal placed the bowls in the sink and rolled another joint. "Free beer?"

It was a few months later, after that first tour, that Walter and Aimee had hooked up.

"I fucked Grandpa." Aimee, laughing, on the phone.

"Wait…Walter?" To Gal, it was an impossibility. Like fucking an amp.

"Yeah, I was shitfaced, I guess."

At practice, later that day, they hadn't talked about it. Gal figured Aimee had moved on, her confession a dismissal. Over and done. Or not done, apparently, as they hooked up again and the news got out. Aimee, Gal figured. Walter was too old-school to brag, and besides, he never talked much anyway, whereas Aimee might toss it out. Trying for a laugh. What she didn't realize, what none of them did, was that even in their libertine world there were some rules.

"T.K.'s pissed." Word had gotten back to her. A bar back's aside. A word to the wise. Their first roadie wasn't with the band anymore. He and Walter still hung out, though, and Gal couldn't think of a good reason for him not to hang backstage, not when so many other friends were always in and out. Better to give Aimee a heads-up. They were all buddies, basically. Everything was cool.

"He's just pissed that Walter has the gig now." Aimee had been nonchalant. She was enjoying this; Gal saw it plain as day. Should have seen more, she realized, in her friend's plain-spoken words.

"Some gig." Gal's mood suddenly going dark. "All the work you can handle, no money, and the beer is usually crap."

CHAPTER 13

"You're being an asshole. You know that, don't you?" Gal throws that out as a rhetorical. The man sitting beside her as she drives hasn't answered any of her other questions. She has no reason to think he'll start now.

To her surprise, Walter nods, although he still doesn't turn to face her. The city traffic demands her attention, but out of the corner of her eye she sees his stone face, staring straight ahead.

"I mean, if you're in some weird grief spiral, I get it." Gal steals another glance at her passenger. Answering his call, she met him outside the lockup not fifteen minutes earlier, somewhat the worse for a night in jail. "But you've got a daughter, you know. And you're putting her through hell."

"I know." His voice so soft that if she hadn't turned the radio off, she wouldn't have heard him. A quick look confirms that he's still fixated on the bumper of the car ahead. If there's anything else, it's nothing she can see.

"I don't understand." Gal isn't the kind to admit defeat. She is, however, confused. "I mean, I get that you didn't want Camille picking you up. Though if you think she's going to go back to school and make like nothing's happening just because you're out on bail, you don't know your own daughter."

That gets him. Walter turns on her with a growl. "Leave Camille out of this."

"You don't get it." That glare almost shakes her, but she's up for the fight. "It's not up to me. You're the one who's left your daughter out, left her high and dry." She swallows. Turns back to the traffic. Rush hour, more than twenty-four hours after Camille's tearful call, and she'd had to wait over an hour before Walter was released post-arraignment and allowed to come home. "Maybe you think you're saving her some kind of bother, not defending yourself." The lawyer had entered the standard not guilty plea, she had gathered, making bail an option. Setting Walter, at least temporarily, free. "Or, I don't know, maybe you think your defense will eat up all your money."

She dares another glance. He's still staring straight ahead, his mouth set hard.

"Is that it?" She plays the idea out in her own head. Envisions a scenario she can work through. It's a favorite technique of hers. A way to avoid being taken by surprise. "Are you worried about Camille's college fund? That she'll have to take another loan or a full-time job? Because you know we could do another benefit—"

"It's not the money." A bark. Pride, Gal figures.

"I mean, I enjoyed playing again. The old songs." Not the old players. She doesn't add that. Better to let the bad blood go. But even as she speaks, she remembers that strange memory lapse. That slip. When she had seen—yes, it had been—T.K. "We could do it again." Her voice suddenly hoarse.

"It's not the money." Sad now, rather than angry, and he looks down at his hands, as if the answer lies in those big, callused palms. Maybe it does. Gal doesn't know the details. Camille had been too upset to answer any but the most rudimentary questions, and Gal doubted the girl knew exactly what her father had been accused of. Living upstate, she'd gotten out of the habit of following the headlines, though in her motel room she had caught an update on T.K.'s death on the nightly news. A possible homicide, they were calling it—a man found "savagely beaten" in an alley. His head hit repeatedly against the asphalt. Hyperbole, she assumed. Even if… Walter might be an asshole, but he was not savage.

Not violent either. She shakes her head to clear it, the idea beyond the pale. She had seen him with his infant daughter, hours after her birth. He had cradled Camille like he was born to be a father, the unplanned nature of Aimee's pregnancy and their hasty wedding all besides the point. Aimee had found a good one in Walter. "He's my refuge," she had told Gal. "My safe place."

"I never liked him." The sad man beside her says the words as if they explain everything, even as Gal puzzles them out. The lawyer? T.K.? As if not liking someone was reason enough to kill. "It wasn't about the money."

"Well, Jesus, Walter." They're at the condo. She pulls up next to a battered Mazda and parallel parks. Some things you never forget. "Then I really don't get it." He doesn't answer. "You've got to defend yourself, Walter. For Camille."

He turns and looks directly at her. His eyes, she would later think, are dead. Haunted, and not simply from a night in lockup. "Thanks for the ride," he says. He doesn't invite her in.

"I'll call you," she says to his back as he walks up to the building. She briefly thinks about following. Grilling him will be easier if she isn't driving. When she can back him up against a wall and put her questions to him face to face. But Camille is waiting for him. Waiting despite his request that she go back to school, that she leave everything to him. And as much as Gal wants to get to the bottom of this, she knows there's a line she shouldn't cross between a father and a daughter. Between family. At one point, Aimee had been family to Gal. She remembers her dream, a memory really—Aimee sobbing as she held her shoulders, as she held her hair. Those days were long gone, though, even before her best friend's death.

Aimee had chosen this man—and chosen to have their daughter together. She had left the band for him, to form a family. Gal didn't often question her own path, the men she had let slip by. The children she could have had with any one of a dozen lovers. At the time, it hadn't seemed a choice at all, her own conviction blazing hot.

These days, the fire has almost gone out. Yes, she had a taste of it again the other night, at the benefit. The rush of the music. Of the power. Something flowing from her, shaped by her wit and will. But go back on the road? On tour? No, she knows that life is over for her now. She knows what it did to her—what it could have done. She remembers Mimi, the day she got the news.

Besides, the magic's no longer there. The songs she writes, when she writes at all, are forced and distant. She's a better craftswoman than she was back in the day. She knows how to structure a bridge, the emotional tug a certain progression will evoke, and when to mix up the pattern to avoid sounding formulaic. But whatever spark she once had? That's gone out.

Walter opens the door of the building and walks in without looking back. Gal sits and watches, engine still running. In her mouth, the taste of ashes.

CHAPTER 14

That first tour, they didn't know what they were doing. Gal didn't want to admit they were on the run, but Aimee had called it what it was: "The great get-out-of-town tour." Of course, she only said this to Gal. During practice, she followed Gal's lead, talking about road experience. Doing something that would help them gel as a band. Honing their chops.

It was true they were kind of all over the place. Dru, their other guitarist, had dropped out even before they fired Shira, seemingly unable to commit to twice-a-week practices. Aimee had muttered about a growing drug habit, the onetime waif beginning to look junkie skinny. But Gal had heard those two were already forming their own band. And although Lina had some friends who could fill in on rhythm, Aimee had put her foot down. Power trio, she said. That was the thing. If only they could get it together.

"Guys, guys, hang on there." Gal wasn't sure when, exactly, she'd become the band's leader, but it fell to her to direct practice. Two nights a week, three if you counted the pub gig, and they still sounded like shit. "We've got, like, three different tempos going."

Aimee had opened her mouth to respond, tempo being her domain. Lina had rolled her eyes.

"Let's try that again." Gal, stepping up. She hadn't meant to implicate Aimee, even if she was the drummer. Then again, it had been Aimee who had wanted to boot Shira. "From the chorus?"

"Maybe we need to take a break." Aimee, making eye contact with Lina. "Take five."

"It would help if we had some gigs." Lina didn't look at Gal as she propped her guitar against her amp, rolling her shoulders in relief. Didn't matter. Gal knew—they all knew—that she had promised the newcomer a gigging band when she'd joined up. Connections in the Boston scene. Something that paid in more than beer.

Even as the newest member disappeared down the hallway, trailing a comment about a smoke and a piss, Aimee had stayed behind. The practice room, windowless and way too small, smelled already, and come summer the stench would be worse. Gal suspected the Gotcha of bringing food in despite all the signs forbidding it. She'd seen the dark shapes scurrying when she turned the light on, and that stink wasn't all sweat and ambition.

"I'm sorry for that crack about the tempo. It's just—"

"Hey, you were right." Aimee stood and stretched, her shirt hiking up to reveal the tattoo on her hip. "We sound like shit. No wonder we're not getting any dates."

"I've been trying." Gal blinked, her eyes suddenly filling with tears of frustration, though the stale and lingering smoke didn't help. "I've sent tapes to everybody. The Call, O'Reilly's. I tried calling again yesterday, Wednesday after five, like they tell you to. Nothing."

Aimee was shaking her head. "It's Shira and her crew. They're badmouthing us."

Gal slumped against her amp. "Yeah, I know. But it's not just that." She looked up. If she couldn't be honest with Aimee, what was the point? "We're just not that good," she said. "Our best song is basically 'I Wanna Be Your Dog' with a spare part added, and our next best is a twelve-bar blues. I thought, you know, with a better guitarist, but it doesn't make a difference if we don't have the songs."

"It's hard to write when we're spending all our time trying to get the set we have into shape," Aimee muttered, poking in her pockets. Looking for the cigarettes that, even then, she was trying to quit. "We need to get away."

"Take a break?" Gal froze, unsure of what Aimee was suggesting. Unsure if this was the end of her dreams, or what she really wanted.

"Get out of town." Aimee dug out her pack, tapped it on Gal's amp, as much for emphasis as to tamp down the tobacco, Gal suspected. "Let's get Lina to make some calls."

"But we're not ready. We're not even getting any offers to play here."

"Touring will make us ready." Aimee's face was grim. "New places, playing every night. If we can get a few weeks on the road, we'll come back as a band. Besides, it's not like you have anything else going on."

"No, that's true." The record store had cut back her hours again. More of Shira's sabotage, she figured. "Could you take some time off?"

Aimee had a real job, working as a staff assistant at the medical school. She shrugged, as if the security, the benefits meant nothing. "I've got so much vacation time stacked up, I'll lose half of it if I don't take it by the end of June. Besides, Lina might not stay if we don't do something."

Gal blinked. This was all coming fast. "She said that?"

A shake of the head. "Didn't have to. I know her, remember? She joined us because she thought we were going somewhere. Tuesdays at the pub don't qualify as 'somewhere.' Besides, didn't we bring her in at least in part for her contacts? I bet we could get a gig in New Haven, then Philly, and then down to D.C. I used to know some people on the Jersey Shore, too, though most of those places want cover bands, and I don't think a rewrite of 'Dog' is what they're thinking of." Aimee leaned forward, a hint of a smile playing on her wide mouth. "The Gulf Coast, maybe. All of those summer places. New Orleans. When things go South…"

"You guys have talked about this." So much for being the leader. So much for being in charge. Well, it was a relief. "You've been planning."

"Someone had to." Aimee shrugged it off. "Come on." She put the unlit cigarette between her lips. "I want to smoke this, not suck it. Let's sound out our sister in crime."

Sisters. Yeah, that's what they'd become. Playing in a strange town for a bunch of drunks who didn't know or care who they were did that for them. Forced them to come together faster than a thousand extra hours in the dank practice room ever could. The time in the van helped, too. Lina getting them all to laugh with her impersonations—she had an eye for details Gal never would have guessed at. And Aimee, the planner, chatting up some guy at the bar, making the calls, and getting them gigs all the way down to Huntsville.

"Show us your tits!" Yeah, they got used to that too. The catcalling, the taunts. You'd have thought that by that time—post-punk, post feminism, almost—the music world would have gotten past the schoolyard shit. In Boston, the comments were subtler at least.

"Girl band?" The look, like they were a pop gimmick.

"Rock band," she practiced saying, punching the word out like a downbeat. That usually shut them up

"You working on something?" Raleigh, some dive. They were crashing at the booker's apartment, and Aimee looked up from the futon, where Lina sprawled. Gal had thought they were both asleep. Knew she should join them—they'd spent most of the night before on the road. But something had kept her up, and she'd found her bass in the darkness, her fingers working silently over the strings. "A new song?" Aimee kept her voice low.

"I don't know." Already, the night was fading, Aimee's features becoming more distinct. She should be sleeping too. "Maybe."

"Good." Aimee flipped over, her head down by where Gal sat propped against the sofa. "You need to let go is all. Let it all out."

"Let it all out," Gal repeated. What she didn't say was why she only tried to write at times like these, the quiet of the night, when she might as well be alone. What if there was nothing to let out? "Maybe," she said. "I'll try."

But she didn't, not then. It took time, she tried to tell Aimee almost as often as she told herself. First, she had to get over her stage fright. Then they had to come together as a band. The songs, they'd follow. Only they didn't. She couldn't. Maybe they never would. The harder she tried, the more she heard her father in her head. It didn't matter that he was thousands of miles away. Too much of a bully before he got sick to let her do anything she wanted. Too mean with it when she finally dropped out, three credits shy of a degree, to even wish her luck. She left home in spite of his anger, not because of it, the echo to every song.

"Too much of a good girl to stand on your own," he said. "Too weak, too stupid," he meant. When he was right, she blamed herself.

At least by the time they'd come home, the rancor had died down. It helped that Shira's other band hadn't come together. That she was badmouthing Dru, this time, rather than Gal and Aimee, the rhythm guitarist's habit having finally pissed off even her old friend. The first night back, out for a drink after the last long drive,

Gal felt the difference. As soon as she walked up to the bar, Frankie was there, a shot and a beer before she could ask.

"Thanks." She slid a five across the bar. Things had been tense before the tour. Frankie was back soon after, topping off her whiskey and pouring one for himself. A Tuesday, and things were quiet. But when Kenny showed up and sat right by her, and Phil and Patti did too, she knew the tide had turned. She didn't have to say anything. Didn't have to ask. Another round, and the stories began to come out. Dru had grown even more unreliable. Spacey as a loon when she was around, and if Gal had a twinge of sympathy—she could remember the panic, the mind-blanking fear—she also felt a bit smug. But it wasn't just Dru. Shira had pissed people off, too, making demands of the bookers and soundmen that burned through the general goodwill in a hurry.

"Everybody was willing to give them a shot." Kenny, giving Gal a sidelong glance. Three weeks away, and the drama had run itself out.

"Frankie? How about a round." It was money she didn't have. A tip—a twenty this time—she couldn't afford. It was a celebration, she told herself. A homecoming with a gig and a party to follow the very next night. No, they didn't have any new songs, not yet. But once everyone heard how tight the band now sounded, the world was going to open up.

CHAPTER 15

Back in her motel room, Gal can't sleep. Her mind is buzzing, as if the morning's coffee has only now kicked in. But it's not caffeine that's keeping her awake, keeping her on her feet. Not the thirst for a drink or the easy camaraderie of the bar. It's confusion that has her on edge. Confusion, and fear for Walter. Decent Walter, acting like he's got no will to live.

"What does he mean, he's not going to contest the charges?" She tries to understand as she paces the small room. Formulates scenarios, none of which make sense, as she walks the narrow pass between the bed and the pasteboard desk and back again once more. "Why would he plead guilty?"

He knows the real killer and won't say so, she posits to the AC unit that runs beneath the window. Camille is somehow involved, she tells the front door with its mixed messages about checkout times and fire exits. But Walter isn't the type to cover up a murder, even if the killer was some kind of friend. Besides, in the life he and Aimee led, they didn't hang with a rough crowd. They were parents and working stiffs. He was a caregiver, in the end, despite those hands, the knuckles thick with callus. The scars she doesn't want to think about. And Camille? The girl was clearly as oblivious as Gal herself. She's been blindsided by her father's refusal to act.

Suicide. The word keeps coming back into Gal's mind, dark and desperate, as she turns once again, her socks sliding silently over the industrial carpet. Walter is in pain; that much is obvious. He's mourning. But why would he volunteer himself in this way? And that comment about his daughter? It isn't up to her to leave Camille out of it. Walter is the one who has dragged her down.

Suicide, she sounds out the word. There is no other explanation. No, she pivots, correcting herself. There is no explanation at all. None of this makes sense.

The uncertainty—the forced inaction—is maddening. She wants to lash out. To grab Walter and shake him. If she'd still been drinking, she might have done just that. Might not have left him to his misery and slunk back to this sterile little room. Might have been the better move, she tells herself, even as she recognizes her own lie. Anyway, she didn't, for better or for worse. And now, instead, she thrusts her hands in her pockets, aware of the need to push against something. To punch.

Only her knuckles don't meet the soft resistance of fabric, the cool solidity of coins, but something in between, and she remembers. She pulls the glossy rectangle out and examines it as the blood rushes to her face.

Shira's card, handed over as she said goodbye. An excuse to leave the party early, probably. Get out of jail free. The spark of an idea as Gal turns it over. If Shira has no love for Gal, she must still feel something for Aimee or Walter. She'd come to the benefit, hadn't she?

Shira, now a lawyer. Now happy, apparently, with the job, the kids, the husband who smiled as he came to claim her. Surely, that smooth, poised woman at the party doesn't still resent Gal for firing her all those years before. Not more than she cares for Walter or

Aimee or—she has kids—Camille. Besides, if she does still hold a grudge, maybe she'll enjoy the one-upmanship of being able to help. Of being the adult in the room.

Gal pulls the chair back from the flimsy desk and studies the card. It's too late to call, but she types in a text, quickly, before she can second-guess herself into inaction.

Hey Shira, she thumbs, wanting to make sure her long-ago bandmate knows the message is intentional, knows that Gal isn't making some late-night drunken mistake. *Wonder if we can talk.*

A row of dots spools out in response. Shira is awake. Or, no, Gal tells herself, she has some kind of autoreply. A professional form that references business hours and emergencies. The dots fade, then reappear. Then fade away once again.

She scrapes the chair back in frustration, hooking her elbow over its molded frame. She's about to leave the phone face down, when the dots appear again. An ellipsis in motion. Waiting.

Of course. To her surprise, the words appear with no tagline. No out-of-office message. *How about tomorrow?*

CHAPTER 16

That first gig after the tour was insane. They may have left town pariahs, but suddenly they were conquering heroes. Or heroines. Babes who could rock. At any rate, nobody yelled at them to take their shirts off. Nobody shouted, "Suck my dick!"

Not that it would have mattered. Three short weeks on the road had hardened them to this shit. Three weeks, and Gal had taught herself how to handle the hecklers. Had learned not to flinch when someone commented on her hair. Her nose. Aimee didn't get the comments. She was blonde, for starters, and the tats up her arm signaled a level of toughness that Gal could only aspire to. And Lina, tall, slender—like a tougher version of the woman she'd replaced—gave off the same take-no-shit vibe. Besides, Lina could shred.

But Gal, well, she was different. Out front when she sang, with only her old Gibson to shield her, she got the catcalls, the stares, almost as if they could see her weakness. The insecurity that had driven her there in the first place. Or maybe she just didn't measure up—too big, too ugly—to what a rock chick should be.

"What are you talking about?" Aimee had turned on her, a quizzical look bunching those dark brows together when she'd tried to explain. "You're a busty redhead. You're hot."

"Thanks." Gal had swallowed any further explanation lest it sound like fishing. Or worse. Had another drink. The buzz helped her stare down those assholes. Made her feel as tight and hot as she wanted to sound. And the practice paid off. The cracks had lessened as she perfected her own version of the dead-eye stare. By Charlotte, she was on top of her game, almost. Anyway, she knew Aimee had her back.

Back in Boston, she found herself quaking again, a familiar ache in her belly as they loaded in. This time, she didn't say anything. Not to Aimee, certainly not to Lina. They were laughing, raucous. Thrilled that the club was already humming as they pulled the van up to the door by the dumpster. This was a celebration. A homecoming for them all.

"Here, let me." Walter had been there, grabbing the drums. It was like old times, but better. Like they were royalty. Hands reached out, lifting her amp, and for a moment she held on. But no, this was home. T.K., too, the hard words forgotten now that they'd been away. Now that Shira was no longer around to bitch and moan. And what with all the help, they had time to socialize. To play the conquering heroes before the opener had even loaded in.

That's what they were. She wasn't going to show them anything else. Not anymore. The shots laid out on the bar—Southern Comfort to commemorate their travels—helped her shake off the jitters. Drown them, as someone called for another round. The floor vibrating as the Sock Dogs began to play.

"Looking good," a familiar voice—T.K.—yelled over the din, and she nodded, acknowledging the compliment. Three weeks in a van, eating peanut butter and convenience store hot dogs, had taken their toll. She felt bigger than usual. Bloated, and the acne on her chin didn't help.

But that was another Gal. The timid girl hiding behind the bass, and Gal felt the change, that magical transformation, as soon as the three of them took the stage. The Sock Dogs had finished their set before Gal had noticed, and it took Frankie grabbing her arm for her to turn and see that her bandmates were already assembling. Strat slung low, Lina was striking a pose, pelvis out. Aimee scowling at the crowd.

For a moment, the disconnect. The distance, the height too far. Then she was scrambling up there, reaching for her bass. A hand she recognized, a man she knew as she made the short trip from the floor to the stage. Three steps, and she was in a different world. She was a different person. A rocker goddess. A star. When she stared down at the crowd, she let herself feel her height. Her power. The heat of the lights playing up the warmth from that last shot.

One-two-three-crash! Lina, first, diving and swirling as the room responded. Gal let herself get caught up in the rush, and starting that eighth-note pulse, almost without thinking. Muscle memory after all those nights, feeling the rhythm rather than counting it. A heartbeat on her hips, low and steady. One of their earliest tunes, a reworking of "Free Zone," the song built on that unison staccato attack, winding up, up, and up.

One-two-three-crash! Aimee and Lina laying out the beat this time, kick drum, and Gal was there on an open A, with Lina's Strat bursting in for that final beat. Aimee and Gal kept the rhythm going, a straight-ahead punk four-four, as Lina took off, fuzz distortion making her solo so scratchy soft and wild.

Two songs in and the nerves were history. The remnant of another time. Another shot, lifted like an offering from the side of the stage, and Gal became positively feline, prowling back and forth. True, she nearly tripped as Aimee rolled through the fill in "Good Time." Goddamn stage monitor snagging her cord when she spun around, making her stumble toward the crowd. But Lina had caught her, stepping forward so Gal fell against her shoulder like they'd planned it, power chords stoking the throb, the pulse.

Next song, she was ready. No more nonsense, no patter, just the intro, Lina laying it out, all wiry and hard. Gal could hear her, even over Aimee, and, more than that, feel her, the way those jarring notes played against her bass line. And Aimee. God, that girl was good! Somewhere on the second week of the tour, she'd added that syncopation, plugging the beat double time and vital as a heartbeat. By the time it came to sing, Gal could feel it surging through her body. Like a pulse, it strengthened her. Fed her blood. And so, powered by the beat, by her sisters, she stood, stance wide and steady, staring out at the floor. Her song. Her crowd. Her band had come home.

Chapter 17

She wakes early the next morning, having slept badly. Walter, Aimee, and, yeah, the idea of talking to Shira again. Her former bandmate had suggested they grab breakfast near her office, naming a onetime diner that had been refurbished to cater to the financial crowd, and Gal gets there early, unsure of what the traffic would be like before opting for the T.

Taking a breath, she checks herself out in the window. The woman who looks back is trim, if weathered. Not drinking has helped her with her weight, which ballooned while she was in rehab. Too much boredom, hospital meals, and no more access to blow. She should feel good. Fit and healthy, at least compared to the last time they hung out. Still, she cowers like a kid as she slides into a booth. A kid or a tourist, unsure of the turf. This area had been warehouses, back in the day. Artist squats and cooperatives by the time she had left.

"Coffee." She takes a seat facing the door, and to her relief recognizes Shira when she walks in. Her old bandmate sees her and comes right over, a half smile on her carefully made-up face. "Thanks for meeting me," Gal says.

"No problem." Shira turns and orders a cappuccino while Gal

sips her own dark roast. "I'm glad you got in touch," she says. "I've been wanting to talk, but I wasn't sure. Different worlds, and all."

She makes a gesture, like she's shooing a fly, and just like that the tension is gone.

"Please." Gal almost chuckles with relief. "I'm the one who's grateful. I mean, I wasn't the most together, back in those days. But I really could use some advice."

Shira takes a breath, and they both wait as the server sets her mug before her.

"I don't even know the rules, the etiquette," Gal begins again. She sees Shira gather herself, about to explain the boundaries. Or back out, she fears. Make some polite excuse about not offering legal advice to a friend because of ethics or billing or something Gal never had to consider, and so she dives right in. "Did you hear about T.K.? He was found behind the Ballroom. He's—he was killed."

Shira's face is blank. Has she really forgotten? But no, it's coming back. Gal can see the memories, like a shadow passing over. "T.K.'s dead?" The lawyer's voice is thoughtful, her face unreadable. "That must have been a shock."

Gal waits for more. For the grief, the horror, but Shira has fallen silent. It has been years, Gal reminds herself. A lifetime ago.

"It's Walter I'm really worried about," she says finally, taking her cue from the other woman to move on, to keep calm. "He's been arrested and, well, I don't know the details. But I spoke with Camille, and she's freaked out. She says Walter doesn't want to defend himself."

Shira opens her mouth and then closes it, and Gal feels the weight of their history as she waits for the other woman to speak. It isn't friendship or concern, she thinks. Shira is expecting an apology. An explanation after all these years.

"I'm sorry." She stumbles over the words, so long in coming.

"You weren't—you didn't come here for that."

"No, please." Shira reaches across the table to take her hand, like you'd calm a shying animal. There's no sign of a guitarist's calluses under the careful manicure, but her touch is gentle. Warm. "I knew you wanted to talk, but I thought that maybe… No, really, it doesn't matter. Please, tell me what's going on with Walter."

Relief, like a cool breeze on a hot night. "It's crazy." Suddenly, Gal can breathe. She outlines the situation for Shira: the arrest, the unwillingness to defend himself. The strange defensiveness when she pushed. "I don't know if he's acting out in some way." She doesn't want to say "suicidal." She wets her lips. "You know, because of Aimee."

"Because of Aimee." Shira's voice is flat. She's watching Gal, watching her eyes, and Gal remembers again that this woman is a lawyer. "And you're sure it was T.K.? Was he at the show?"

"Yeah." She chuckles to hide her nerves. She doesn't want to look down. "You remember him, don't you? He used to roadie for us back then." She wants to say, "back in the beginning," but she stops herself. The beginning was all Shira had with the band. Those early days.

"I remember." The elegant woman sitting across from her is cool. Her voice doesn't betray a thing.

"I was surprised to see him." Gal thinks back to that night. There was something…a moment. "I mean, I guess a lot of people came out. People really loved Aimee."

Shira is nodding, and it occurs to Gal that she's not taking notes.

"I'm sorry," she says, not sure even how to phrase the question. "I don't really know what you might be able to do. I just couldn't stand the thought of Walter giving up."

"What you said was that he didn't want to defend himself." The lawyer speaking, not the old friend. "That his lawyer entered a pro forma plea of not guilty but that Walter was going to change that. That he wants to plead guilty."

"Yeah." Gal nodded. "Isn't that the same thing?"

"I don't know." A faraway look in her old friend's eyes. "People often have complicated reasons for doing what they do."

"Yeah, but…" That sounds like a rationalization to Gal. The kind of thing that gets said about drunks or addicts. "Can you talk to him?"

"I may be able to speak with him. Maybe make some inquiries." Shira speaks slowly, as if explaining to a child. "But unless he asks me to represent him, there isn't much else I can do."

It's maddening to feel so powerless. As if all the air has been taken from the room. Maybe that's why she can't speak. Why she can't argue with Shira, or, as she really wants, with Walter. Gal takes a breath, surprised to find she can do that still, the pressure is so great. If only she could release that breath into words. An argument to shake them into action. Into getting up to fight.

"Are you okay?" Shira's brows drawn in worry. Her voice softer now, less professional.

"Yeah." Gal looks down at the table. There's a slick of oil on her coffee, the drink gone bitter as well as cold. "I just—it's frustrating, you know?" She pushes the mug back. Wishes it were heavier. Wishes she could shove it away with all her might.

"I do." Shira draws out the last syllable, waiting. "But like I said, there are limits as to what I can do."

Gal turns away. Stares out the window to the street outside. Limits. That's why she went on the road. What she worked so hard for. She never wanted to be bound by anyone else's rules. And for a while she wasn't. She was free to define her own life.

CHAPTER 18

"This is it! The big time." It was Aimee who'd broken the news. "Hold Me Down" was charting. The album, what they still called a CD back then, was going gold. Maybe platinum. Maybe more. "We can write our own ticket now."

"Think we'll get a day off?" Gal's comeback. "A spa day?"

She didn't mean it. Not really. They'd been back on the road by then, their first big tour with the label—with Gus and his crew—and the relative luxury of hotel rooms, of a bus big enough to sleep on hadn't yet worn off. Besides, Gal was proud. The song was good, she knew that. And if she was a little nervous about writing a follow up, well, she'd learned not to show it. Still, something in her wanted to counter Aimee's enthusiasm, almost as if they'd changed places—her friend's girlish glee bringing out the cool and pragmatic side of Gal.

"Oh, come on." Aimee threw a pillow. They were in a motel outside Syracuse—or was it Scranton?—an hour to kill before the show. "You love it."

Gal let her face relax into a smile. "Yeah, well, I always knew we were good. That we could be good," she corrected herself. "Why not?"

Lina had come in then, Gus and his boys in tow. The guitarist had only just heard the news and was bouncing off the walls. Gus had helped, of course, laying out lines on the Formica dresser top as if they were party favors.

"Enjoy the rush, girls!" Barrel-chested—barrel-bellied, too—Gus tried for avuncular and they let it go. "The ride doesn't last forever."

"This is just the first stop." Gal, growling, even as she took the bill, a rolled-up twenty, from the road manager.

"Come on, do another," when she tried to hand it back. "Don't you want to be good tonight?"

She shot him a look. She'd been working on her dead-eyed stare for a while by then, but he only laughed and nodded toward the blow.

By the time they hit the stage, she was flying. Not just the coke, though Gus always had access to the best, but the music. The scene. The venue was packed, as if the news had already spread. Not a stadium, but not a basement club either. Some old Depression-era theater with the seats torn out to make a dance floor. From the stage, Gal looked out over a sea of shining faces. In the balcony, too, above the metal scaffolding that held the lights, suspended from the peeling plaster medallions.

Okay, not everyone was watching her. Someone—a member of Gus's crew?—was fussing with that scaffolding, and Gal had a flash of foreboding. The jury-rigged setup could come down in a moment. She turned away. A couple was making out in the corner. Three girls were vying for the bartender's attention. It didn't matter. None of it did. She inhaled deeply and felt as much as heard Aimee and Lina waiting, breath bated, beside her.

"Ready, girls?" She turned back to them, her sisters. This was their time. Their world.

"One, two, three, four!" Aimee shouted out the count. A crash of the cymbals as she and Lina came down hard. Bass and guitar, and everything in sync.

CHAPTER 19

She hates to feel so powerless. She needs to do more. That much is clear as Shira finishes her fancy coffee drink and prepares to leave. A lawyer, she has a day to see to, and so Gal swallows her protest. In its place, she gives her old bandmate Walter's contact info, a little surprised that their former colleague doesn't have it already.

"I thought maybe you two had been in touch." She waits while Shira punches the numbers into her phone.

"Not in years." She tucks the device into a neat leather bag. "But I'd spoken with Aimee, of course."

Of course? It's on the tip of Gal's tongue to tell the woman before her that it was Aimee who wanted her gone, who wanted her out of the band. But that's ancient history, and besides, her friend is dead. She nods, as if it all makes sense.

"That's why I was wondering." Shira is fussing with her bag and then with her coat, and it occurs to Gal that the other woman is avoiding meeting her gaze. As if she could hear the thought, the lawyer stops and looks at Gal. "I thought, maybe, you wanted to talk about those days, and everything that happened."

"Me?" She laughs and hears the nerves in the brittle sound. This is what she'd been thinking of, what she'd feared. "I was hoping that was all under the bridge," she says. "I mean, it seems like everything worked out, right? You look great. You sound like you're happy."

"I am." A satisfied half smile, as if remembering some moment of domestic bliss. "It's you I was thinking about."

"I'm grand." It's reflex, but that doesn't mean it isn't true. "I mean, I'm sad about Aimee and all."

"And T.K.?" An unreadable expression on her face.

"Yeah, that's a bummer, huh?" It's time to go. This trip down memory lane is turning into a drag. "I wonder what happened to him. I mean, I didn't keep up with him. Did you?"

Shira only blinks at her. "No," she says at last. "I didn't."

Gal remains unsettled, even once Shira leaves. Without a job, an office of her own to go to, without even a practice space, she finds herself out on the street. What's going on with Walter? She ponders calling. Wonders if he expects her to finish up the benefit accounts, still. They seem unimportant now, what with everything else that's happening.

Maybe she should just go home. Her cat, her man, such as he is, are expecting her. But while waiting for the elation or even simple relief that thought should bring, she realizes it only makes her anxious. She can't leave, not yet. Not with so many loose ends still hanging, the tension of an unresolved chord.

"Hey, Walter." Her call goes to voicemail, for which she's suddenly grateful. "I wanted to know if you still want me to finish up the benefit paperwork." She pauses and then decides to plow ahead. "I'm sorry if I went too far yesterday. But maybe you could tell me what's going on?" This time she waits too long and the voicemail cuts her off. Well, she tells herself as she tucks her phone away, it wasn't like she had anything more to add anyway.

Without a definitive answer, she doesn't feel free to leave. Not that she wants to, exactly. What does she have waiting for her? There's no drama with Russ. He'll keep Honey as long as necessary. Keep her house from burning down, too. And so she starts to walk, her feet taking her by habit from the financial district down toward the water. Toward where her old haunts used to be.

The streets are the same, for the most part. The old bridge is blocked off. Well, it was a death trap anyway, the pavement open to the water in spots. But a new bridge takes her over the channel, over to the point where the confusion kicks in.

"Is this...?" The sound of her voice stops her mid-question. Because there is no doubt, this is the same roadway—Necco Street—the way it bends off to the right. If it weren't for that curve, she'd never have known. Sure, the area had been changing even back then. The old factories mostly gone south or busted. Artists had begun moving in before she came to town. The big freight elevators made toting oversized canvases almost easy, and the light... Those big windows, the water nearby. She can clearly recall someone talking about the light.

The block-like brick buildings weren't approved for occupancy. Everyone knew that, but so much space in a town that was already losing rent control? Already going to the yuppies and the college kids and their trust funds? The old factories had electricity and running water, and, really, what else did you need?

If the artists were the first urban pioneers, the bands came soon after. Space for everyone, and cheap at a hundred, two hundred a month. Maybe it was Squiggly, converting that basement to rehearsal cubicles and charging what he did that gave everyone the idea. She remembers their old practice space a couple of blocks south, the one they shared with the Gotcha. Man, the landlord had really raked it in. Down here, they could have had a room of their own. A place to live, too, if they'd wanted. Her and Aimee... She brushes over that one fast. Time lost. Other bands did it, though. Nobody complained if you practiced late in some industrial space, concrete floors and brick so thick. If you crashed there after. Moved in. Throw a few parties for the neighbors, and people might even come to your gigs.

Gal closes her eyes, the dizziness is so bad. That world is gone, no matter if she can walk the curve of the street blind. If she knows without looking that the engraved stone above her says EST. 1874. Her history might as well be as long ago, and no trace of it remains.

"You all right?" A man half her age in a slim-cut suit is standing before her, an iPad tucked beneath his arm. "Do you need some help?"

"I'm fine." She manages a smile. The guy is cute, if a little young. "Just a little disoriented by all the changes."

"I understand." A patronizing note in his voice. "The old Starbucks being converted to a co-working space throws a lot of the older crowd."

Ouch. Gal manages to keep the smile in place. "Thanks."

"There's a new Peet's around the corner." He points and she nods. He points and she nods, as if more caffeine is what she's after.

Two blocks on, the queasiness has lessened, if not entirely disappeared. Small landmarks keep asserting themselves, throwing her sense of time and place into disarray. A stone curb she once tripped over, drunk out of her gourd. The gray granite still rounds the corner by a street drain. The sidewalk has been repaved. Brick, but new and even, to match the upscale office set back on it. Three names and no profession. An architect, she guesses. Or something to do with tech.

She stops to kick at the curb, for old time's sake, then reaches down to run her fingers over the stone, its corner worn smooth. The drain no longer smells like vomit, at least, a memory of being this close. The stink. She stands, another wave of nausea passing. Maybe she's getting the flu, she thinks. Maybe all the stress, the travel. A virus of some sort. She's not used to being in a city. Not used to being in a crowd, not anymore.

The coffee place sounds good, suddenly, and turning her back on the old corner, she makes her way there. Mid-morning, she expects to find the usual crowd of writers, artists, and students hogging every table. Spying a seat by the window, she drops her jacket to claim it before heading to the counter.

"Cappuccino, please." A whim, Shira on her mind. A buzz and a whir and she's sipping at the hot milk, waiting for the bitter. Feeling, instead, the foam on her lip as disorienting as the room she now sees is half empty. Either this area hasn't caught on the way the developers had hoped, or nobody comes to coffee houses anymore.

A woman rushes in. "Hey, Paul."

"Hey." The barista has her order ready: four tall takeout cups and a bag that smells of butter and cinnamon. "Oh, wait, I forgot the muffin."

He leaves her there, and she reaches over. Gal sees she's browsing a paper, left on the counter, as if it were a relic of an earlier time. Perhaps it is. Paul returns, two oversized muffins in his hand. He makes sure she sees them, Gal can tell, before tucking them into the bag. "By this time of day…" He shrugs, a stage move that matches the shit-eating grin. It works. A dollar goes into the tip jar. The paper stays where it was.

"May I?" Gal never got the hang of reading on a screen, and with her head this way, she doesn't want to start now.

"Sure." Paul doesn't even turn. He knows the type that tips, and Gal's not it.

She takes the paper back to the window, enjoying the luxury of feeling affronted. Politics: nothing has changed. The Sox still make the front page, and so she flips inside, through pages of business news—the Seaport District, yeah, that's what they call this area now. The paper's thin. Who buys ads in print these days? Before she knows it, she's at the back, the obits, and a photo stops her. Thomas Kennedy. T.K. She blinks and tries to see the younger man in the lined face. The rusty buzzcut gone, the dark eyes hooded and flat.

Mr. Kennedy was known as a pillar of his community. A deacon at his church, he helped run the Excell Mission...

Recovering alcoholic, she translates. Can't work, or doesn't want to, but can't stray too far from his higher power, she figures. Too aware of wanting to drink again.

Mr. Kennedy leaves behind his wife of fourteen years, the former Julia Clowe, vice-president of marketing at Landers and Clowe. "Thomas was a loving soul," she said. "His outreach gave him his reason to live."

Didn't have to work, then. A corporate wife in what sounds like a family firm, T.K. probably served as a house husband. She imagines a suburban home filled with kids. The mission a substitute once they'd gone off to school.

The image bothers her more than it should. She never wanted that, the house and kids. Actively avoided it on at least one occasion. Then again, Aimee hadn't either, until she did. Getting pregnant changed her. Made her get serious about her relationship with Walter rather than the other way around.

Which was fine. Clearly, it had suited her, and Walter loved being a dad. Still did, despite his odd refusal to make any effort to remain free for Camille. For Gal, that choice was not an option. She lived for the music, for the band. Giving up either of those, even giving up the road, would have seemed like death to her. Slow and stifling and final.

But T.K.? Well, she's been away so long, who knows how people change? Julia Clowe, she makes a mental note of the spelling. Clowe, not clown. Not claw. And then she pulls out her phone.

CHAPTER 20

She thought of that night as the real beginning. The night everything changed. Before the big tour, the gold record. The hits and the videos that followed one on top of each other, at least for a while.

The homecoming gig had been wild. The headlining slot had been a gift. An apology after all the shit with Shira and Dru. The band had the chops then, sure, after three weeks on the road, but they still had no songs. She hadn't written "Hold Me Down," that first big hit, yet. They didn't have anything on the radio. They hadn't gotten into a studio even.

Still, something was different. She'd felt it—seen it—in the way everybody reacted. Sure, she felt bad about Shira, what with her own band falling apart and all. But the skinny guitarist had been deadweight. She knew it that night. Shira never could have kept up, coming back for an encore that turned into another set. That turned wildly, crazily acoustic when the sound guy cut their power.

"Closing time!" he'd yelled. Over at the bar, Frankie was clapping his hands, like they were all stray cats that would scatter at the sound. "Come on now."

She can still hear the buzz and thrum of her A string, no power left in the amp.

"Let's boogie," said Lina, laying a hand on her arm. That's when she noticed that, yeah, the room had emptied. Closing time in this dead-end town and this crowd? Wimps. "We can take it to the Fargos.'"

And so they had, rolling their amps the three blocks to the other band's loft space. Gal's tipping as she maneuvered it over the big stone curb, and her almost doing a header after it.

"Here you go." Someone helping her. Taking the amp and steadying her. T.K.? Maybe she's conflating gigs, the memories running together. All those times he'd roadied for them, back before they went on tour. The streetlights weren't that great down here then. A well-thrown stone, when someone wanted privacy, or maybe just the city's general disregard for the drunks and artists, the riff raff, who frequented the area at night.

"I got you." An arm around her waist. The smell of vomit from a street drain.

One-two-three-crash!

She almost lost it in the elevator. The upward lurch had her grabbing for the walls. The hands supposed to steady her now too close, hot and wet. She pushed away and swallowed, the sickness settling as soon as the door opened. The crowd, the noise. The Fargos' loft as big as the club they'd just left, it seemed. Bigger, as people came and went from the back rooms, the floor-through loft partitioned into living space by someone with a plan, a set of tools.

Aimee had set up by the time she made it to the stage area, back against the windows. It felt like swimming, the air as thick and hot as a bath. The faces like the sparkle on the waves, shiny with sweat and anticipation. Most she knew, the club crowd reconfigured. Some from the gig earlier. Diehards like her, back for more. Aimee reeled her in. "You good?"

"I'm great." Gal reached for her amp to steady herself. Let someone drape the bass over her shoulder, let its weight anchor her to the ground as she turned to Lina, then to Aimee. They were waiting, she saw that now. Solid figures in the crowd. "Dog," she said. One word, the set she barely had to list. A countdown beat and Lina's feedback shriek, and the music took control.

That's what Shira didn't get, and never would. The sheer joy of playing in impossible situations. Of the same changes over and over because they felt right. On the road, they'd learned to love it. Drunk, sick, tired—none of it mattered once Aimee counted off the beat.

"Adrenaline and beer." Gal was shouting. She could hear herself, in the break. Lina turned to look. Was this a song she didn't know? And Aimee, always game, began to slam her sticks. *One-two-three-crash!* A blues progression, made-up lines. By the second time around, the band had all joined in, shouting along with the improvised lyric. They lived for this. They'd play till dawn, if the crowd could stand it. Someone put a shot glass on Gal's amp, and she grabbed it, thumbing open notes while she slugged it down. "Beer!" A new lyric, a request. It didn't matter. This was the fire that forged their rock and roll.

Chapter 21

To her surprise, the widow is eager to meet. Curiosity, as much as anything, had prompted Gal to reach out, under the guise of a condolence call, but the newly bereaved woman responds with an invitation that throws her off her guard.

"I'm so glad you called," she says to Gal. "I've heard so much about you. You were important to Thomas, you know. He often said he should get back in touch. Would you like to come over? Or I could come to you."

"Really." Intentionally noncommittal, Gal feels herself drawing back. Disturbed—no, disapproving of the impromptu invitation that caps off the unlikely rush of words. How desperate is this woman? Is she flailing in her loneliness, and will she drag any poor sucker down?

"Yes. I'm—well, everyone from the church has been wonderful, but I'd love to talk to some of the people who knew him back then." She sounds ardent, rather than anxious. Strangely enthusiastic, even. "I assume you'll be at the service?"

"I'm sorry. I didn't make plans to." Didn't think about it at all, is more like it. Of course there'll be a service, a full-bore funeral with kids and mourners. T.K. was married. A deacon. "I don't know if

I'll be in town by then." She doesn't know when it's going to be, but figures this is as good an excuse as any.

"Of course." The widow consoling her, as if that were the natural thing. "In that case, could we meet for tea? Or lunch, perhaps? I would dearly love to get out of the house."

She can't refuse again, not without feeling like a heel. Not when the invitation is so open-ended. And so plans are made for later that day. Better to get it over with, Gal thinks. Get it done.

Gal sits for a moment after the call has ended, vaguely queasy once more. A little, she wishes herself sick. A fever, a flu. It would simplify matters. She could go home, hole up, and recover. But the feeling passes, as she knows it will. Besides, she wants to help Walter. She calls Camille.

"It's Gal," she says to the voicemail. "I wanted to check in." There's too much to explain over the phone. "I thought I'd come by and finish the paperwork," she says. Walter never responded, but she had promised, what feels like eons ago. "And, well, I may have someone who can help us." Better to explain in person.

The promise, vague as it is, energizes her, and she hits the street, her mood picking up as she crosses the fancy new bridge on her way to the T. Better to be active, to be doing, than wallowing in the past. Gal thinks back to her touring years, the craziness. She kept going by never stopping, same as any of them. Until, of course, she did. But that's beside the point. She has a task to complete, a task she assumed freely in order to help the family of her old friend. If, along the way, she can be of assistance to Walter in this current mess, well then, so much the better.

"Hello?" She lets herself in when no one answers the bell. "Camille? Walter?"

Silence. She tries to take heart in that. Maybe they're with the lawyer. Maybe Shira has already called and weighed in. Gal tries to picture her friend here, Aimee hard at work among these neat piles of papers. The office feels so much like Walter now, it's hard to see any trace of the wild-child drummer, though, of course, Aimee wasn't by this point. Was a mom, instead. A freelance designer, too, working on projects between PTA meetings.

Gal wanders over, scans the desktop once again. Maybe there was another reason Walter didn't want to talk to that lawyer. Maybe he was Aimee's advocate in the divorce. Pending divorce, Gal corrects herself. She's not sure it was ever finalized.

The news that they were splitting had surprised her. Gal wasn't one for long-term commitment. "Too much rock and roll in my blood," she had told more than one lover. Even Russ is essentially a convenience. The fact that he knows to back off is a big part of why they're still an item. That, and the lack of options in the small upstate town where she spends most of her time these days, the way the days and months have turned to years without her noticing. But Walter and Aimee had seemed stable. Settled into the kind of comfortable routine that, if she was being honest, filled Gal with dread. Maybe it was inevitable, she thinks now. Everything fades away.

The bigger surprise had been their marriage. Sure, Aimee had slept with Walter. In retrospect, his pot belly, the receding hairline, matter less now that they're not in their twenties. He was around, and he was a nice enough guy. Why not? But when Aimee had confided about her pregnancy, a month or so into their third tour—North America, their biggest yet—Gal had expected her to terminate it. Had offered to go with her, in fact, figuring they could use one of their rare break days to fly back to Boston if the drummer didn't want to schedule something in LA or Cincinnati, or wherever the timing was right. This was their second time out with label support, and Gal had the routine figured out. Gus and his crew handled everything but the playing anyway.

"Yeah, maybe." Aimee had sounded distracted when she brought it up.

"Just don't wait too long." Gal spoke from experience. It was so easy to let the nights turn into weeks, and she'd been lucky to come in under the wire of her own abortion less than a year before. A week or two later and it wouldn't have been an outpatient procedure, back on her own sofa that night with some movies on video and a bottle of Jack to augment the pills.

Two weeks later, she woke in Cleveland to the sound of Aimee heaving. They were staying in motels by that point. No more crashing on the sofas and futons of other bands or someone's cousin's friend, those days long behind them. They still shared rooms, though, and even though Aimee had closed the door behind her, the sound of her retching had been enough to break through Gal's restless sleep.

"You okay?" She'd rapped on the door. "Aimee?"

"Yeah." The choked response, and Gal realized, with a sinking feeling, that her drummer, her friend, had been hiding something from her.

"You want to talk about it?" She'd waited till she heard the water running. The sound of spitting in the sink.

"Not particularly." And that was it.

Twenty-odd years later, she sees the results. Photos of Camille are all over the office. Two on the desk from her childhood. One shows the three of them, the unlikely perfect family, somewhere with a lake. They're all smiling, but Walter in particular is beaming. Maybe he never expected something like this to happen to him. Maybe he never expected it to last.

On a whim, Gal pulls the desk chair back and takes a seat. She's not looking for anything now, but she can't resist trying it out. What it must have felt like, to be settled. A home office, a husband, a child. The neat stacks that Walter has assembled. Not his home anymore, but still his family. More his responsibility now that Aimee is gone, but he's been respectful of his ex-wife, even in death. All his papers are piled here, on top of the desk. Gal thought, at first, that was for her. Maybe it was for Aimee.

She pulls open a drawer. Sure enough, more papers. An old date book, the kind you leave open on the desktop, has been shoved inside. Out of the way or, more likely, too painful to peruse. A reminder of everyday life before the end.

Gal opens it, curious about what she missed. The last few months are blank. Hospice care taking the place of doctor's appointments, the burden shifting to other shoulders. Before that…it's too much. She doesn't want to know, and so Gal flips to the year's beginning. Aimee's illness came on swiftly, she'd been told. But looking at the first week of January, then the next, Gal has to wonder if her friend had her suspicions early on. *TEST 10:30*, she reads, *BWH 1030*. A hospital address. *BWH* the next week, and then again, four days later.

Aimee knew. But what Gal reads next is what snaps her head back in surprise: *Shira*, she reads, followed by a phone number she now recognizes.

Gal shrugs off the shock the notation provokes. Takes a breath and shakes her head. Of course they were in touch. They knew each other, and they both still lived in this city. That explains why Shira made the concert, most likely, although Gal can't remember her former guitarist mentioning an ongoing friendship when they reconnected over coffee. Then again, she'd monopolized the conversation, going on about Walter and his case. And, yeah, that decades-old guilt had played a part—it's rearing up again now—bringing with it an overlay of jealousy. So Aimee and Shira had been in touch. Had Shira known that Aimee had been the one who wanted her out of the band? Did they talk about it? Did she care?

Gal tells herself it's idle curiosity as she turns back a page and then another. She's looking for more mentions of Shira's name, for more of a sense of what they meant to each other. If they were truly friends. Gal should have been here more those last months. She knows that. Boston isn't that far away, but it felt like such an effort. Maybe she's become a country mouse after all.

When she finds the card, tucked into a page three weeks before that notation, it gives her an absurd rush of relief. *Shira Goldstein, attorney at law*, the same card the lawyer had handed Gal, and clearly Aimee had taken her time before calling. Funny that she should feel so possessive of Aimee, almost protective. Her nightmare flashes in front of her—the sickness, the tears—and she shakes it free. Just then, the sound of the front door opening causes her to look up.

"Hey, Camille." Relief washes over her at the sight of Aimee's daughter, so like her but healthy, young. Alive. "I was just going over the benefit receipts and I found something kind of curious."

A tilt of the head and a smile invite her to go further.

"I gather your mom and our old bandmate Shira were in touch." Gal's mouth has gone dry and she licks her lips. "Did you know her at all? Were they close?"

A shake of the head sends her dark curls bouncing. "No, I don't think so. What was the name?"

Gal repeats it. "Shira. Shira Goldstein. She was our first guitarist. I gather she became a lawyer. I saw her at the benefit, and she and I have been in touch."

"No, sorry." It's Camille's turn to look a little embarrassed. "My mom gave me a list of all the people to contact, her closest friends." A pause. They both must remember the morning Camille had called, but the young woman can't know that Gal was home at the time, staring at the phone as her friend's daughter stammered out her number on the voicemail, the message so vague and at the same time so undeniably clear.

"Anyway," Camille swallows, her own version of the memory stuck in her throat. "I don't remember a Shira. Maybe Dad does."

Gal is about to tell her not to bother, the matter is minor, when Camille turns and calls back into the other room. "Dad? Do you know a lawyer named Shira? Gal says she and Aimee had some connection with her?"

Suddenly, he's there, filling the doorway with a face like a thundercloud. "What? No." He barks and strides past his daughter. "What are you doing in here? Those are Aimee's things—my things. You've got no business."

"Sorry!" She slams the chair back and stands up, heart racing. "You weren't here, and I didn't know. I was trying to finish up." It's weak, she knows it. Walter has organized everything so neatly. All the benefit papers are out on the dining room table. She looks past him, to that table and the door beyond, and realizes how time has flown.

"Look, I've got a lunch appointment." She grabs her jacket, grateful for the excuse. "I'll come back and finish later, if you want, and I'm…I'm sorry." He steps back and lets her by. "I didn't mean to overstep."

He's silent as she heads to the door, but Camille tags along, stepping outside and closing the door behind her.

"I'm sorry." Aimee's daughter looks so much more like her than her glowering father. "He's just hurting."

"I know." Gal manages what she hopes is an understanding smile. "Please don't worry about it. Besides, you answered my question."

Camille beams. "Please do come back." She nods toward the

door. "I'll handle him."

Gal's grin widens. "Yeah, Aimee always said you had him wrapped around your little finger."

CHAPTER 22

"I'm so glad to finally meet you." The widow, Julia, is waiting when Gal gets to the diner, a few minutes late and somewhat flustered after the scene at Aimee's. "Thank you for coming out."

"It's no problem." Gal slides into the banquette across from the widow, a round-faced brunette. The Peter Pan collar of her pink-sprigged blouse does her no favors. "And I'm sorry for your loss."

"Thank you." The widow's face lights up. "He's with Jesus now."

Gal nods, unsure how to respond. The T.K. she remembers was not big on religion. Or marriage either, she would have thought. But as they order—a burger for Gal, a salad for Julia—she tries to reconcile the hard-partying roadie she remembers with someone this prim woman would marry.

Something of her thoughts must show on her face.

"Of course, you didn't know him recently." The woman opposite her speaks with a warmth pitched to counter any sting in her words. "He's—he was—a deacon in our church."

Gal nods. "I read that." Too cold. "I mean, yeah, we'd not been in touch. Do you have any children?" As soon as the question is out of her mouth, she regrets it. She's out of sorts, confused. A woman like this, married to T.K. A shadow has fallen over the widow's face.

"I don't," Gal adds hurriedly, hoping to soften what is apparently a blow.

"No." It appears to work. "I'm sorry. I was remembering. For me, it doesn't matter much. I come from a big family and have a dozen nieces and nephews. But Thomas always regretted not having children. We married late, you see, and, well, it wasn't God's will." The smile returns, a little more tentative now.

Gal does her best to put on a sympathetic face. A Jesus freak. Somehow it seems fitting, though she can't exactly place why. Already, she's regretting the seating arrangement. The banquette, up against the wall. Not that this round-faced child woman could block her if she really wanted to bolt, but she feels hemmed in. In her pocket, her phone vibrates. Someone is trying to reach her. She thinks of Camille, seeking support, or even Walter, ready to apologize and talk, but she resists the urge to fish it out. She can hold her own here. She's not going to run. It's only lunch, she promises herself. She can deal. She will.

"How did you two meet?" A safe topic, and it helps to talk. Another buzz, an angry bee urging her to respond. It wouldn't be Russ. That's not his way, not unless there's been an emergency. No, even then, he'd manage. Figure it out on his own. But maybe—no, before she can renege, their food arrives. Besides, the woman across from her has already started to answer.

"—the church." There was more, but that's all Gal catches. "Thomas was always a seeker, but in Christ he found peace."

"Ah." Gal nods at her burger, suspicion confirmed. "When I knew him, he was a bit wild."

"I gather." The widow picks at her salad, distracted. "I believe that's why Thomas so wanted to speak to you."

Mouth full, Gal can only shake her head, confused. She's taken too big a bite in her desire to get through this lunch. Her mouth is dry, and she struggles to swallow.

"He'd had a lapse recently." The widow doesn't seem to notice her discomfort and keeps on talking. She sounds so matter of fact it's like she's talking about her late husband forgetting to take out the trash, but Gal can well remember T.K. drinking. Lining up the shots. "And he'd been very keen on working the steps. You must know them?" A look Gal can't interpret.

"Not firsthand." She has managed to swallow and pushes the plate away. The burger has no flavor, and this woman is growing tiresome.

Julia seems to sense her desire to leave. She strains forward, her eyes opening wide. "I believe that's why he wanted to reach out to you. He was quite…emphatic."

Gal looks beyond the widow for the server. "Well, he didn't." That sounds cold, even to her ears. "I'm sorry. I don't live in town anymore, and we haven't kept in touch."

The server sees her. A nod, but she's brought back by a touch. The widow's hand is on hers, as if she wants to restrain her.

"I don't know the details, but I knew my Thomas," she is saying. Gal fights the urge to pull her hand away. "He would have wanted to know that you were going to be okay." The urgency as she leans in. "He would have wanted to help."

"Help?" It's all Gal can do to choke the word out. "How?" That's what she means, but she can barely ask.

"He wanted to help you, but only you can take that first step." The widow's voice may be soft, but she has all the fervor of a missionary—or a madwoman. "You have to find it within yourself."

That's it. Gal stands, knocking back the table, which hits the other woman in her ample midsection. The stout woman pulls back with a start and stares up at Gal like she's the crazy one. And at that, Gal relents. This woman has just lost her husband. She was trying to reach out.

"I'm sorry." She is, more than she can say. "But I have to go." She pulls a twenty from her wallet then adds another. Money she can't afford to spend. But it's worth it for her conscience, and she throws the bills down on the table and strides toward the door as quickly as she can without breaking into a run.

As soon as she's outside, she finds she can breathe again. She continues around the block and collapses against a building, the wave of relief out of all proportion to the discomfort of the meal. One sad lady, peddling her faith—her late husband's agenda. Gal really needs to get a grip. T.K. Shit. So T.K. wanted to get in touch. To get her in the program apparently. Shit.

She shudders. It's getting cold again, and she shoves her hands in her pockets. Her phone. Grateful for the distraction, she pulls it out. The number isn't one she recognizes. Not Russ, then. Not Camille either.

Her finger hovers over the voicemail, not wanting to engage. *He wanted to help you.* She shudders again and hits play.

"Good afternoon, Ms. Raver. This is Detective Bixby of the Boston Police Department. I'd appreciate it if you would call me back at your earliest convenience." He repeats the number, which matches the one she can see on her phone. A throwback to another era. A habit that dies hard.

The police. Shit. She thinks of T.K. and all the trouble they used to get into. She thinks of Walter. Of Camille and Aimee. Her thumb finds the redial and she starts to walk as the phone on the other end begins to ring.

CHAPTER 23

"Detective Bixby?" As soon as the words are out of her mouth, she kicks herself. A man has answered, but he sounds young. The message had been left by an older man. Wearied, weathered. She's jumpy, and she blames the widow. "I'm sorry, I'm returning a call?"

Even as she speaks, she's regretting her haste. She wants to protect Walter, but she can't just rush in. She should have reached out to Shira first. Gotten some advice.

"Ms. Raver." She's put through to the detective, who sounds as gruff as she expected. Only she's on the defensive now. Too many years on the road to be comfortable around authority, especially when one of her own is in trouble. "Thanks for calling me back."

"No problem." She wants to ask. She won't, holding onto her slim edge.

"We'd like you to come in. Answer a few questions."

"About what?" Giving an inch. Already stalling. Should she ask Shira to accompany her? What would that cost, exactly—and can Walter afford it? That couldn't be why he is refusing to mount a defense, could it? Gal flinches at the thought, even as the voice on the phone answers.

"You are probably aware that there was an incident outside of a venue where you performed a few nights ago," the cop is saying. Incident? "We're talking to several people in our attempt to discern what happened."

"Ah." She exhales. Maybe Walter hasn't been arrested, hasn't been arraigned in connection to T.K.'s death. Maybe it's all gotten confused somehow. Another issue. A misunderstanding and Camille has panicked. Twenty is younger these days. Twenty-one? Whatever. Maybe she's the one who misinterpreted. Walter might have… well, she doesn't have time to figure out his role in all this, only maybe… "You mean with T.K.—Thomas Kennedy?"

"We'd like you to come in and talk with us."

She nods. Perhaps it was an accident, after all. "Of course," she says. "When were you thinking of?"

"As soon as is convenient. Today, if possible." A pause, and she imagines him shuffling through papers. Marking names off a list. "I gather you don't live in the area, and we'd like to speak with you while you're still in town."

"I could come by this afternoon." Better to stay away from Walter for a while. Better if she could go back to him with some good news. Laughing over the confusion. "Maybe a half hour from now?"

"That would be great, Ms. Raver." Another item checked off that list, she imagines. Something routine. "See you then. "

As soon as she hangs up, something like reality kicks in. An old reflex, the training she got on the road. "Never talk to the cops." Gus, lecturing her like a child. There'd been a brawl. Damage to a club. Had Aimee been with her? Aimee was never one to shirk a fight. "Never. Talk. To. The. Cops." A hectoring tone, as if she'd still been drunk, that next morning after he'd bailed her out. Just her. After Aimee, then. End of that third tour, or maybe the one after.

"That's what I'm here for. What we're here for. You call us. Now say it."

"Never talk to the cops," she mutters, and makes herself laugh at the memory. Yeah, she'd been trouble in those days. But the road crew hadn't helped. Hired by the label to ferry them around, they'd acted like they were the talent—the adults—and Gal and the band were simply product. An animal act, or, no, fresh fruit that had to arrive unblemished. Over time, Gal had come to accept it, not like she had much choice.

Well, she's not that fresh now. Something to be handled, and, besides, she's helping out a friend. Actually, she's grateful for the distraction. What else was she going to do this afternoon? She's not ready to return home, not yet, not with all that paperwork left to do, and better to let Walter cool off before she heads back to Aimee's place—his place—again. Shoving any last misgivings aside—drowning them out, rather, by humming a song—she turns back into town.

"Ms. Raver?" The cop isn't what she'd imagined. Despite his voice, he's young enough, forty, maybe, and slim, with grizzled hair a shade longer than expected. The kind she'd go for in different circumstances. Still might, she muses, as she follows him down a hall. Something about his long, easy stride. It's not like she's twenty anymore either.

"Thanks for coming in." He opens a door and steps back, waiting for her. Ushering her into a private room.

"My pleasure," she purrs. Been a while since she felt like this, she muses. Maybe she's been away from Russ too long. Maybe she's been needing a change.

"Coffee?" His voice is still gruff, but it's warmer than it was on the phone. Gal smiles up at him as she sits. Holds his gaze a moment too long.

"No, thanks." She's rewarded as he looks down, discomfited even as he takes his own seat across the table.

"Ms. Raver—"

"Call me Gal." She can't help herself. Doesn't want to. It has been too long.

He nods, a hint of a smile. "Would you tell me about your relationship with Thomas Kennedy?"

She sits back, suddenly winded. It's almost like she'd forgotten why she was here. T.K. dead and Walter up on charges. There wasn't a mistake. "My relationship? I don't have one, not with T.K." She catches herself. The flirting has got to stop.

As it is, the man across the table is waiting. He doesn't have to ask. She knows what she said.

"Not for years," she says. "T.K.—Tom Kennedy—was around when I lived here, in Boston. He roadied for my band when we were first starting out."

More silence, but the raised brows are urging her to say more.

"That's about it." She punctuates her statement by putting her hands on the tabletop. She's not going to push off, not yet, but some gesture, some action, is necessary. "I hadn't spoken to him in years."

"That's interesting." A shift in the mood, or maybe it's just her. She meant to stop where she had. She doesn't know where that last detail came from. It's not like it matters, but it bothers her. A loss of control. "Because he seemed to consider your relationship still active."

A statement, not a question. Still, she feels the flush rising. "The wife. Widow, I mean. Julia Clowe? I had lunch with her today." Now she has to explain. "I looked her up because I'd heard, of course. I'd never met her before. I gather he'd changed quite a lot."

"In what way?" An innocuous question from anyone else.

"Well, he was kind of wild back in the day. Heavy drinker. I mean, we all were." She thinks of Walter. "That can't be why you—" Catches herself. Maybe she's not supposed to know. Maybe there's been a mistake. Anything's possible. "Anyway, she told me that T.K.—Tom—had wanted to get in touch with me. She seemed to think he wanted to help me. Save my soul or something." Surely, he can see the humor in that. "But he didn't."

The man across from her nods and does not smile. She was wrong about him. The pleasant buzz is gone. "To be clear, you're saying he never got in touch?"

"Right." She wants to be clear. To be gone. "I never heard from him."

This silence is becoming tedious. Plus, his eyes are cold. "What does this have to do with Walter?" She kicks herself. "With anything?"

"Thank you so much for your time, Ms. Raver." He stands and walks to the door. He's a gatekeeper, not a gentleman. "We may contact you again."

Gal's cheeks burn as she walks by him. The flush rising further as she struts back down the hallway, conscious all the while of his eyes on her. Of his body behind hers. Crazy stupid, feeling like this. Like she hasn't taken the stage in front of several thousand staring knuckleheads. Like she can't command them to their feet. Bend them to do her bidding. Shoulders back, she tosses her hair. So what, it's not as full as it once was. A little wiry, the color a little brash. She's a fucking rock star, not some victim to be hauled in for questioning.

She catches herself and almost stumbles. Forces herself to keep on walking. *Victim.* Where did that come from? She's walking out under her own power. As free as she ever was. It's T.K. who was the victim here, killed behind the club where she had once again been front and center. T.K. who's dead, and Walter, her friend, Aimee's widower, who has been arrested for it. Whom she came here to help.

She's reached the end of the hall before she stops and turns. Surely, there is something she can salvage from this stupid meeting. Just because she got distracted, because she hasn't gotten laid in way too long.

"Hey." She summons up that smile, the easy one, and tilts her head. "Seems like I'm owed a little something for coming in." Might as well make him think she's still interested.

But the man behind her is humorless. A greying slab of wood. No, granite, like that curb. "I'm sorry, Ms. Raver." His voice holds no regret. "I'm afraid it doesn't work that way. You should know I can't comment on an ongoing investigation."

Ongoing? The word stands out. Maybe there's some hope. Maybe Walter had a lead to share. Did something to clear his own name. Maybe the case isn't cut and dried. But just as quickly, another thought springs to life, like a flame blazing up inside her. *It should have been me,* she thinks.

She turns to hide her face, her confusion. The flush that burns like shame. And as fast as she can without running, she makes her way to the street.

Chapter 24

There's no chance of going back to Walter's after that. There's no way she wants to face him, not yet. Not until her own thoughts, her confusion, settle back into the cool and clear. What she really wants is a drink. Something to settle her. The peace of her own bed, alone, with the cat.

She's come too far to backslide, however. No matter what she told the widow, what she almost told that cop, she's quite aware of how alcohol affects her. She doesn't do programs. She doesn't have to. But on days like this, she almost wishes she had that crutch.

"Fuck this shit." She's thinking crazy, that stupid refrain echoing in her head. What she needs is a friend to talk some sense into her. If only Aimee or even… She could call Shira. The thought springs open like an escape hatch. No, that's nonsense. Lina, maybe. The benefit had gone so well. But she can't stop thinking about how it all ended. Those last days, the last tour? She'd been a handful. Of course, she'd been the star. Not that that was a good enough excuse. She knew it then, if she's being honest. Probably. Knows it now for sure. They all got along well enough, now, though. Didn't they? The memories. No, she'll tough this one out alone.

What was she thinking? What was she *doing*, going to the cops without a lawyer? Gus, the label, they were all right. She needs managing. Not fruit, maybe an animal. Feral, un-housebroken. Ready to be put down.

No, she catches herself. She made a stupid move, but nothing fatal. She just needs to hold herself together. She didn't do anything, right? She pauses. No, she wasn't drinking. She doesn't drink anymore. So why, then, does she feel culpable somehow, as if she did kill T.K.? As if she could have?

She makes it back to the motel on autopilot and turns on the TV. The noise helps distract her and she considers a hot bath. She knows what can happen when her nerves get this jangly. If she could talk to a friend…but Aimee's not there and Walter, well, she doesn't know what's up with Walter. Only that he's not the one to call. Not now, anyway.

Russ? No, he's too mellow, with his aging hippie vibe. Plus, he didn't know her then. Fuck it. She grabs her phone, but not to call. Instead, she texts a message. *Me again. You free tomorrow?* She waits, weighing the words. Weighing what to add, but then hits send. Gal was never one for caution, never one to sit still.

Her phone buzzes while she's in the tub, skittering across the floor like a beetle on its back. She's half asleep by then, lulled by the steaming water, by a day that has turned unexpectedly exhausting. Barely dark, and she's ready to crash. To crawl into the motel bed and sleep till noon. Another buzz, rattling along as the phone does its little dance.

She could reach it from here. That's why she left it so near by. She could dry her hand on the towel and pick it up. Maybe it's Russ, with some sweet calming nonsense. Or Walter, calling to apologize and invite her over. Camille has made dinner. She should bring wine.

She closes her eyes and sinks under the surface, feeling her hair float around her. Dark red once more, like back in the day. Like blood. The phone buzzes again, the sound strange and muted by the water. It's quiet by the time she surfaces, but she stays in the tub until its steamy heat is nearly cool. And then she's ready for bed.

CHAPTER 25

One-two-three-crash!

She wakes with a start, the music still pounding in her ears. Struggles to get up, weighed down by heat, by pressure. A voice, close to her ear. Someone is shouting, right nearby, and then fades out as her body goes with the rhythm. The music, the beat. She always loved this song.

A moment—could be more—and she starts, jerking up, again. This time, it's serious. Her stomach spasming, she pushes her way free. Makes it to her knees before heaving, the sour taste of whiskey and bile, and then her head, heavy on the floor. Another voice, hands that hold her firm. That take her arms and lie her down, and she feels herself falling backward. Into the dark.

When she wakes, everything aches. Her head throbs, and her throat is raw. To sit up, she must lean on one arm and catches sight of a purpling bruise above her elbow.

"What the hell?" That's when she notices the rest. She's naked, or nearly so. Shirt bunched up around her throat, tangled in her bra, jeans on the floor beside her. She's lying on a hardwood floor. A loft, a party…it begins to come back to her. The puddle of sick makes her stomach writhe and she grabs at her jeans—she missed them when she puked, thank God—managing to step into them as she runs down the hall to the bathroom.

There's little in her belly to come up at this point, but the cool of the porcelain feels good against her cheek. She's on her knees, her eyes closing. If she could lie down for a moment, it would help.

That bruise, the one on her knee. She fell. She remembers that now. She was running, shouting in the street. On the way to the after-party. A homecoming for the band. Fell again in the loft, dancing with friends. She stumbled over some records, a pile of vinyl stacked by the stereo, only dimly aware of the earlier bruise, the soreness distant. Funny, somehow.

"I'm okay!" Hands gathering the records. Ducking down to help. Laughing as she nearly went down again, off balance, tripping over the stack. More hands, handing her another drink.

"Turn it up!" Talking Heads, or was it Bad Brains? All she remembers is the beat. A pounding like the pulse she can feel in her neck and in her head. Yeah, she was dancing, wild. Alone, like the rock star that she was. Spinning around like that record until she fell again. The place was a mess. Clothes everywhere. A fire hazard, same as always. Crowded, too, at least at first. Too hot from all the bodies. The drinking, the dance. Someone handing her a drink. Pressing her fingers around the red plastic cup even as she spun. Something cold, this time.

"Whoa! Watch out!" Laughter, as she spilled it on the floor. On herself. A hand with the wet shirt, her sleeve soaked from the wrist on up. What the hell, it was a party. When she closed her eyes, she could see the music. The beat throbbing with the heat. Another drink. Held, this time, right up to her lips, and voices cheering.

She was home, back on the scene. With her people. Her father had died while they were on tour. She'd gotten the message but hadn't told anyone. The man had been gone from her life for years.

She was free now. Happy. High.

Another drink. "Oh, why not?" Only she's falling this time, and hands are reaching for her. Helping her up. Helping her. The party has just started.

CHAPTER 26

Startled awake, in the motel room this time. Face down on a damp pillow, she pushes herself up in a panic. In disgust, and then relief, as she catches herself, stiff-armed above the mattress, staring down at a tangle of cloth, mashed into submission, a wet spot darkening one end.

Her pillow and a towel, shed during the night. She's here now. Sober. A nightmare, nothing more. She takes a breath. Rolls over to stare at the motel room ceiling. The red light of the fire alarm flashing once, flashing twice, flashing again. She times her breath, holding it as she waits. As she feels her heartbeat steady and slow.

The red light is a reassurance, she tells herself. Not an alarm, but a sign the system is working. Regular like that, once a minute, she thinks. Something Russ has told her. Something she'd never noticed. All those nights on the road but not until she has a home of her own does she find herself staring. Anxious, wondering what the slow cycle—*flash*, wait, *flash*—means.

The dream has left her sticky with sweat, her heart racing. God, she was wiped, collapsing like that. She barely made it into bed after her bath. After that weird, hard day. The widow creeped her out. What an odd choice for T.K., she can't help thinking. Hard-partying

T.K., her roadie. Her buddy. She tries to remember how they lost touch. Why.

Shira comes to mind. Shira drinking with him, that first night at the pub. Whiny Shira, and now she's a lawyer. The world is strange. Shira—she reaches for her phone and then decides against it. Yeah, she needs to talk to her again. Follow up, make sure she's on the case. Funny how the balance changes. Poor old Shira, unfit for the rock life. Shira complaining about everything. Whining. And then Aimee…

She closes her eyes as the loss hits her once again. Aimee never whined. Tough as nails, that girl. The memory of tears, of vomiting, of her dear friend sobbing in her arms. But they'd been drunk then. The road was hard. The stress. Shira couldn't take it. Even Aimee left, pregnant with Camille. A home with Walter. A life.

Why had Aimee contacted Shira? Camille said they weren't friends, but does a daughter always know what's going on with her mother? Yeah, she catches herself, closing her eyes. When your daughter is planning your funeral, then, yeah, she does. So, why the card? The appointment? And what the hell is up with Walter, anyway?

Times like this, she wishes she smoked again. If she can't have a drink, she'd like a butt. A reason to lie here, staring at the ceiling. Watching the smoke rise in hazy swirls up to the ceiling. Not that she'd be allowed to smoke in here. Another rule to break. The red light in the ceiling blinks once more. That dream creeped her out as well, she'll admit it. She'll feel better once she's washed the memory of it off her body and had some coffee. What do the twelve-steppers say? It's time to start another day.

Thank God for Starbucks. She walks to the corner, where the old El Pueblo used to be, glad to stretch her legs, her mood picking up with the air and the promise of caffeine.

Good coffee is her drug of choice, now that it's available. Maybe it would have been then, too, back in the day. Only then, it was only Dunkin', and once you left New England, not even that. If she tries, she can summon the bitter aftertaste: acid and iron filings. One part truck stop coffee, the pot left simmering until it was done. One part, if she's being honest, the drip from the speed and coke.

"Wakey, wakey." Gus, the crew boss, would hand out pills like candy, getting them up and ready to play. "Morning, children."

Not that it was morning. Not usually, she thinks as she feels herself relaxing in the warmth of the sun. No, the pills, the wake-up call—these were for the show, a boost to get them revved and ready. To get them wired, regardless of whatever debauch they'd indulged in the night before. That was Gus's job, as much as getting them to the venue and making sure they got paid. He had underlings to deal with the other shit. The vendors selling knockoff T-shirts. The promoters who wanted a little more. Gus saw the big picture, he said.

"That's what I'm here for." It became his mantra. "You girls just get up there and play."

That was what they'd wanted, of course. What the label had promised, when the suits came courting. One local radio hit, and another that was already generating buzz. The local fans, the grind and heat of that Southern tour, had paid off, and between the gigs and the partying, Gal had learned to loosen up. To take the stage like she owned it. Now, when she wrote, she went into a fugue state, or something like, anyway.

"Where did this come from?" The first time a writer asked her that, she'd started, taken aback by the question.

"From me." She covered pretty well, she thought. She'd perfected the shark-like smile by then. He was a pretty boy, after all. "What do you think?"

"I mean, the pain in it. The anger."

She'd laughed him off. Told Gus, "No more interviews." Not that he listened.

"Sorry, girls. Part of the gig." He answered to the label, they were realizing, as that second big tour was extended. Twelve cities. Fifteen. Crossing the country and then back again, the middle this time, then back up north. Cleveland again. Scranton, two nights at the old theater. Not quite arena ready. Working every night, but Gal didn't care. She loved it. For Aimee, though, it was getting difficult. She and Walter were becoming serious. Their last break—five days and twice as many parties—she had changed, somehow. That next month on the road would be her last.

"Come on, girls. Wakey wakey." Gus shaking a pill bottle like it was full of cat treats. And like kittens, they'd all lined up. All except Aimee. Gal should have seen it then. Should have known. A month later, she was gone.

The Starbucks is more what she's used to. Brighton's not the Seaport. Not yet. A student crowd—young people with their laptops, a few older women who could be retirees—and Gal finds a seat, settling in with her dark brew. No milk, no sugar. Not for her. Yesterday's cappuccino a silly indulgence. Only then does she take out her phone. It's discipline, she tells herself. She's not one of those automatons, glued to their devices. Besides, it's easier to face the day with a strong cup of joe in her hand.

The first text was the one she expected: Shira. What surprises her is the timing. The lawyer had texted her back before ten, less than a half hour after Gal had reached out. *Yes*, she'd said. *Call me.*

Funny, Gal smiles to herself. She'd figured her old bandmate to be an early-to-bed type now. She certainly hadn't taken to the rock life. But there she was again, a half hour later: *We should talk.* By then, Gal realizes, she'd been in the bath, half dead with the stress of the day and in no mood to wrangle about Aimee, about their past. Funny to think that she'd become the early-to-bed one. Funny how things work out.

She drinks her coffee and thinks about returning the call. Not here, of course. There's no privacy here, never mind the generic soundtrack of yuppie tunes, the kind of pop that her band was supposed to prove extinct. Besides, she really ought to respect Walter's wishes, at least as far as she can. He's the one who matters in all this. Him and Camille.

Despite yesterday's confrontation, she feels good about this decision. About playing her part in their mourning. Dials Camille's number as an ice breaker. A way to work into her day.

"Hey, Camille?" Voicemail. She couldn't have timed it better. "Gal here. I don't want to get in your dad's hair, but do you think I could come by and finish up those expenses?" She makes a quick mental inventory before the service can shut her off. "I really only have about a day's work, and, well, I think it would be easier for me to finish than explain it all to someone. Anyway, thanks, hon. Let me know."

She rings off and considers a refill. That wasn't hard. Camille is a good girl, and for the briefest of moments, she has a twinge of regret. The road not taken. Then again, Aimee had Walter. Camille might have been an accident—there was no other way to explain the timing—but she was wanted. She was loved. And Walter had come through. He'd dropped his hard-partying ways, his old gang, like a hot potato, once he and Aimee decided to keep the baby. She gave up the band. Her music, but he gave up something too. Well, he couldn't be a roadie forever, but becoming a parent had made him an adult. That edge, that anger that Gal had run up against yesterday, that had started around then. He'd become…protective, the word jumps into her mind. Yeah, protective of his baby girl, and protective as well of the woman he married.

That explains it. She finishes her coffee. Decides against a refill. Aimee'd had a partner. A man who'd stepped up to be with her, when her body went rogue. Gal tilts the paper mug up to get the last bitter dregs. She'd made the best of her own options and look how far she's come.

CHAPTER 27

"Where the hell did that come from?" It wasn't just that pretty-boy journalist. The suit from the label had asked, too. All of them knocked back on their asses when they heard what she had done. That song, "Hold Me Down," had been their breakout. Their hit, even in the rough four-track version they'd recorded down at Randy's, burning up the college stations with a waiting list for the single, fans asking at the record store whenever she dropped back in to pick up a shift. It was why the suits had come calling, taking the shuttle up from New York to hear them at the Rat, the Channel, Taji's.

"Can I do it again, you mean?" She had stared the fat man down, unafraid. This one had stuck around, waiting by the door. Knowing that they'd come out—the so-called backstage a windowless supply room—to drink. To bask in it.

Aimee had been anxious. Gal could hear it in her voice during their quick, huddled confab before they'd opened the door. And Lina, well, Lina always wanted to be a star. She wanted to believe, but her dreams had become smaller. Even after the song hit, she'd been scared. A little desperate, wanting them to go on tour again, like the first time, to couch surf to the coast as soon as they had a case of vinyl to throw in back.

Gal saw it another way. This old man, with his jowls and his tired eyes—he was the suitor. He needed what they had. Their youth, their energy. Their—*her*—genius.

"'Course I can." She had smiled, the slow, tight-lipped smile she'd call on when she wanted to chill someone out. "You think I don't know how it's done?"

It had worked, that smile. Well, that and the song—"raw heart's blood," some wag had called it in that weekly zine. The kind of rocker that only got better live, the anger and the energy tearing through. She could see that from up on the stage. Just that night alone, she wanted to tell him. The couple making out in the corner, all tongues and loosened belts. A tall figure propping up a slouching girl, hands reaching around to fondle her even as he helped her off the floor. And the eyes! Those eyes staring up at her, wide with wanting. She knew desire when she saw it. All those boys, some of the girls, too—the way their lips parted as they stared up at her. She recognized that look in the suit, even after the set as he waited, hot and restless. The wet mouth, the glow of sweat. Tried to explain to Aimee that they'd have a deal before they knew it. That she didn't have to worry.

It was almost like they'd changed places, then, for a bit.

"You still on antibiotics?" Aimee, anxious, asking. The suit had finally taken off with promises to be in touch, licking his lips at the prospect. The party afterward.

"A few more days." Gal shrugged, slamming the glass down while she waited for a refill. For the real question. They were fine. She was fine. "It's all good."

Hell, she'd finally fucked Frankie only a few nights before. A week early, sure, but the bleeding had stopped by then. She hadn't told Aimee that either, Aimee being friends with Frankie's girlfriend and all. But now she looked out at the crowd with a new confidence, a warmth that didn't just come from the tequila. And Frankie had jumped to pour another.

She'd been right about the suit. He had an offer for them by the time she woke the next afternoon. The second, and better than the one from that British indie. Full tour support, a cut of the merch. Shit like that, and although Aimee had wanted to hang back, to hire a lawyer or maybe a manager, Gal had pushed the deal through.

She had to, really, because she knew the truth. For all her confidence on stage, she'd been bluffing about being able to grind out songs like that one. "Hold Me Down"? She had no idea where it came from either.

"Holy shit." Lina had been the first to respond the day Gal brought it into the practice space, nearly a month before. "So that's what you've been up to."

Gal had looked over at Aimee, then, her best friend's gaze steadying her. They didn't have secrets, none of them. But Aimee had gone with her. A stupid screw up. Too much to drink and not enough to think, she'd said. And, no, she didn't need anyone to talk to.

"Yeah," she said in response, eyes locked on Aimee all the while. "Maybe I need to get laid more often. Gets the juices flowing."

Something had, though it felt more like panic at the time. Or maybe an infection. Something inside her that she wanted to get out.

"I just feel so stupid," she'd said to Aimee, trying to put her finger on it. "What was I thinking?"

She'd been at Aimee's when the sickness hit, barely making it to the toilet before the wave of nausea had her doubled over, heaving, even when there was nothing left. It was Aimee who'd asked, who'd suggested that maybe it wasn't just the schnapps or the burritos they'd picked up on the way home.

"Such a fucking girl." The words as bitter as the taste in her mouth, still bent double, as she acknowledged that, yeah, maybe she'd fucked up.

"Occupational hazard." Aimee had held her hair back, run her cool hand over her forehead. Like that dream, only backward. Her eyes stung—maybe it was the stink—but Gal didn't cry. She was furious, instead. How could she have been so careless? So goddamned soft?

"Cut yourself some slack, Gal." Aimee, practical. Gentle, even, once the truth had sunk in. "We've been partying pretty hard since we got back."

"This isn't going to stop us." She'd sat up by then, leaning back against the tile. Wiped her mouth with the back of her hand. "Nothing is."

Still, it had slowed her down. Taking care of it, of herself, especially when the doctor told her she'd have to wait two more weeks.

"Fuck that shit," she'd bitched to Aimee as soon as she'd gotten home. "I want this off my chest. Out of me. Now."

She'd waited, of course. She'd had to. But while she did, she'd planned their next tour. Called the clubs they hadn't hit. Reached out to bands in Cleveland and Cincinnati, desperate to be out on the road. To be touring, to be away.

"We've got a tape going out to the college stations," she'd lied, ready to sell her soul if necessary. "Here in Boston, we already have a buzz."

And, then, like magic, it happened. One morning, the sun making everything look bleak, she'd picked up her guitar. The nausea was constant by then. Whoever called it morning sickness didn't know shit. Forget saltines, the only thing that helped was playing. She hadn't even thought she was concentrating. Hadn't been able to focus on anything except counting down the days until she could have it done. But the music was there, and the words followed, flowing like blood from a wound.

"*Gotta get it out. Gotta get myself free.*
Leather tough, steel cold, nothing left of me.
You can't hold me down, hold me down no more."

Okay, so the lyrics weren't brilliant, but they had a drive that played right into the surging rhythm, a force she could feel even as she worked it out, the first verse forming a rhyme before she knew what she was doing. Grabbing up a ballpoint, she dashed off those lines and the changes, happy for the first time in weeks. Or, if not happy, then distracted—no, *directed*. She'd tapped into something creative, and she knew not to let it go.

"It's fucking brilliant." Aimee wasn't humoring her. Gal knew that when she called her up to play it for her. Called her not to cry or whine for a change. "You've got to bring that in for the band."

"We've got to record it." Gal hadn't told her bandmates about her pitches, the calls to out-of-state clubs. She hadn't been sure they wanted it enough, needed to get away like she did. Even Aimee, at times, seemed okay with being a Boston band. Was she seeing Walter then? They were friends, they all were. Walter hanging out. Helping out. Was T.K. still their roadie then? God, it was all so long ago, Gal can't even remember. Once she had the song, it didn't matter. She stopped calling clubs. Scrapped the push for another bare-bones tour. The hell with convenience store hot dogs and sleeping on floors. She had other plans.

"We're going into the studio?" Aimee had sounded incredulous. "Who's paying?"

"We've got to do something." Gal, growing frantic. Needing this. "We can do it on the cheap, at that loft. We just have to have something to send around."

"You don't want to wait?" The appointment was scheduled already for a week from Tuesday. Aimee knew because she was going with her. "You might want to take some time."

"Fuck that." Gal felt like she was recovering already. Getting stronger. Harder. More kick-ass rock and roll. "One day, Aimee, and that's all. I want to finish this, see if I can sharpen the bridge. And then I'm going to come up with a B-side. Something better than 'Hard Ass.'" She named their current closer. "I'll call Randy. Set something up. This is it, girlfriend. We are out of here."

And so they were.

CHAPTER 28

What sealed it was the B-side. "So Fucking Stupid" was a crowd pleaser from the start. Everyone loved to sing along with the shouted gang vocals, and the rowdy rocker had that chorus that nobody could forget. Even in the radio edit, the one that made it onto their major label debut, there was something raucous and, yeah, racy about it. Very Boston rock: rough, funny, and a perfect counterpart to the tear-your-heart-out rager that "Hold Me Down" could be, especially on nights when Gal was really feeling it.

True, the song wasn't half as powerful as "Hold Me Down." But just when the negotiations were beginning to get complicated, when Gal was starting to worry she'd overplayed her hand, it really helped to have another hook-filled song. A second local hit to cement their reputation as a band that had a draw. That had legs.

"And you've got more of these?" The label rep wasn't wearing a suit when he came back. The black leather jacket didn't work with how he rolled, showing up at the Worcester gig in a town car with a driver. Didn't do him any favors either. Not with that belly, but Gal saw how he wanted to present himself. How he wanted the fantasy, as much as the music.

"As common as cunt hairs." Aimee's eyes had opened wide at

that, the negotiations bringing out her wary side. But Lina had laughed, and the fat man had, too, a beat later. A shade off balance.

"As the wrinkles on your ball sack," she added, in case he'd missed the point. She could take it to him, and she would.

"I love you girls," he'd said, his grin a bit unsure. "If I were twenty years younger…"

She smiled her evil smile, relishing the sight of him uneasy like that. As long as she had the edge, she was content.

That edge, that was the thing. Part of it was the radio play. Having two songs in rotation made her feel good, even if the station had, as one promo ran, "less power than your toaster." That airplay got their names on the college charts, which meant better gigs when they decided to tour again. Other offers, too, whether they signed with the fat man or not. Maybe he saw that; maybe they really were that good. The contract came through the next week. The suit wasn't stupid. He had the idea for the "adult" pressing—a re-recorded version even more profane than the original—paid for and distributed while the album was still in the works. Limited edition blue vinyl, it sold out in a week and got them a feature in *CMJ* to boot. Sure, it was marketing, but Gal liked it. Rock was supposed to be dirty. Besides, it whet the appetite for what was to come.

"*So fucking stupid!*" Some of it was the label interest, sure. Some of it was knowing that she had it—had *them*—under her control. Ever since that first night back, things had been different. She swaggered now on stage, so sure and sexy. Hips forward, against the bass. Making them think about her fingers, about where that rhythm was hitting her. What it was doing. Even as she sang, stalking the stage to the limits of her cord. Growling as much as singing. Seducing. Commanding. In charge.

"*What was I thinking? So young and dumb.*" It was that contradiction—the tough-as-leather delivery against the self-deprecatory, hell, self-lacerating lyrics—that made the song work. Nobody wanted to hear a sob story, but everyone had drunk too much and done something, well…the song title, that shouted chorus, said it all.

"Cunt Hairs." She wanted to call their next single that. Wrote a tune that fit, with lyrics about how finicky people could get, always wanting to parse every single little thing. She brought it to the band the week before they were to start recording.

"Come on," she'd said. "We can fit it in. 'Shot Put' is old, anyway. Everyone's heard it."

"Everyone in Boston." Aimee had been the voice of reason. "But this is for the label. We need tracks that we know work."

"Anyway." Lina, intimidated by the suit, by the time already booked at a studio out in Western Mass. "Shouldn't we be practicing the songs we've already agreed on?"

Gal had looked at her band mates in disbelief. "Is it the money?" she asked. "Is that what's got you so cowed? We're the talent. We're what they want. And as far as practice goes, shit, haven't we done this set a thousand times in the clubs? Can't we play these tunes shitfaced and half asleep?"

They'd compromised. Aimee winning Gal over with the promise that they'd try the tune out once they had the track order down cold. Gal agreeing that, yeah, the bridge to "Outhouse" could use some work. She would try to figure out something a little more nuanced for the middle eight before the recording date, before the clock started running for real.

Still, they'd found time. Besides, Lina and Aimee had liked the song. Gal had been working on it, nights when she couldn't sleep. What she'd first envisioned as a light-hearted number, poking fun at fuss, had taken on a darker, nastier turn as she wrote another lyric and, thinking of "Outhouse," an inverted bridge that had her pushing her range. Only after she'd played it for Aimee, always her sounding board, did she realize just how nasty the lyrics were, lashing out at the prim and the meek. The whiners who couldn't handle real life.

"This about Shira?" Aimee's question had startled her, coming out of nowhere.

"Whoa, what sparked that?" She'd laughed, shaking her head, her default gesture. "You mean, 'cause of the whining?"

Aimee had shrugged. "I don't know," she said. Not meeting her eye.

"Hey, you were the one who wanted her out of the band." Gal didn't know where this was headed. Aimee had always been her friend first.

"Yeah, she was a shit guitarist." Aimee had been setting up her kit, though Gal thought the attention she was giving to tuning her snare was a bit much. "But you were the one who was always down on her for her complaining."

"She was a little pussy." The words sounded harsh, even to Gal. "I mean, we're a rock band, not a nunnery."

Aimee only grunted at that and bent lower over the drum. Fuck it, thought Gal. Maybe it was about Shira, but maybe it was about the world. Touring—hell, life—was rough, and if you couldn't hack it, you shouldn't be on the road. Besides, she'd gotten a good song out of it. Even the label agreed, though they made her change the name.

"No." The fat man, not so flirty now. But Gal had laughed and played along. The suit versus the band: the eternal tension. But she had changed it. "Split Hairs," it became, the third track released to radio. She should have known then what would happen.

CHAPTER 29

She needs to call Shira back. Her old bandmate has been great, responding to her text right away. Gal knows that, but that memory—that song—makes the tips of her ears burn. She shouldn't be embarrassed, not really. It was all so long ago. What did Shira say? A different world. But, well, she really had been a bit much in those days. She'd had to be. Kicking Shira out, bringing Lina in. Going out on the road.

T.K. had wanted to tour with them. The memory comes out of nowhere as she walks back from the coffee shop. Maybe it's the setting. Brighton hasn't changed that much. As she passes a storefront advertising halal meat, she remembers him asking. Coming up to her after a gig, maybe even in that blues place that used to be on the corner there. Eager. Pushy, even, offering to drive as well as roadie. To handle things as they came up, as he put it. Basically, he wanted to be what they'd learn was a road manager, to be a Gus, not that they knew that then.

At the time, it just seemed a bit much. Especially with Shira out, after all her complaining, they didn't want to be seen as playing favorites. As being anything more than they were, Gal not yet comfortable with the spotlight. And so that first tour had just been the three of them, which might explain why T.K. had been so excited to see them that first gig back. Why Walter, his buddy then, had ended up getting together with Aimee. Only, Gal remembers reliable old Grandpa as gone missing. Out of town—was it a funeral?

No, she decides, settling on the memory. The halal place fading in her mind's eye into the Vietnamese noodle shop where they always hung. That was the next break, after they'd signed. After that second tour, the big sweep of northern cities, made easy with label support.

Once they were under contract, bringing along their own crew wasn't an option anymore. They'd not realized, fully, what tour support meant, but they found out. A proper bus, with a proper driver. Doug, that first tour. Or, no, was that the guitar tech, Gus's right-hand man? Gal couldn't remember any of the other names. Didn't have to, not with the crew in charge. Get on, get off. Play, sleep. It didn't take Gal long to learn that if she had problems with either of those, Gus could help. Coke, if she wanted. Something to relax, if not, and the driver always had speed. That made sense, considering the miles they logged. He also had a gun, which should have made her feel safe. "It's a cash business, darling." She hadn't asked again. Gus got them anything else. And once the single hit—"Hold Me Down" by unanimous acclaim—they were wanted everywhere. They took any boost they could get.

It got so it was almost boring. Load in. Play. Pack up, or watch Gus's crew do the work, and hit the road. Drink, sleep, play cards, play guitar until they reached the next town. Then it was the promo. Radio stations, especially the morning shows, were big on bands in studio. The DJs wanting to flirt and joke around. First thing in, they'd hand you a drink. A smoke.

"How about a little pick-me-up?" Well, why not, if you had to be witty at eight in the morning? Or ten or twelve. Besides, they loved it when you got wild. All the morning shows were the same.

After that, it was over to the other station—in the towns that had two—or the college station or the in-store. Signing promo copies of the record before she had her own, Gal had been a little freaked at the photo the label had used. The fans liked it, though, especially the boys. Yeah, well, they would. She remembers asking Gus when they were getting their own copies, at least she thought she did. She doesn't remember him answering. Someone would hand her a phone—some reporter full of questions. Talking until Gus would break in, announcing that time was up. Sometimes they met with the reporter, Gus or one of his boys watching over them like hawks.

The noodle shop reminds her. Spilled pho and a beer. On the good days, they had some down time before the gig. A chance to chill with Aimee and Lina. To laugh and have a drink, and then a little something to get geared up. The gigs, though. Those were the best. Venues she'd never heard of, and for all his gruff exterior, Gus knew how to direct a crew. Everything was there for soundcheck, and no hassling about the pay. Then back on the bus and moving on. It's amazing she remembered how to walk.

Poor T.K. Her mind skips back to him. Brighton, Allston, the gigs here, and over in Southie. The parties. But what she told the cop was true: they didn't stay in touch. Walter, though. Yeah, she remembers. That next time back, after the first big tour—their first with the label—he wasn't there. Aimee had been looking for him. Gal could picture her talking to T.K. Asking questions, the image of them huddled in the corner of the bar strangely vivid in her memory.

Walter. Shit. Her imagination's been running wild. She needs to go talk to the man, at least to clear things up. She can't just call Shira back. Go behind his back when he'd asked her not to. That wouldn't be fair.

It's a relief to have something resolved, and so she stops in her room just long enough to grab her keys. Sure, he got upset. He's got a lot on his plate, and she wasn't helping. But that's why she came back to town, right? To help.

"Hey, there." She opens the door but calls out before entering. "Walter, you here?"

A shuffle, and for a moment she panics. Someone's hurt. Someone's down. Aimee, crying, and she steps in before thinking. No, of course not. Her memory is simply running wild these days. But by then she's standing in the living room. Facing the office, where Walter is sitting where she had sat only the day before. He's looking up at her with a face like a train wreck. Mouth agape, hair messed, his eyes red and swollen. That sound she'd heard. That's why it was familiar. Walter had been sobbing.

"I'm sorry." She is. Her heart could break again. Aimee. She loved her so.

"No, it's fine." He raises a hand, absolving her. Wipes his face and then fishes around for a handkerchief so he can blow his nose. "It just hit me. You know?"

"Yeah." She goes to him and takes a seat, pulling the spare chair closer to the desk. Grief is the great leveler. It's not like she hasn't seen him cry before. She remembers now. The funeral, it was his mother's. He'd gone back home—Burlington? Lewiston?—and missed their triumphal return. The song had hit, and they were stars, coming back to town with label money and that bus and all. But she'd seen him three days later, sobbing in her drummer's arms. Maybe that's what she remembered. Walter, not Aimee, crying fit to break your heart.

"You want me to get lost?" Another idea hits her. That memory. Aimee crying, too, as they held each other. God, they were young. "You want to talk?"

He shakes off the idea, to her immediate relief. "Nah, thanks, though." Wipes his face again. "And, hey, I'm sorry I blew up at you. I know you're just trying to help."

She waits. She is trying—she wants to help, but how? "You know I'd do anything." That sounds awful. "I mean, I've already talked to Shira."

"How dare you!" The change is immediate, the tears replaced with ice. Those big hands clenched into fists. "You have no right."

"Hey, I'm sorry." She jumps up, her own hands high, though whether in surrender or to ward him off, she doesn't know. "I saw her at the reception, and I hadn't seen her in ages."

"Sorry." He deflates, tired now. Defeated. "This has all—it's just too much."

"Please, Walter." She pulls the chair back and sits once more, leaning in. "Let me help."

He looks around, as if hoping for an escape. "I don't know, Gal. You're already handling everything with the benefit."

"That's nothing. I'm almost done." If she cracks down, she'll be through the paperwork by the end of the day. "The guy who did the shirts, the venue, everyone's been paid. I'm only waiting for some of the legal stuff."

He tilts his head. She can see his temper start to rise.

"The bank," she explains. The ghost of a grin twitching in the corners of her mouth. "I've learned—I've had to learn a few things since, well, you know. I want to put the profits in the right kind of account for taxes and everything. We did well, Walter. There's going to be money left over, for Camille."

The air goes out of him. "Good." He collapses back into his seat. "That's good to hear."

She wants to ask. Of course she does. What she doesn't want to do is get him all riled up again. If only he knew how much she cared. If only he saw her as family.

"I think you're doing great," she says. She doesn't, not now, but it's an in. "I mean, we've all been through some stuff." She pauses, trying to think of herself crying. She can't. "I remember when your mom died."

He actually smiles a little. The memory, she thinks. Maybe crying serves a purpose. "You do?"

"How could I not?" She warms to her story. "You and Aimee had just started seeing each other. Yeah, I knew." He'd tried to keep their relationship quiet. Not secret, exactly. But not rubbing it in people's faces either, like Aimee sometimes did. He'd been a roadie. They'd all hung out together. Things could get weird. She remembers Aimee crying in her arms. Puking her guts out as Gal held her, both of them too drunk. Holding her hair back and then cradling her sweating body in her arms. Her muscular drummer had felt so vulnerable then. Soft and warm, like the child she never had. Damn, she loved that woman.

"It was that same weekend." She hears herself and comes back to the present. "The weekend we came back from our first big tour. Aimee and I got really wrecked."

"No." One syllable, and she realizes her error.

"She didn't drink like that usually. Not like I did." It's an apology, an explanation. "I think we'd been on the road too long and gotten into some bad habits."

"No, it wasn't then." He's shaking his head. "It was later. I remember that night. The party. I was there."

"You're probably thinking of the night we came home from the first tour. The three of us stinking from the van. I think we went straight to Taji's. I remember Aimee telling me you two hooked up not long after that." That should be a happy memory, but she can't quite summon it. It's been too long. That gig—the party after—it's all a blur. "I mean the next tour, the first real one, with the label behind us. We were gone for, like, months."

"No." There's force behind the word, the ones that follow. "I know the gig you're talking about. The record had just come out, and it hit while you were on the road. You'd left town as hopefuls and came back rock stars."

"Rock stars." She laughs. Had Aimee told him about the drugs? About the night the driver pulled his gun? Threatened them all if they didn't get back on the goddamned bus that minute? "They packaged us like animals. Like a circus side show. Carting us around and telling us what to do. Every minute accounted for, and a chemical spur for whatever the occasion."

Walter's looking at her. She can't read his face, but she can hear herself. How hypocritical she must sound.

"Hey, I'm not complaining. It's given me a good life, but Aimee was smart to get out when she did." The one after, the second tour with the label. That was when the drummer had called it quits. Chosen Walter and Camille over the band's burgeoning fame. "She had you waiting for her."

He looks away, but she can still see the pain. The way his brows gather, his mouth pinched like he's trying not to cry. Aimee. An infant in her arms.

"Oh my God," she says, almost laughing at the realization. "Camille must have been conceived during that break. After you got back, I guess."

"I was never away." He's staring at her. "Aimee and I were together that whole time. What was it, three weeks?"

"That sounds right." She thinks back. "Then they flew us out to LA to work with Fischer. Fischer the hit maker." More drugs.

More wake-up calls. Publicity. A print-out handed to her each day, as if she cared. It didn't matter. They got her when they needed her, awake in the studio. For the most part. "But I was sure—" She can't shake the idea that he'd been gone. That Aimee had called out for him that night, crying in her arms.

"I should know when my own mother died." Curt, like he's angry with her. Grief was funny. "Besides, I should get back to work."

"Of course." She doesn't know what she said, but she can tell she's been dismissed. "I'll be in the other room."

A nod, and when she steps out, she closes the door behind her. She should be used to this by now. The way she's lived has taken its toll on her memory, events sliding together. Aimee crying. Walter, too. She sits at the table and pulls the papers toward her. The bank forms, applications for nonprofit status. A trust. It's all there, only she's been stalling. Wanting to make this last. Her final connection to Aimee, to the band. She should call Shira back, she tells herself. Reconnect with someone who was, at one point, a friend. But first, she'll file for the new account. Get something tangible done.

An hour later, she's done. Walter's still in the office, and so she thinks about knocking. Instead, she leaves a note on top of the forms. "Sign here, and we're done," she writes, and adds a smiley face. He's so touchy. No, she understands that. It's the bigger questions that bother her. Why isn't Walter defending himself? And why does she think he's lying? *It should have been me*, that refrain again. No, that makes no sense. She grabs her jacket and heads out.

CHAPTER 30

After Aimee left, things got really crazy.

It wasn't that Aimee didn't party. At least, up until those last couple of weeks when, Gal realized in retrospect, the drummer was deciding what to do about her pregnancy, Aimee had been up for anything. But even when they were wired up—coke for the energy, pills and booze to level off—Aimee had been Gal's rock. Her mate. The one she told everything to. Almost.

Gal stops herself at that thought and shakes her head. She's back in her motel room, and although she meant to get some dinner hours ago, she finds she's still on the bed, bass in her lap, working out the changes of what might just be a new song. Something for Aimee or Camille.

"Damn." She flattens her hand over the strings, realizing what she's done. She's playing "Hold Me Down" again, lost in the memory.

She'd been worried when Aimee dropped out. Unsure if the magic would continue. The timing couldn't have been worse. The album was a hit, and they were heading out again. A big tour this time: national, Canada too. Gal was writing; Aimee was as well, or would be, Gal recalled. When they started that third tour—after Walter had returned from his mother's funeral, Gal was sure of that—she had thought they were on the top of the world.

The memories flood back. The bus, the big one this time, pulling up to the compound to load in. Gal ready to defy any comment on the size and smell of their practice space. Walter shunted aside as Gus's crew took over. She remembers the shaky smile on his face as he stood on the curb, taking Aimee's hand. Bummed that his girlfriend was leaving, unsure of what would happen to their fledgling romance, probably. Bummed that he was no longer indispensible, not even here, in town. But did he know then that she might be pregnant? Or was he simply mourning, a rocker suddenly transformed into a lost boy with the death of his mom? Gal wracks her brain. Too much partying, and she no longer can be sure what she remembers.

Not that the partying hurt them, not at first. She remembers how easy it was, this time, to fall into the routine. Walk into a radio station, drink in hand, greasy jeans hanging low like a dare. Unshowered, still high from the night before. Not only did it not detract from her appeal, it enhanced it. This was rock and roll, after all.

Besides, none of that mattered. What mattered were the shows. God, they were great. She was on fire. Gal looks back now and can't imagine how she did it. Fearless and wild, even after Aimee called it quits and the label sent them Britta. Someone Gus knew, her own band in disarray. Seattle's drug scene crazier than theirs.

True, Britta wasn't Aimee. Wasn't as sane or stable, in retrospect, and maybe she wasn't the best choice as a bandmate, considering her predilection for the various substances available on the road. But she was a rock-solid drummer, a monster on the trap, and she knew the material. Even when they moved to the bigger venues, with the booming stage sound, Gal could count on her, could *feel* that rhythm. Even when Britta was flying high. Even when they all were.

Gal closes her eyes, remembering. Was it Cleveland? Yeah, how perfect was that.

Cleveland. They'd come in late, after dark, all the pre-show press done by phone the day before. They could have slept, that meant, as the bus rolled in, straight to the venue, but Gal doesn't remember sleeping. Barely remembers sleeping at any time during that tour. Just the theater—the Beacon or the Orpheum. One of those tumble-down places built first for vaudeville. The kind with a deep stage and a pit for the orchestra. Gal loved those ratty old theaters, the gilding peeling from the ceiling. Loved the decadence of the musty velvet curtains, even though the backstage would be as drafty and narrow as an alleyway.

She remembers the smell of them. Dust and sweat, a hint of ozone from the lights. Remembers waiting there, gearing up for the show. Gus warning them that it was a full house. Restless, wild.

"What else is new?" An extra toot as she visualized the crowd hanging off the balcony. Reaching from the boxes toward the stage. The album had gone gold. "They love us."

"They're crazy here." Saying it as a warning. To egg her on. "Last band here were some death metal freaks. Pyrotechnics and everything. Nearly burned this old dump down."

"We don't need that fake shit." Another line, going down easy. "We *are* the fire."

It was their standard banter. Gus pushing and Gal pushing back. So what if they weren't playing the larger venues yet? That Gus had brought in Mimi to play bass, telling Gal she needed to become more of a front woman. To be free to move around. Not a discussion, the word from above. Fuck it, they were punk. Rock. A better fit with the faded velvet and down-at-heels glam than any death metal headbangers, any stadium bands. They didn't need fire pots or lasers, no dancing clowns to make their mark. But Mimi? Gal had bridled at that, a little. Bristled at giving up her bass.

"You want to play stadiums?" Gus's point. Always the same. "You've got to give them a show."

"We'll give them a show." Gal growled to herself. A losing battle. Next tour, if they got the stadiums, they'd have fireworks going off and strobes popping. As inevitable as Mimi on bass. The label would make sure of it.

"Hell yeah, we'll give 'em a show!" Britta burst in. Gal remembers how bright her eyes were, the electricity coming off her like the blue tips of her bleached-white hair. Almost Aimee, like the label had her dyed to order. "Fuck that shit!"

Britta was loaded. High on something other than what Gus and Gal were sharing. Even as she passed the CD case, one of theirs, to Mimi, Gal remembers wondering. What had her new drummer gotten into? And how could she get some?

She doesn't remember asking, but Britta—or maybe it was Gus again—knew. A bottle, a pill, and then they were on, wobbling into those filthy curtains on her way to the stage. Dark, of course. This might be rock and roll, but who didn't like the element of surprise?

"Hey, Cleveland!" A roadie, one of Gus's crew, had guided her to the mic stand. The dust, the coke, made her hoarse. Made her sound sexy, she thought, laughing into the night. "How you doing?"

Nothing. It was Cleveland, right? In the glow of tech lights, she could see Lina to her right and, beyond her, a crew member gesticulating. "How ya doing?" She fumbled with the mic. No switch. There hadn't been a switch to turn on since they signed. Since Roddy started doing their sound. Her own mic every night, but no control to go with it. Then again, the Shure she pressed her mouth up to didn't smell like vomit and stale beer. She leaned in, lips on the cold mesh head—and that's when it hit. The lights—

white-hot kliegs—blasted the stage like lightning that didn't fade, and Gal, startled, stumbled back, the mic still in her hand. Only then did Britta's sharp-stick count kick in, and she remembered. A cold opening. Dark to light, blasting the crowd like a shot of—

"Cleveland!" Recovering, she ran forward. "We are here for you!"

And that was it. Lina's wiry intro loud in the stage monitors. Her own vocals deep and throaty in the mix. Yeah, she wasn't in Boston anymore. Wasn't playing in basement dives for drunken Massholes. She wrapped one leg around the mic stand and bent it over. Bent it to her will. Maybe it was good to have Mimi on bass. Singing—fronting the band—that was Gal's strength. Making them want her. Making them scream.

Two numbers later, she was positively tripping. What had been in that pill? No time to wonder. She was flying. She was in charge. "Stupid as fuck!" Singing or screaming, it all worked. The stage lighting had shifted. Not warm, but not blinding bright, illuminating the wide, sweaty faces screaming up at her. Those eyes, those open mouths, so hungry. She wanted to feed them. To smash them, towering over them as she was.

It was the old theater. The pit too far down. In a club—the Rat, Taji's—those faces would be right at her feet. Close enough to crush. Grabbing the mic, she stalked the stage. Part Iggy, part Mick, hot and hard with the sound, and the crowd was loving it.

"Hold Me Down," and she heard the screams. Looked up to see the wild eyes and open mouths in the boxes, reaching out to touch the stage. That's when it hit her. This old dump, it wasn't made for a sound like hers. The amp stacks on either side barely fit. And so she started climbing. Hanging from the speaker even as Lina soloed fast and mean.

"*Down!*" she screamed when the guitarist hit her cue, pitching her wail to that one held note. "*Can't hold me down!*" She was going to make the box. Outstretched hands desperately reaching, ready to pull her up. Pull her off the stage to freedom.

Only Gus's guys got to her first. Firm hands on her hips, and she collapsed, laughing, as they lowered her to the stage. Spun around, once they'd released her, nearly tripping over the cord but perfect in her abandon.

"One, two, three, four!" Britta shouted out the count, and Gal took a swig of the bottle she found in her hand. Dying of thirst, of laughter, she spun again, and Lina caught her. She hadn't dropped her mic, though, and she growled the opening of "Bad Way Down" like she always did. Rough and ready, and fearless in the service of rock and roll. Even as the liquor steadied her, she ranged the stage like something feral, loose limbed and sexy. Gus, barely visible in the shadow, had his arms crossed, and she could imagine him shaking his head, pissed off at the excessive theatrics. At the risk that didn't calculate reward.

Fuck Gus, she thought. Maybe even said it, her mic still on. The label controlled everything they did twenty-three hours of every day. When she was up here, though, she was in charge. If she wanted to climb out of herself, she would do it. She could sing, and she could make them scream. She was rock and roll, and when she was on stage, she was free.

Chapter 31

"I think T.K. wanted to save my soul." She's on the phone with Russ. It's like talking to herself, only she feels a little less crazy knowing he's there. "I gather he found Jesus along the way."

"Whatever works for you." Her own personal Buddha, albeit with a better body. He's working, she can tell. Distracted but happy enough to hear her voice.

"I guess." Sometimes his nonchalance pisses her off. "His widow was creepy as fuck."

A laugh. The Russ she misses, almost. Which reminds her of that cop, Bixby. All-business Bixby, she tags him, and recalls what he said.

"He must have thought I really needed saving." She's thinking aloud, really. That's all. Still, it would be nice to have some input. "The cop in charge says he was trying to get in touch with me. His widow said that too."

"Maybe he just wanted to touch base." The distance making itself felt. "I mean, when was the last time you saw him? When you were last in town?"

"God, no." A shiver of revulsion. She pokes at the takeout container. Noodles congealing in their brown sauce—the good

Vietnamese place long gone—and pictures dinner with T.K. and his wife, their heads bowed in prayer. Overcooked vegetables and no wine. She'll take the noodles. Fishes out a peapod and eats it, thinking while she chews. "I hadn't seen T.K. in…years."

She pauses, not that he'd notice, and tries to remember. Things had been so crazy there for a while. That first tour they'd done by themselves, just the three of them in that van. Then the second tour, when the label hooked them up with Gus and his crew. Harnessed them, really. Looking back, it was pretty clear that Gus had begun running the show even then, doling out portions of freedom each night on the road. With a radio hit and another on the way, they hadn't cared. They had each other. By the next tour—the big one, the one Aimee left—even the illusion of choice was gone. Dates added, the schedule unknowable as Gus brought in Britta, brought in Mimi. Brought in anything to keep them—keep her—going night after night after night.

"Well, if he went into the program, and you were still drinking…" Russ doesn't even finish the thought. It's too much like confrontation.

"No, no way," she fires back as if he has. T.K. wasn't avoiding her. She dropped him, she's sure of it. Isn't she? "I mean, I don't think that's what happened."

Another chuckle. "Hey, no offense." Goddamn Russ and his mellow humor. "It's just, well, you got yourself pretty wired up there for a while."

She doesn't respond. Doesn't have to. They both know how they met. She was in rehab, a quiet place upstate called Vale Acres, though whether the "Vale" stood for valley or as an exhortation to be well, she never did find out. He was the local handyman, the only person she could stand for quite a while. She'd begun taking long walks by then and would swing by his truck to chat him up.

Being with him, the exercise, helped to clear her mind more than the mandated group-think sessions. Before long, she'd found him receptive to other forms of exercise as well.

"I thought you weren't supposed to get into a relationship with anyone for, like, a year or something?" She remembers him saying that, one lazy afternoon. She was out on her own recognizance for the day. They were used to her rambles by then—she wasn't sneaking out nights anymore—and seemed to understand they kept her sane.

"Who's talking about a relationship?" She felt a bit of the old power coming back. But she wasn't a rock star, not there, and he'd only laughed and reached for her once more, like he probably did a different woman every ninety days. Something they had in common, she figured. The comfort of the flesh.

By the time she'd finished treatment, she'd developed a habit. Russ, for sure, but also those long walks along country roads, with ditches instead of sidewalks and the mountains in the distance. When she asked, he'd said, sure, he'd show her around. Of course, he happened to know of one old, ramshackle place that might be available—his neighbor's, naturally. The old man had died a year before, and his nephews happy to unload it. She figured he got a cut, but she didn't care. The royalties were still coming in back then, and she liked to think of herself as free with cash. That he would help keep it up, get it back into shape, was unspoken. That he'd share her bed was, too.

Where else was she going to go? She went back to her mother's house briefly, after she was discharged. Found her bass in the cellar, covered in cobwebs. She remembers taking it out of the case—that broken clasp—and cradling it like a long-lost friend, heavy in her lap. It was pretty much all she took with her when she went back to Bearsville. To her own home, at last.

The years had flowed like water. A month would pass, maybe

more. Then the slow season, and he'd show up with the sticks and the mud. Soon he was staying, and she saw the grey creep into his hair. Most times, the informality of the arrangement—no rules, no strings—kept her from bolting. Sometimes, like now, she wondered how laid back her rustic paramour actually was.

"You knew I was a heavy drinker from the get-go." He hates it when she goes straight at him. She doesn't care. "That's why I was up there, off the road. Stuck in rehab."

"Hey, I didn't mean anything by it." Skittering off, as usual. "Just that, well, I thought maybe this T.K. might have felt the need to break away."

Felt the need… Gal frowns. For all his hippie ways, at times Russ sounds like one of the shrinks at the facility. "He didn't." She would set the record straight. "I did."

"Got it." His voice, as usual, warm and soft, but for a fleeting moment she wonders if he's humoring her. "It was your choice."

"It's always my choice." She hears the edge in her voice. "Sorry, Russ. It's been tense. What with Walter and all." She thinks of Shira, of that cop. That niggling voice in the back of her own head. Why did T.K. want to talk to her?

"I get it." The casual indifference gone. "Look, babe, why don't you come home?"

"I—" She catches herself. This isn't how they talked. *Babe? Home?* "I don't want to leave Walter in the lurch." And something more, too.

"Sounds like he doesn't want to be helped." Russ, sounding more reasonable, more focused, than she expects. "You've got to let people find their own way, Gal."

Was that what he's been doing with her? She brushes the thought away. "This isn't about giving up drinking. This is about going to jail. About murder."

Silence on the other end of the line.

"I want to find out what T.K. was up to." The words are out before she's even thought them through. "Why he was there, at our gig. It wasn't because of Aimee," she says before he can interrupt. "They didn't—they'd had a falling out."

That came from nowhere. An excuse, but it sounded right.

"You think he was there to see you?"

"Yeah, maybe." She draws her knees up and hugs them close. The idea is strangely disconcerting. "Creepy, huh? He came to see me, and he got killed."

She says it like a joke, but in the pause that follows, she hears that Russ has taken her seriously. "Gal," he says, "do you think you might be in danger?"

"No." It's reflex, the denial. *It should have been me*. She wraps her arms tighter around her knees, until her fingers sink into her upper arms. He was there for her, she knows.

CHAPTER 32

Camille. That's who she needs to talk to. Someone who cares as much about Walter and maybe can talk sense into him.

"Hey, Camille." Voicemail, of course. "I'm sorry about the other day. I had some ideas, though. Call me?"

She should have mentioned Walter, the talk with the widow, but at the last minute it seemed a lot to dump on a college girl, especially in a voicemail. Camille is only a little younger than she and Aimee were when they started the band. She's seemed even younger recently—the shock, the loss. But there's resilience in the girl. There has to be. She had Aimee as a mother, didn't she?

Scrolling through her messages, she pauses on Shira's. The one from the other night, her thumb hovering over it before she moves on. She and Shira have gone in such different directions, whereas Shira and Aimee were both mothers. Both still living in town. There are tons of reasons they might have been in touch, and what right does Gal have to ask? It's not like she and Shira have anything left in common. A lawyer and a—what?—a washed-up rocker? Besides, Shira would have said if she had any ideas about Walter. This was only her returning a call. A courtesy to an old colleague. Nothing that she'll miss.

Speaking of old colleagues, Gal thinks of Lina. The guitarist still has that edge, a dissonance that pits funk rhythms against punk's stark shards. It felt good playing together the other night. It hadn't been seamless—she remembers that memory slip and shakes it off with a shiver. Seeing T.K. had been, well, it had been a shock. But overall, the gig had been good. Playing with her girls. She'd missed it.

Before she can overthink it, she scrolls through her phone. Yeah, Lina's there, from the days before, when everything had been chaotic and no one was sure how it would all go. The calls after, with the news.

"Lina? It's Gal." Suddenly self-conscious, as if her guitarist wouldn't recognize her voice. The number on her phone. "I was thinking about the other night." Now that she's talking to her onetime bandmate, she feels shy. She should have checked the time. Texted first. "The gig."

"We were smoking. Weren't we?" The pleasure in Lina's voice is encouraging. "For old gals, we've still got it."

"Yeah." Gal laughs at the description. Old? Well, maybe. "But you're still playing, right?"

A snort. "Once a month at the Plough," she says. "And happy to have that."

Gal starts to say something. To compare Lina's gig with those first days, when she remembers—Lina wasn't in the band then. That was Shira. T.K. hanging around. "I know the feeling," she says. The words sound foreign. Nonsensical. "I mean, I've been sitting in at a local coffeehouse sometimes. Back up in Bearsville."

"A *coffeehouse*?" Surprise ratchets up Lina's voice, before she catches herself. "I'm sorry. It's just…that's so not how I think of you."

"Yeah, well." Gal doesn't know how to feel. Knows she wants to move on. "Hey, did you hear the latest about T.K.?" Silence. "The cops are investigating. They asked me some questions about what happened. You know, the night of our show."

"Wait, what? So they think someone meant to kill him? I thought it was an accident. I guess I was hoping…" Silence for a moment, but she's still there. "I'm sorry. I don't really remember him very well. I didn't realize he was a friend of yours."

"A lifetime ago." Gal waves it off, like an annoying fly. "But that's not why I called. Actually, Lina, I was wondering. Would you want to get together again? Play some more of the old tunes?"

"You mean, another reunion gig?" Surprise, pleasure maybe? At any rate, Lina is happy to move on, and so Gal explains.

"Maybe something more informal. For us." She's already thinking about Bobbi Jo. Lina's drummer had been good enough for the benefit, but does she want to deal with an outsider? "I mean, hey, when am I going to get to play Aimee's song again? Besides, I kind of messed up 'Hold Me Down' the other night."

Silence, and she remembers. Other nights when she messed up. A tour cut short. The stadium shows that never happened. It was her band. Hers and Aimee's, and she'd been the star. Only—

"Hey, why don't you come sit in?" The voice snaps her back. "Tomorrow at eight, the Plough. This is one of our weeks. I mean, it won't be much…"

"I'd love to." She laughs at her own eagerness, and maybe a little with relief. "Hey, maybe some of the old gang will come out one more time." T.K. staring up at her. "Or, well, maybe it'll just be fun."

They trade information. There's no load in, per se. All she has to do is show up, Lina says. Gal stops herself from asking if the sound guy knows what he's doing. If the house mics are any good. This is a friendly gathering. Casual. And more, Lina's doing her a favor. Neither one of them has said it, but Gal feels it now, the awkwardness. The debt. Was she really that awful—that last tour?

It doesn't bear thinking. At times like this, she wonders what the program would say. Something about forgiving yourself, she figures. Maybe she should have joined up, all those years ago. Only now it seems a little late. She doesn't drink. She's in control. All she needs is absolution for all the bodies in her wake.

CHAPTER 33

It was the fourth week in rehab, maybe the fifth. Time had kind of disappeared by then, almost like she was on the road again. She remembered being taken aback by the shock of autumn, and the annoyance of having to explain that she wanted her hoodie. Needing permission to go back in early from her walk, back when they were still watching her. Back when they'd had reason to.

The weather hadn't bothered her on her nights out. Her roamings, as she called them to herself. Those few nights when she'd exit through the kitchen, after a smoke with the cleanup crew. The last of the kitchen staff. It was easy enough to do, the place more country club than locked ward. A beer in town, once, maybe twice. A couple of shots shared with that one guy on the late shift, a dishwasher who smelled as much of sweat as he did of whiskey. A brief escapade in his car, less fun than she'd expected. Had that been the last time? Maybe. Once she knew she could, she hadn't bothered. Instead, she'd let herself fall into the patterns of the place. Time must have gone by. It always did.

Not that it mattered, she told herself, as the chill turned to frost. Five weeks, maybe. Maybe more. Another layer under the hoodie. Another morning, woken for meetings. For a mandatory meal. She wasn't paying for it. Or, well, yeah, she was, the royalty statements would bear that out, she realized at some point. A sign of her clearing brain. Her drying out. Cheaper than a lawsuit, she figured, remembering the blood. Cheaper than jail.

"Why do you think you drink and get high?" Not group this time, but the private shrink. The twice-weekly sessions that were as mandatory as the piss tests. "What are you trying to bury?"

"Bury?" She'd chortled, ever the wordsmith. "Don't you mean drown?"

"Drown, then." The shrink, a quiet, pudgy man, eyes like a spaniel's, bigger even, behind his glasses. "What is it?"

More laughter, bursting out like vomit, and about as pleasant. "I'm a rock star," she'd explained. She'd tried to, anyway. "It comes with the territory."

All a big joke, until she'd heard about Mimi. The TV in the common room, usually set to game shows or some endless ongoing soap had been left unguarded. A celebrity news program had come on. "Rocker found dead." The crawl had caught her eye. For a moment, she'd wondered. They know I'm here, right? But no, it was Mimi. She saw the photo—their last publicity shot—and turned the sound up, not too loud.

Poor girl. She must have been lost without the band. The TV report was brief, barely touching on her work before. But Mimi'd been a pro, been on the road since she was sixteen, Gal knew. Did studio work, too, until her habit made her miss some gigs. Screw something up. But she knew Gus, and he'd brought her in. Did he know she was using? Had she been, before joining up with them? With Lina and Britta? With Gal?

Too much to think about. She'd made her choices; they all had. Still, it shocked her. Mimi had been twenty-seven, the TV said, before moving on to some actress with fake boobs and a lawsuit.

Of course she was. Join the club, Gal said to herself. The last bit had been something about the pending autopsy. Knowing in advance what they'd find.

Knowing, as well, how lucky she'd been. That the night she didn't like to think about—the incident that had landed her here—was a gift from the gods. So that night, Gal had snuck out again. Only this time, she'd gone to that tattoo place, the one the kitchen guy told her about. He was open late, not that nine was late by real-world terms. An old hippie who barely raised an eyebrow when she walked in, head swiveling to make sure she'd not been followed. "An F clef," she'd said, drawing one on his pad to make sure he understood. "Here."

"You sure?" His brows had gone up when she'd turned her arm over, revealing the soft pale flesh of her wrist. "It'll hurt."

"Good," she'd said.

CHAPTER 34

When the phone wakes her the next morning, she's afraid to answer. It's Lina, calling to cancel. She'll make some excuse, but Gal will know. Her bandmates don't want her around. She's too much trouble. A prima donna. The out-of-control control freak, as some wag in group therapy had dubbed her. But as the device buzzes for a third insistent time and her head clears from another round of confused, disturbing dreams, Gal recognizes the number.

"Camille." Gratitude makes her effusive. "Thanks for calling me back."

"You're welcome. But I'm not calling because you did. That's not—" The young woman's words are clipped, strangely formal, before dropping away entirely into awkward silence. As Gal waits, she tries to remember why she reached out to Aimee's daughter. What had seemed so important. Shira, she recalls, and she tries to work out how she can rephrase her query, explain her curiosity about that long-ago appointment. Before she can find the words, Camille starts speaking again. "I—we—we're meeting with that lawyer. Me and Dad."

"Shira?" She catches herself, remembering Walter's anger.

"What? No, Dad's lawyer, Albert Gallegio." Her voice is tight, the name awkward in her mouth. "The one whose number you

168

found for me."

"Oh, good." Relief like a wave washes over Gal. Still, it's no wonder Camille has been tense. Bigger issues than Gal's own guilt trip are at stake. "I'm so glad he's finally taking these charges seriously."

"But he isn't." Before Gal can interject, Camille keeps talking, the tension unspooling into words. "He's still not going to fight it—fight them. I guess he's told the lawyer, and now neither of them will talk to me about it."

"So, wait, what are you doing there?" Gal's missing something. Confused. "What's going on?"

"Dad asked me to be here because he wants to sign everything over to me." Camille's voice is clipped. Gal can hear the strain in it. "I mean, the condo. All his accounts. Even the publishing rights to Mom's songs."

"The publishing rights?" This isn't making any sense.

"Yeah, that one hit? It still pays. I guess some TV show used it in its soundtrack? Anyway, Mom signed it all over to him when she got sick. Now he's signing everything over to me."

"I guess he wants to take care of you." Gal speaks slowly, trying to think this through. Grief and a desire to protect…

"But he isn't." The tension breaks, and Gal can hear the tears gathering. When Camille speaks again, her voice is choked and high. Twenty isn't what it used to be. A grieving daughter, still a child. "Why is Dad doing this? He should be working on his defense. Not, I don't know, giving up like this. I'm scared, Gal. I'm afraid he's going to do something. That he's going to hurt himself."

"I'm coming over." Her response is immediate. Instinctive. "Where are you? At his office? Are you at the condo now?"

"No, I-I don't know." The girl stammers. "Dad says I should go back to school. He told me to take the first bus out. That I should leave before the court date, before he changes his plea. But I don't want to leave him like this."

Damn Walter, dropping this on his daughter and then sending her off. "Don't worry, Camille." Gal is in charge now. In control. "I'm going to speak to your father, and I'll talk some sense into him. We'll get this straightened out."

Her first call is to that detective, Bixby, and it goes to voicemail. She leaves her name and number but nothing else. What can she say? A man has been arrested, and she wants to talk about him. She'll be told to talk to the lawyer. She's seen enough shows…hell, she's signed enough contracts. Not that it matters. She no longer has this Gallegio's contact info. Never copied it from the Post-It she gave to Camille.

Her first thought is to call the girl back. But even as her finger hovers over the number, she remembers Camille's choked voice. Aimee's daughter so close to tears. Besides, it'll be easy enough to go back to the condo and get the lawyer's info again. Give the distressed daughter a few moments of peace, of thinking that Gal is, as she'd promised, taking the burden off her back.

Ten minutes later, she's knocking on the door. Nobody answers. She hadn't expected Camille to be there. A little, she hopes the girl took her father's advice and went back to school. But as she lets herself in, Gal realizes she half expects to find Walter sitting at his desk. Fuming over his papers. To see Aimee, laughing at the fuss.

No such luck. And though Gal would like her friend's ex to be there—to be handling all the hoopla without her—she's on her own. As always. As Gal goes once more into Aimee's office, now Walter's, she feels the weight of this.

A moment of panic. The pile of papers—the sticky notes with numbers, the lawyer—is gone. A wish fulfilled? No, she never really...

A little breathless, she rushes over. Takes a seat and opens drawers, trying to be methodical. Not to panic, not to feel guilty about the relief that has flooded through her. Not her fault, of course. The lawyer, the meeting, Walter would have taken everything over to his office. A planned and considered move.

Pushing the chair back, she breathes. Wills her racing heart to slow as she places her hands, palm down, on the desktop. Sees, as if for the first time, what has replaced the piles of paper she'd expected to find here.

To her left, a crayon drawing. The peak-topped house the family never had, a yellow-haired mother and a dad, for some reason, with a pipe. Camille got Walter's hair right, at least—that mess of brown curls now grayed and thinning—and colored herself with a big smile, lips as red as her childhood hair. Beside it, a stack of cards, folded inside each other.

She opens the innermost. Cartoonish and bright, larger than the ones enveloping it. The signature is a childish scrawl that doesn't match the "Dear Dad" on top. She can picture Aimee and Camille browsing the stationery rack, the little girl reaching for the biggest one there, brilliant blue with a red bear on the front.

Sheepish—this isn't what she's here for, this is personal, Walter's—she flips through the rest. A wheeze from one of the later ones, a musical chip long since played out. A bad pun referencing a Top 40 song from a few years back. What did Aimee think of its repurposed pop? Were she and Walter still living together then? Gal weighs the stack in her hand. Resists counting, looking for the gap. Camille loves her father. All families go through hard times.

Not that she knows, not from this side of it, her own father a bad memory fading fast. She makes herself put the cards down. Stop her snooping. She's not going to find the lawyer's info here.

Walter's taken everything, taken care.

Tidying the pile back up, she admits to a melancholy mix of confusion and regret. Never one for coupling up, she wonders once again how Aimee and Walter managed for as long as they did. As she closes the door, locking the condo up behind her, she lets herself remember. She and Aimee were so much alike, or so she'd thought. Independent, free-spirited. Straight, sure, though they both had their moments. She tries to conjure up her friend back at the beginning, when they'd first met—those muscles. The tattoos.

Gal remembers one night, early on. She'd been dating someone—God, the idea is as foreign as the word. Jake, a bass player in another band. Sweet, but flakey, and for some reason she found his spaciness annoying. Gal shakes her head at the memory. It feels like a different world, but yeah, she can still hear herself, complaining because he hadn't shown up at their gig. Hadn't called, and she'd felt hurt by that. She and Aimee drinking at Aimee's apartment afterward. Hiding out, she admitted, in those pre-cell phone days, in case Jake came by. Let him worry, she remembers Aimee saying. Let him wonder where you are.

Had she really cared that much? She had, remembering the tears if not the emotion they sprang from. Realizing, not then but sometime after, that Aimee was her soulmate, the one she could rely on. And yet she'd let her old friend go, just like Jake and all the others. Somewhere in there, she'd stopped caring. Some of it was the life—Jake never did schedule time for romance. And yet, Aimee and Walter…

Well, that was different. She thinks of Camille. That was fate. And Walter was home. He was here, always hanging out. Helping out, at first, with T.K. The romance blossoming despite the old friendship. Despite the tension she had warned Aimee about—Walter not wanting his old buddy to know. Not wanting to upset their group chemistry by pairing off. By getting serious. Growing up.

She stops in her tracks outside the building. Was Walter seeing anyone recently? Did he have a new relationship? Gal never knew the details of the breakup. She and Aimee had drifted too far by the time her old friend had told her they were separating. It had sounded amicable, and Walter's certainly taken on the widower's portion, cleaning out Aimee's condo and putting her affairs in order. That didn't mean he didn't have someone else, a lover who has taken a backseat during the crisis and its aftermath. That's what adults do, she knew in some corner of her mind. What non-rockers do, in any case.

If that's the case, she has no idea where to find her. For a moment, she visualizes a scene: Aimee's estate settled and daughter safely back at school, Walter returns to his new home. His new love. Only, no, there wasn't anyone around when Walter was arrested, and Camille hasn't mentioned a third party in all the talk about her father's arrest. Besides, if he had a new life, would he be so willing to give it up?

There isn't anybody else. Never was. The thought strikes with the certainty of truth. Walter may have moved out, but he hasn't moved on. That's why the fussing over Camille, over Aimee's affairs. He's still hanging on to her, any way he can.

"Walter?" Gal remembers laughing the first time she and Aimee really talked about it. Early autumn, they were in limbo. Off the road, waiting, the pending deal making everything more serious and more casual all at once.

"Yeah, crazy, huh?" They were drinking out back. The lot behind their practice space on a hot September night. "He's just so calm."

Gal bit her tongue. Or, more likely, took another swig. "Calm" wasn't much of a recommendation. It didn't seem likely either,

considering how crazy she and Aimee could get. Then again…
She thinks of Russ. Calm has its advantages, and there have been
times recently when she's found herself relaxing into a routine with
her handyman neighbor. If she were someone else, she thought, it
might be nice.

If she were someone else… But it's all luck of the draw, isn't it?
Aimee and Walter had found each other. Gal had her music and the
road. And now, well, now they've all ended up alone anyway. And
she has a job to do.

She'll get the lawyer's number. She can ask Camille for it. The
girl wants to know about her father's case, and there's got to be some
time. Even if he's not fighting, there'll be some kind of a trial. Won't
there? But as she's about to call, Gal finds herself musing over what
Camille didn't say. What she doesn't know.

Did Camille ask her father about what happened that night?
About why he's fussing now with Aimee's catalog, with the rights?
Something went down, she figures. Between Walter and his former
colleague. Between Walter and Aimee, too, at some point.

Not that it's any of Gal's business, except, of course, the business
part. That she knows. Well, she should know, anyway. She's certainly
been through it all.

Gal never paid much attention to her publishing contracts. Not
until the money started to dry up, at any rate, and Russ cajoled her
into meeting with another of his clients, a retired lawyer who spent
summers up in the hills. Good thing he did, too. Chris Ecmont had
called her deals a mare's nest, with more of her rights signed away
than she had ever thought she owned. He'd been able to straighten
her affairs out, though the money gone was gone. And wanting to
be part of the community—she thought Russ might have had a
hand in that—he had refused all but a token payment for what must
have been a dozen hours of his time. She'd played a house concert,

one bright summer night, for him and his city friends. Russ had probably set that up as well, she'd realized a year or two later.

One thing that strikes her now, though, is how the assignment of rights worked. Ecmont had been after her to make a will. She still had his worksheet at home, gathering dust somewhere. But he'd been so earnest, talking her through the contracts, the new ones he'd drawn up, that he'd gotten the labels to sign, that she remembers why that mattered, or could for someone like Aimee, anyway. Her publishing went to her, via her attorney of record, in lieu of an agent. That, for once, was clear. And once she died? To any heirs. All very cut and dried, though once she was gone, she wasn't sure why she should care.

Aimee, though—she had Camille, still in college, too. Surely she had taken better care of her publishing. Even if she'd let things slide, once she'd gotten her diagnosis, she would've set her own affairs in order. And if Walter were named as executor or co-heir, or whatever a child's father was called once the parents had split up, what did it matter? It seemed straightforward enough. Unless, Gal thought, Walter was trying to hand property over that he thought might be forfeit if he went to jail. Only, it wasn't like he'd committed some kind of fraud. It wasn't like he was trying to profit from what still seemed like an impossible crime.

Mostly likely, he's simply anxious. Trying to cover all the bases. Maybe he…no, none of this made any sense. She's promised Camille she'll talk to him and clear it up. She needs to talk to his lawyer to get there. But first, she has to get some understanding of what exactly is going on.

With a feeling of dread as deep as that first morning of rehab, she flips through her recent calls. There's too much she doesn't know, and too few folks who can help her out. She needs to talk, once more, to Shira.

CHAPTER 35

A dry drunk. The words pop into her head like a bad memory as she drives. One of those rehab catch phrases that was supposed to make things make sense. Make you understand the need behind the abuse. Gal never got that. The abuse *was* the need. The hunger for more—more excitement, more volume. More, yeah, rock and roll. If she could have kept going, she would have. In a minute.

Only now, what she craves is control. Two lost years—maybe twenty-six months—of Gus, the label, calling the shots, the lack of it now drives her crazy. Her grip tightens on the steering wheel, her knuckles white with the strain, and she takes a breath. Tells herself to relax. It's an overcorrection. A pendulum swing, like those first nights, when her body was readjusting to food and water and even to sleep by being wide awake. Nauseous and fighting the sleep aids—the good drugs, they called them—that would help her over the first bit. When she thinks back, she can still feel herself fighting, her mind racing like a speed-metal riff. Maybe she is a dry drunk. She sighs and makes herself breathe. Russ, again: his voice in her head. Or maybe she's just a middle-aged woman with a shit ton on her mind.

Coffee? She had texted Shira back. A cop out, telling herself this was all too much to discuss by phone. Her old colleague had responded immediately, almost like she wasn't a lawyer with a life of her own, naming the café by her office. Suggesting a time twenty minutes on.

Only Gal hadn't heard the ping of the response, lost in her thoughts outside Walter's. Lost in her memories, if she's being honest. And now she's late and she hates herself for it. Asking a favor and then not showing up. What kind of friend—what kind of sober adult is she proving to be?

It's no use, she tells herself. Makes herself pull over half a block away and catch her breath. Shove the hair back from her forehead and brush down her shirt, shedding imagined wrinkles. It's not like she and Shira didn't just meet a few days before. Only this time what she wants to ask her is personal. Could this be what the lawyer was hinting at, the topic she thought Gal was going to raise? Gal doesn't know. She can't know. And in her current state, that's what grates.

Shira doesn't look angry when Gal walks in fifteen minutes late. Doesn't look surprised either. But she stands and reaches out to Gal with a smile that only emphasizes the difference between them.

"Gal. Good to see you again." Two hands out, her former bandmate reaching for her. She takes one and holds it awkwardly. "I'm glad you called me back."

"Mind if I grab a cup?" She nods toward the counter, and Shira immediately lets go.

"Of course," she says. "Join me when you're ready."

Almost like a therapist, Gal thinks as she waits for the barista. That smile, the voice. *She can't think I've hired her.* She starts as the thought intrudes. She doesn't have the money for a lawyer, not anymore. And Walter's been clear about his wishes, plus, he's got his own guy, even if…

No, she orders, willing herself to calm down. She's made

no agreements. Signed no contracts. And these days she would remember. Not like back in the day. She's almost laughing by the time her dark large arrives. Yeah, she made some crazy moves back then.

"Thanks for seeing me again." She starts right in, wanting to be clear. To be in charge. "I want to make sure there's no confusion. Walter does appear to have a lawyer, another lawyer, that is. That's not why I'm here."

"Of course." Shira dismisses her concern. "Please, you can just start by telling me what's on your mind." That must be her trick, Gal realizes. She inspires confidence, as if she were a friend, and Gal realizes she has to push back. She's not a client. She's not going to be billed because of a misunderstanding.

"But this isn't just personal. I mean, it may have a bearing on what happened with Walter, but I can't be sure."

Shira nods, urging her on, and Gal imagines her talking to Aimee, those last few months. Counseling her. *I should have been there*, Gal thinks, a pang of guilt. Of jealousy. *It should have been me.*

"I don't know if it's any of my business." Might as well go for it, she figures, brushing her misgivings aside. "I mean, things would probably have been different if Aimee had still been around."

Shira waits. A lawyer trick, thinks Gal. The best response to her own leading statement: ignoring the bait. But then the well-groomed woman sitting opposite her leans in again and asks, her voice soft as a whisper.

"Do you want to tell me what happened?"

What happened? Gal sits back, blinking. Her question, only Shira is the one doing the interrogation. A lawyer at her core. Again, that flash: *It should have been me.* Guilt, or something like. She reaches for her coffee to cover. Takes too big a sip of the hot drink and has to force herself to swallow.

"Well, that's just it, isn't it?" Enough of the foreplay. "I need some advice about how to proceed. And I think you might have some insight. I gather you met with Aimee those last few months." Shira starts to speak, but it's too soon. Gal holds up one hand to halt her. She needs to explain. "I'm sorry. This isn't just me being nosy. Camille has asked me to look into things. To try to figure out what's going on with her father, with Walter. Legally, I mean. He has been charged—I don't know if it's murder or manslaughter or what—and she says he's still insisting he's not going to defend himself. He's got his lawyer on board and everything. For now, he's out. I've seen him, I picked him up. But that can't last, right? I need to get him off."

The last words aren't what she meant. Not in a long while, but the woman seated opposite doesn't seem to notice the slip, so deep in her own thoughts.

"You think he's innocent? Or do you want to give evidence that whatever action he took was justified?"

"I don't want to be involved at all." *It should have been me.* "I mean, I was nowhere near there." She thinks back to the night of the benefit. The time she spent backstage, waiting, before joining the crowd. Time alone. The cops can't think that she…

Gal feels her pulse quicken. Her throat tightens as that refrain echoes in her head. *It should have been me.* Shira is an officer of the court. She may have heard things. Gal has been a blackout drunk. She has a reputation, a record.

Focus. She brushes the panic aside. The past is past. Speaking carefully, articulating every word, she tries again. "I want to understand what's going on. The process. I mean, is there a chance that this is all a mistake? That they've just let him go?"

"He was arrested?" Shira's voice is serious now. The business of law at work. "He's been charged, arraigned?"

Gal nods, then corrects herself. "I think so. He was locked up overnight and, yeah, his daughter said he's out on bail. But it's been a while. A couple of days."

"And he's not going to contest the charges?"

"No." The word sticks in her throat. "I don't think so."

Shira shakes her head. "I know the DA, Jack; he's a good guy. Even if the defendant is waiving his rights, he'll do a thorough investigation. Maybe more so because the defendant isn't contesting the charges." She holds Gal with a look. "He'll want to understand what happened, and not just so he doesn't get sued down the line. It is in his interest to understand the chain of events."

Gal nods, suitably reprimanded.

"So how much time do we have?"

A shrug this time. "Who knows? If they gave him bail, they don't consider him a flight risk. From what you've said, that's why he's settling his accounts. It's the smart thing to do. And from the sound of things, he'll have some warning. He, or his lawyer, will be notified. Even if he intends to waive his right to a trial, his lawyer probably filed a not-guilty plea at the arraignment. That's standard; it gives you some room to maneuver. So next will be a pre-trial hearing. That's when he'd change his plea, and then the judge would schedule his sentencing hearing. He hasn't been given a date for the pre-trial yet, has he?"

"No." She answers automatically. Would Walter tell her? Does Camille know? The stab of guilt. "That's good, right?" All this legal talk is making Gal fidgety. *Not a friend of authority*, she thinks.

"It is good." Shira nods. "Jack actually believes in justice, not just the law."

Gal starts to laugh. To make a joke, but Shira is serious, she sees. That shuts her right down.

"So what can we do? For Walter, I mean?"

That look again, her eyes wide and searching. "Do you want to talk to the DA?"

"Me? No." Her voice squeaks. Man, doesn't Shira remember anything about her? Doesn't she remember anything? But no, it hits her. Shira was out of the band before then. Before the drugs, the guns. Before the crazy hit the fan.

"Sorry." She raises her hand, to wave her off. To hold her back. "Old habits." She wheezes out a laugh. "Things got…I was kind of crazy for a while there."

Surely, Shira must know. Must have heard. She was friendly with Aimee afterward, wasn't she? Those dates in the calendar. Camille didn't think so, but then a daughter wouldn't know everything.

"I get it, Gal." A sad half smile. It's not going to get better. Gal thinks of her friends in the program. A searching moral inventory. "Believe me, I understand."

"Look, I'm sorry." Gal can't look up. Talks to the mug instead. "I really am. We were—I was a kid then. I didn't know, and, man…" Looks out the window. The city, once again. So many years have passed. "I wasn't always at my best then. To be honest, I was really messed up."

Shira is silent, but everything about her says she's waiting. It's been years. It's time.

"I'm really sorry we fired you. That we—that I—kicked you out of the band." One rush of breath, and it's out. It's over. Only Shira hasn't taken it like Gal expected. No relief or glee. Only a strange, confused look on her face, her brows knotted together like a question mark.

"What are you talking about?" She's got her normal voice back. A little louder, pitched higher for the question. "You didn't fire me from the band. Nobody did. I quit."

CHAPTER 36

"The fuck?" The words slip out before Gal can stop them. Never mind that she's sitting in a public coffee house. Never mind that she's talking to a lawyer, a woman whose business suit looks like it cost what Gal's Toyota did, tailored for a body that's not been living hard, out on the road. As the woman opposite her draws back in surprise, this all hits her. Shira's soft. A civilian. And Gal? She's forty plus and cursing like a teen.

"Sorry." She shakes her head. "I just…" She has no words. Shira must not remember. Must have made up some story to ease the pain. Then again, that lets her off the hook.

But Shira is talking. "No, it's my fault. I'm sorry," she's saying. "I thought that's why you wanted to meet today. The inappropriate behavior. Why you wanted to talk."

"About why I—" Gal swallows. Her mouth is dry. *Inappropriate.* Well, shit, yeah, that was one word for it. "How you left the band?"

An emphatic nod. "Yeah, kind of." A weak smile. So it must hurt still. "I mean, I remember how disturbing it was. How angry I was. After what Aimee went through, I thought you wanted to talk."

What Aimee went through. The words burn like a slap. How does Shira know? This smooth and polished outsider. She wasn't there, on the road. The craziness. She wasn't the one holding her friend as she sobbed and puked. Gal opens her mouth, about to tear the woman in front of her a new one, when it hits her. She's got it wrong. The cancer. That's what she's talking about. It must be. Shira was here for that—living in Boston, anyway, and Gal wasn't. That date in Aimee's calendar. They talked, at least once. Gal didn't come to visit. She didn't call, not often enough. And now? She has no words.

"Aimee." She looks away, toward the window. It's not the tears that have suddenly sprung up, making her eyes smart. It's the shame. The knowledge that each time she put her old friend off, she lost a little of what they'd had. She lost another chance.

Seconds pass, and she reaches for her coffee as much to clear her throat as because she needs the dark and bitter brew. "So you and Aimee, you talked?" Aimee had been the one to deliver the news that Shira was out, all those years ago. The one to swing the axe. What had she said? Gal hadn't wanted to know.

Shira's not saying. Not the details, anyway. Instead, she nods again, the gesture accompanied by a sad smile. "Yeah, she'd kept so much to herself, I think it did her good, especially toward the end. She was concerned about Camille, of course."

Of course. Gal should want to follow up. Here's her chance to get the details, the confidence she wasn't privy to, but she doesn't. Only isn't this what she came here for? To help Camille?

"I don't blame her." Rallying around her friend, around her daughter. Letting the past go. At this point, what else can she do? "That's why I'm so worried about Walter."

Shira doesn't respond, and when Gal glances up from her coffee, she sees that her old colleague is staring at her. Her face is unreadable. Blank. *That should have been me.* Gal swallows. Twenty years earlier, she'd be blushing. Shame? Guilt? Awareness of their changing roles? It doesn't matter. She was a rock star once, and this woman—this lawyer—she did something else.

"I guess it's good you went to law school, huh?" She has to say something, right?

"It was the right choice for me." Shira, so composed. "And, really, I'm happy to help out Walter any way I can. I do have some ideas about this. I'm sorry I haven't followed up yet, but I will. I'll talk to Jack. I can't promise anything, but maybe I can find out what's going on."

Gal nods. This is what she wanted. Not the touchy-feely. The confession. Only Shira's not done yet.

"I mean it, though, Gal. If you want to talk, I'm here."

Gal throws back her coffee. The grounds like sand in her mouth. "Thanks, Shira. You've been great."

A hand reaches out for her, and Gal has to fight the urge to snatch her own away. "I was there, Gal. I mean, yeah, I got out, but I remember. We were so young."

That's it. Gal's on her feet, her best rock star sneer standing in for a smile. No wonder Shira can't remember the truth. She's soft, just like always. Shira the whiner. Useful, but not someone she could rely on. Not like Aimee. And so she backs away, the heat of Shira's touch like a burn. Heart racing, she reaches for the door.

It shouldn't bother her the way it does. Shira's got her story. Gal knows how it goes. She didn't need to spend three months in rehab to learn that memory is selective. It's human nature to smooth over the rough spots, and if her onetime guitarist wants to pretend she quit the band, well, that makes things easier.

Funny thing is, Gal was all worked up to apologize. To admit that just maybe she'd been hasty. Shira wasn't a bad guitarist. Not as sharp as Lina, maybe. None of that speed metal zippiness that, to be honest, brought them more of the mainstream fans. The boys. But Shira did have that punk funk thing happening before anyone else, all wiry staccato and odd interval jumps.

No, the problem with Shira was her attitude. Out on the street, Gal feels her heart rate slowing. Her breathing returns to normal. There's something anxious about that woman, she thinks. There always was. Gal remembers her constantly going on about some bullshit or other. A lack of privacy. Of "personal space." Well, fuck, they were a rock band. Everyone was up in each other's business. It was just as well they jettisoned her sorry ass. Gal can't imagine what she'd have been like on the road.

Not like Aimee. God, she misses her. Aimee was a rock. No questions, just there for her. Especially in those dark few months. Aimee kept her sane. And she? The pang cuts like glass. Yeah, she was there for Aimee, wasn't she? A memory of a bad night. The tears in the bathroom. But later?

That was different. She had Walter by then. She had Camille, and the band had been broken up for so long. How old was Camille? Twenty? Twenty-one tops? Yeah. Aimee had been out of the band since her second trimester. Still, they'd remained friends.

And Shira? Had she been there? A comfort at the end? Gal feels her guts churning, the coffee gone bad, when it hits her. The publishing—the rights thing that Camille told her about. That's what Gal should have been asking about. That's why Aimee had reached out to Shira. Who better to handle that kind of thing than a former bandmate turned lawyer. Only, Walter had a different lawyer. Some man.

Gal tosses it off. Aimee and Walter had separated by then. Walter moved out, and Aimee wanted someone of her own, at least for a consult. Most natural thing in the world. Had Aimee said anything when Shira had spun her tale about quitting? About Gal acting— what was her word—inappropriate? A sting of shame heats up her cheeks, and she ducks her head even as she walks. Well, fuck, they were in a rock band. Not much older than Camille is now. What? Twenty-three? Twenty-four?

Gal stops and looks out at the city. Sees how much it has changed. No, some of that shit was real. The whole point of rehab, right? She was inappropriate. Scary, people said. She'd gone a little wild at times. They all had.

CHAPTER 37

She missed the bass at first, almost like she missed Aimee. A part of her, surgically removed. Having the heavy solid-body up against her pelvis like a shield had been a comfort. A constant, always there. Plus, in the early days, the bass had been a distraction from her stage fright. Something to focus on, an excuse. By the time Gus brought in Mimi, that part didn't matter anymore. She didn't care if she fucked up a lyric. Didn't worry about hitting a note. She never wanted to be a chick singer, though. This was rock and roll. And her battered Gibson was familiar. A friend. Once Aimee left, she felt just that little bit more alone.

Still, she had to admit it was liberating. Gus was right about that, and as the tour progressed and the stages got bigger—she was dimly aware of the announcements, the changes in venues—she had relished that freedom.

"How we doing, Tampa?" Yelling out into the lights, the room finally so big she couldn't see the corners. Couldn't see the mischief brought on by the dark and the drink. "This is Tampa, right?"

She was joking, at least in part. Draping herself over the mic stand as if she were David Johansen. As if she were Mick, turning toward Lina to let her know she could take the next eight. Waiting for Britta, poor old Britta, to start the count.

Mimi she had trouble warming to, at least at first. Some of that was envy. The new girl got to step right in, play her lines with her band. Some resentment. Mimi wanted to get close, Gal could see that. Wanted to replace Aimee, she couldn't help thinking, whereas Britta knew it was a gig. The dye job, a part she had to play.

One week in, and none of that mattered. Gal had talked Mimi into partying with her, daring her to match her drink for drink. Line for line. She'd taken the new girl's bass from her then, bringing it out after the show. She remembers the night. An after-hours club, somewhere in West Texas. Tequila shots and speed. Britta and Lina crashed out hours before.

"Damn, girl, eat a sandwich." The bartender pushing a plate toward her. White bread soaking up sauce.

"That's not what keeps me going." She'd nodded toward the bottle then, even as she strapped on Mimi's bass.

"Whoa!" Hands reaching out to steady her as she stumbled back. The weight of it. How could she have forgotten?

"Give it here." Gus, always there. Always watching. "There's no amp for you to plug into, shithole like this. Besides, Gal, you're a rock star. You don't play for free anymore."

That was then, a long time ago. Now she's looking forward to the gig with Lina. Playing for nothing, playing for fun. She's eager to have this day behind her. She's allowed, right? Shira's looking into Walter's case. Talking to the DA. Gal has done what she said she'd do, in terms of the paperwork. The accounts. Maybe Walter will come out, like he used to.

She pictures him at the side of the stage, ready to grab a mic stand if she kicks it over. To right Aimee's cymbal, the one she always knocked off balance. Walter and T.K., standing by.

That's not going to happen. She shakes it off, just as her phone begins to buzz. Shira can't have anything so soon, can she? No, she takes the call even as she recognizes the number. It's the Boston police. Dread falls like a curtain over her hopes for the day.

"Hello?" Remembers that she'd left a message. Tells herself to chill.

"Ms. Raver? Detective Bixby here." The voice on the line is neither worried nor angry. Cool as an ice cube, she thinks, and envies him. No wonder she was hoping to heat him up a bit. "I've been meaning to return your call. Would you have a few minutes to speak with us again today?"

So polite, but Gal is wary. What had she been thinking, calling him for advice? Flirting with him? Cops don't ask for favors. "What do you want?"

"It would be helpful if you could come in." Pause. "Or we could come to you."

"What is this about?" Her back is up, and she lets him hear it.

"We'd like to know more about Thomas Kennedy. About his social circle. His friends and acquaintances."

Relief bubbles out in a laugh. "You've got the wrong gal, then." She chuckles at her own pun. "As I've told you, I haven't lived in this town in more than twenty years. T.K.—Thomas—wasn't hanging around with our old crowd, from all I've heard. He'd moved on."

She's about to tell him about the church. The crazy widow, but the voice on the phone cuts her off.

"We're aware of that, Ms. Raver." Still calm, but she's on alert now. "It's Mr. Kennedy's associates from that era who we want to speak with. Besides, I gather you have some questions for us or some information that you would like to share? You could come in and speak with us, if you'd like. Or should I send someone to you?"

Choices. Another thing from rehab.

"I'll come by," she says. It's all about control.

CHAPTER 38

She means to go down there. Really, she does. At this point in her life, she's not going to run from the cops. Hey, it's not like she's holding. Only, for the rest of the day, whenever she makes a move in that direction, she stops. Keeps on putting it off.

Some of it is Walter. She knows what Shira has told her, but reading between the lines she assumes they want to make a case, one that will stick. *Justice, my ass.* Why should she help them convict her friend? Maybe she hasn't figured out how to get him to defend himself. That doesn't mean she's going to speed the prosecution along.

The funny thing is that she is still curious as to what the cops know. What they want, not that she's expecting them to give her anything that will clear Walter, not now. Those days. It's not that her memory is that shot. Yeah, there were some nights—okay, quite a few—that she might never entirely get back. But really, what else could have been happening? They were kids then. Camille's age. And back when T.K. was on the scene, the drugs were minor league. Kind of like the money.

Gal's heard the stories. The club manager who disappeared, his body found only decades later, a reputed mob hit. But running a club, that must have been big bucks. Gal and her friends, they were lucky to get a hundred for the night back when T.K. was their roadie. Yeah, they drank for free, but that was it. And drugs? Until they were on a label, none of them could afford that shit. That's why they all drank so much.

Doesn't matter. She can't shake the nagging feeling that there's something in their line of inquiry she should be aware of. Until she can pinpoint it, she'd rather not be caught off guard with more questions. That, and her concern for Walter, of course.

"I'll come by." That's what she'd said when presented with the choice. "I've got some things to take care of, but I'll come by later." That had been vague enough.

Well, so, her day got busier than she'd anticipated. With one thing and another, it's time for her to go meet Lina and her band. Time for another trip down rock and roll's memory lane.

She gets to the pub early. In part, she wants to check it out. Figure out the sound, the layout. In part, she admits, she's a little self-conscious. All this dwelling on the past has reminded her of how she was, those last days with the band. Yeah, Lina has asked her here, and the memorial show went great. Only Gal still feels a little on edge, like she has something to prove. A history that she'd rather leave behind.

The place itself might as well be in a time warp. The bar, the pub tables. The little stage up by the front windows. She's almost tempted to check for a dart board, over by the kitchen, only she's half afraid that if she finds one, she'll start laughing so hard she won't be able to stop.

Instead, she takes a seat at the bar. Orders a club soda and waits.

"You here for the band?" The bartender couldn't be more than twenty-five. Still, Gal feels the old glow and lets her smile grow wide.

"Something like." She tilts her head toward the stage, where she's left her bass. Lina's got her own band, her own setup, but a girl gets used to having her gear with her. Maybe she'll play a song, as well as sing. "What gave it away?"

His answering grin is warm. "Lina usually gets here around seven thirty," he says. "Good luck."

He's moved on before the shocked bark of laughter breaks out. He thinks she's *auditioning*? Well, she catches herself. Calms herself down. Maybe she is, after a fashion. Yeah, that would explain her nerves.

She doesn't say a word when Lina comes in. Still, she's gratified to see how her old guitarist's face lights up when she sees Gal. No, she's relieved.

"Hey, Gal!" Lina strides over to embrace her. Holds her at arm's length to look at her before she calls over to the barkeep. "Boyd, do you know who this is?"

"Lina, no." Gal wants to save the boy some embarrassment. Save herself, but it's too late.

"This is Gal Raver." Her voice a little too hearty, a little too loud. "You know, 'Hold Me Down'?"

"Yeah, yeah." He's nodding, like he's heard this before, even as he brings over an Amstel. "I remember that."

"Kids." Lina, loud enough to be heard, even as he walks away. "No respect for their elders."

"Hey, did we have any?" Gal glances back over her shoulder. He's not that young.

"Come on." Lina nods toward the makeshift stage. Her drummer is already setting up. "Let's show 'em how it's done."

192

CHAPTER 39

The first song is easy. They start with a blues. "Get everybody warmed up," Lina says. But Gal knows it's for her. Lina's band does this once a month. Knows the room, knows the crowd. Plus, when the guitarist was putting together the set list, she kept looking over, eyes dark under that suburban-mom fringe. Watching her, Gal knew. Being careful, as if the memorial was the exception and Gal was likely to go back to her old habits. To go off the rails.

"You call it, I'll sing it." Gal had tried to deflect. Left her bass in its case. "Whatever you want." And Lina had offered a friendly grin in response. Still, she'd made a point of consulting Gal as she wrote out the list: "Baby, Please Don't Go," in Gal's key, up next.

"That'll get us going," said Lina. "Everyone gets a chance to solo."

Gal had acquiesced with a nod. This was Lina's gig, after all. But when she suggested working in some of the old songs, their hits, later in the set, Lina's reaction caught her off guard. Eyes wide, brows shooting up. Gal almost expected the guitarist's hair to spike once more.

"What?" She wanted to push Lina. Give her a friendly punch, like back in the day, but she held back. "It's not like they're that complicated. I mean, I can write out the chords if you want."

"It's not that." Lina withdrew, studying the floor. "Marie and Bobbi, they're good. It's just—I was thinking about what happened. Your old friend." She peeked up at her old bandmate. "Are you sure you want to go there?"

"We just did them. The songs, not T.K." Gal felt like she was talking to a child. "Hell, Lina, you pretty much promised that boy up there that we'd do 'Hold Me Down.'"

She heard herself and tried another smile, this one more a grimace than a grin. "All right, then," said Lina, once again meeting her eyes. "I'll put them on the list."

She was regretting the invite already, Gal realized as she fetched a bottle of water from the bar. Well, maybe she was auditioning after all.

Two songs in, and she's done. Served up her best Delta drawl. Tried to channel Billie, but now she's getting pissed. Why did Lina have to say that? It's not like she and T.K. were close. Not after all these years. And, as she'd pointed out, she knows these songs cold. The memorial had been only a week before. Only after the easy lope of those blues—circling round for chorus after chorus as Lina improvised a slide with that Amstel bottle—the raw rage of the old tunes feels a little out of place.

"Pig brain." She recites the line rather than singing it. Rather than shouting it out as the *cri de coeur* it once was. The dozen or so who have gathered look more like shopkeepers and accountants than the punks of old. Friends or family, she thinks, seeing the smiles and the nods. "Pig brain!" They're here for Lina as much as the music. She knows that, and yet it all feels wrong. Strangely rude. But wasn't that the point, once upon a time?

"*Pig brain!*" She goes a little louder when the chorus comes around, hoping the volume will push it through, will push *her* through this odd awkwardness. It's no good. The song is soft. Dull. She should have said something to Lina. Made her leave it out. The drummer has no sense of the rhythm; the bassist is playing flat, her A string out of tune. Did this crappy little bar band really do these songs? Her songs? Here? Before she can reason it out, the bridge comes around for the second time, and then they're out.

She glances down at the set list, even though she knows what's coming. What Lina printed out in marker not forty-five minutes before: "So Fucking Stupid," the song that proved she had more than one hit in her. The B-side that got them signed. Only then, it was a rousing cry: brassy and bratty and full of spunk. Even last week it felt good to sing it. Good to let it out.

She looks out at the room, such as it is. Twenty people, maybe twenty-five and a few more by the door. Lina's regulars, or maybe she spread the word. Gal, the surprise guest. Sees a woman who could be Shira walk over to a seat and feels again the hot blush of shame. For firing the guitarist? Or, no, for letting Aimee do it, and then for never following up to see what her first guitarist, her first drummer had done with their lives.

She catches herself. Where did that come from? She stayed in touch with Aimee. Always, except maybe at the end. Besides, this is Lina's band. Lina's night. Everything would have been so different had Shira stayed. Was it Lina who made the difference? Her presence that pushed the band into full punk mode? Into this screaming anger? The song kicks off—*one, two, three, four!*—and then she's on, her feral growl as much a centerpiece of the song as the shouted chorus where they all join in. Only here, with this crowd, Gal can't do it. The room is too small. Too *nice*, and Gal finds herself holding back. Singing the radio edit, as if the bar were full of toddlers or nuns.

"'Cause you were so... You were so..." She can't find it. That sweet spot where the song just flows without thought, the music and the words bursting out as one. It's this place. This pub is all wrong, the song too punk for a cozy beer and burger joint. She feels herself holding back and that makes it worse. Makes her self-conscious and awkward. Every word an effort. It's almost like those first gigs, before she learned the trick.

And yet they get through it. Lina winds through that last arpeggio and with a quick drum roll, they're done. Gal takes a sip of water and reaches back, putting the open bottle on the bass amp behind her. Catches a movement out of the corner of her eye—a hand—and she remembers. Not her amp, not her band. She smiles and moves the bottle to the floor beside her mic, as Lina leans over.

"You okay?" Her voice, her face, tight with worry. She looks so old now, it's hard to believe.

"Me? Hell, yeah." Gal forces a chuckle. Fake it till you make it. "It really feels good to do these tunes."

"Whipping Post!" Someone in the crowd calls out. The old joke they all know, and someone else laughs. Lina seizes on it, though, and plays the opening riff, and then there's no choice. They all have to go along. "Whipping Post" it is.

Gal eyes her guitarist, wondering. In the old days, sure, sometimes they'd pull a stunt like that. Do covers of anything the crowd called out, half-assed versions of oldies or whatever was on the charts at the moment. Half the time, they were wasted, and the covers disintegrated into sloppy fun. An excuse for a break and another beer. Tonight, though, they're all sober—*too sober*, the thought sneaks into her mind—and Lina's been so careful with her setlist, checking in about every song.

She's worried about me, Gal realizes, and the wave of fury that follows almost chokes her. The chorus is coming around again, a natural for a break, a little improv with the tempo. Only Lina won't catch her eye.

But she's here. She's Gal Raver, and she's forgotten more about real rock than these fucking civilians will ever know. Stepping up to the mic, she howls, her voice loud, discordant—a departure that makes everybody turn. Shuts the cover down like a slap. And with a smile, she starts to sing again, slower this time. A snarling, bratty take on that hit from long ago.

"*You wanna, you wanna hold me down.*" Her song, the one that broke them out. That broke her out, anyway. Leaving these losers in the dust. "*You wanna wear my crown.*" That's what this song could be about, couldn't it? All the wannabes and pretenders who tried to hold her back.

She closes her eyes as the band joins in. They know the song. They were waiting. Heading into the verse, she listens for something—for Aimee, it hits her—and she stumbles. Almost loses it, but Lina steps up and starts to solo, something tamer than what Gal longs to hear but good enough. When she opens her eyes again, she sees what she's needed. The crowd is staring now. Transfixed. Their suburban complacence shattered.

"*You wanna hold me, hold me down...*" She growls into the chorus, reaching deep to power through. Feels the music building up within her. Getting louder, getting wilder, and her voice is cracking. Everything is breaking, but that's good. That's the way—the opening that will release her real voice. The song. If only she can just keep on.

"*Hold me down!*" A woman stands, her face white and staring. Shira, here tonight. The crowd has grown. Forty now, maybe more. And just like in the old days, she finds herself trolling for the men. A figure—tall, broad in the shoulders—is moving up. Reaching for a woman slumped against the wall. "*You wanna wear...*"

She swallows. Those shoulders, broader than she'd thought. It's that cop, Bixby, the one she blew off today. "*Wear my crown.*" She stumbles a little, but makes it work. A Jagger-esque growl pushing the missed beat into blues territory, into something rough, just like they want it.

No, it's T.K. Like that night at the memorial. Only, no, the chorus ends and she's not singing. The verse lost like it was before. Lina jumps in again. Her guitar cries out, as if in pain. In shock. And suddenly Gal's scared. Her body liquefies in terror, and she turns away, afraid to face the crowd again, and when the chorus comes back, it's Lina who takes it. Who gives the drummer some kind of signal because they wind up then, before the final verse.

"You okay?" She hears someone talking to her, but she can't look up, doubled over by the drum set, dizzy and as sick as she's ever been. "Gal?"

A hand on her arm. She feels the fingers clenching, and she reacts. "No!" She lashes back. Throws it off and turns to see Lina blinking, one hand up to her lip, where a bead of blood is forming.

"I'm—" Gal shakes her head and steps back. It's all too much. She's going to be sick.

"Let's take five, everyone." The drummer's on the mic. "We'll be back." Only Gal is gone. Pushing through the crowd, to the back. The bar, where someone has lined up shots. Three of them, like T.K. used to do. She grabs one, downs it, even as someone yells out, "Hey!" The whiskey burns, and through the fog she realizes what she's done. She's not an alcoholic—not her. But she knows herself. She hates herself. The weak, sad, mewling thing that she's become.

Dropping the glass, she staggers over to the bathroom, barely making it in before falling to her knees. She wants the whiskey out, and she hardly has to try. She's puking, coughing. Sick as a little girl in her first trimester, but it's better then. It's gone. And while she's kneeling there, head resting on the cool porcelain, she hears a voice both soft and low.

"Gal, it's me." She nods, or thinks she does. She's never been so tired. Shira. "I was afraid something like this would happen," the voice says. She has the sense not to touch Gal. Not to get too close. Instead, Gal hears her shift and settle, as if reading the graffiti on the wall.

"What the hell is wrong with me?" She doesn't mean to ask out loud. Barely forms the words. But from the way that Shira sighs, she knows the other woman has heard her. "What happened?"

"I think you know," she says.

CHAPTER 40

It must have been Cleveland. She's still not sure. Cleveland sounds right, anyway, the butt of every parody of every arena band ever. Not that they were playing arenas. Not yet. Not quite. So maybe it was Cincinnati. That was possible too.

By that point, every city looked like Cleveland. Every crowd, every club the same.

"Hello, Cleveland!" She roared out at the house, the lights shining off a sea of sweaty faces. "How ya doing?" Hey, they all cheered, though whether that was because she got the town right or 'cause they were in on the joke, she didn't know.

Didn't care, either. She was there to rock, and man, she was on fire that night. Had been since they pulled up. And the band—the band was burning too.

They were at their peak by then. Every song a hit. She could tell during the station visits. The way they greeted her, coke and smiles, like she was fucking royalty. Shitty little places, for the most part. The so-called "alternative" rock stations that were remaking the map. The charts. The scene. Big-time ratings, she was told, but for the most part, the studios smelled like something had died in the walls. Bad headphones and waffle soundproofing that blocked the air, too.

Still, she remembers Cleveland. That was a good day. A golden day, at first. Two stations with Gus and a driver. The label's local rep who took one look at her and knew to keep it shut. Morning guy teams of wise-ass jokers who fell all over themselves when she walked in. Who wanted her—wanted to do everything for her.

"Watch out! Here she comes." She remembers one skinny guy pushing people out of the way. Yeah, fucking royalty, as they cleared a path for her into the studio. Ten minutes on air. A station ID they'd had to do three times, maybe four. W…W…what the fuck. How was she to remember? Same thing at the next, the label rep AWOL by then, and back to the bus. Back to the hotel room for a few hours before the gig. Hours? Could have been days. Bored and busy at the same time, with Gus and his crew hovering. Handing her the phone. The papers. The bottle.

"Come on, Gal. Just two more." Twenty minutes with some zine, same questions from the next. No rest for the wicked. Not that day, although Lina had escaped, moaning something about bedtime when Gus had grabbed her for an in-store. A last-minute add-on, the label rep's revenge. Sleep wasn't a problem for Gal. A cat nap in the car and then the screams woke her. Fans out front, holding up the album. Photos with the manager. Promo for the record was still part of the deal, and the flashes going off as she scrawled her name on a poster. On the wall.

"Come here, darling." She remembers grabbing the little blonde, a shy-looking girl who had actually carried out the case of CDs for her to sign. "You look good enough to eat." But the blonde turned her head, and all she got was cheek as she leaned in for a smooch. The girl wiggling away, as squirmy as a kitten. She didn't mind. She turned and laughed, looking for Lina. For her comrade in arms. Girls were soft that way, that's why she liked them. Sometimes.

Sometimes not.

"What about me?" The store manager, big belly and a sneer.

"Fuck you," Gal growled. Like she'd ever.

"Come on, Gal." Gus, making nice. The soft voice he used when he was offering a toot. A blue for before the show, a bennie for after. "He's just a guy."

"Just kidding." Gal turned and draped an arm over the fat man. There was no point in fighting, and really, what did she care?

"Wow, you're a skinny little thing." His arm around her waist, pulling her close. She laughed. Yeah, she was pared down to the basics by then. Black leather and worn denim stretched tight. "Where'd you get these bruises?"

"Fuck off." She pulled away. Reached for her jacket. She was always cold, anyway. Too long under the lights, her thermostat had been reset.

"Just a few more. Come on, Gal." She turned with a snarl, but it was Gus, pushing the Sharpie back into her hand. "Here." A CD in front of her, the little blonde nowhere in sight. She scribbled something. Another, and she scribbled again.

"Can we go?" The noise, the crowd. This wasn't her scene, and finally, it was time.

"One more shot?" The arm around her waist before she could pull away. Flash and then Gus was there.

"We're good. Thanks, everybody!"

"Fucking assholes." Gal let him lead her to the car and closed her eyes.

"Come on, Gal. Time to rock." She didn't know how long she'd been out. It was dark, and Lina was leaning over her, breath soft in her ear as she pulled her jacket out from under Gal's head. Gal propped herself up, feeling the warm leather slip by. She was on a sofa, somewhere backstage, she figured. Some club in some city. She'd given up trying to tell them apart.

"Sound check?" She sat up, licking dry lips. Her mouth tasted like shit.

"Got it." Lina forced a smile. She looked as worn out as Gal felt. "Gus did your mic for you. Figured it was better to let you rest."

"Yeah, maybe." She tried to stand. Steadied herself with the wall. "I could use a little pick-me-up."

Lina's mouth opened, but then she turned away.

Gus, out of nowhere, with a beer. A pill. "Down the hatch."

She threw it back. The beer too. "That all you got?" Just words. Attitude, mainly. But he nodded and reached into his pocket for the little glassine bag.

"Hey, what happened to those folded pieces of paper?" Gal's mood improving by the second. "The party origami?"

"Seriously?" Gus tapped out a small pyramid onto the back of his hand. Held it up so she didn't have to strain. "That's for small fry. Here we go now."

"Yeah!" The burn woke her, and she dabbed at her eyes. "Hey, what about a drink to go with? I've got to sing, you know."

"Roddy?" Gus to one of his ghosts. His henchmen. The skinny one who was always hanging around. "Get the lady a beverage, won't you?"

"Jack." She was feeling it by then. Like she could take on the room. "Get me the bottle."

"A shot and a chaser." Gus's voice, soft, is the one he heard. She could tell by the way the minion nodded before he ran off. "Let's save something for later, why don't we, Gal?"

"My ass." She turned away, the high turning surly. But then she laughed. No good came from crossing Gus. "Sure thing, Roddo," she called after the departing lackey. "And hurry it up! I can't sing when I've got cotton mouth."

Damn lights. She stumbled climbing onto the stage, the black paint making that last step up invisible. The crowd was chanting already. They did that now, and she loved it. That's why she waits until it's built up. What Lina and Mimi didn't understand.

"Make 'em want us." She mouthed the words, knowing Lina couldn't hear her. She'd said it before. Told them all, but her guitarist was staring at her like she had two heads. Standing at her mic like they hadn't done this a million times.

No wonder, Gal realized with a rush of annoyance. "Get On It" had already started. It's that metal chick Gus put on drums. Britta, she remembered. Someone he knew. Someone who could jump in when Aimee dropped out mid-tour. Last tour? Whatever. A pro, he said. Bass drum like a heartbeat. Like a headache was more like it, more bombast than beat, and not enough sense to wait until everyone was strapped in.

"Here we go!" Gal at the mic, breaking in. A smile to Lina, to Mimi. Fuck Britta and that *pound-pound-pound*. "*Get on it!*" She leaned into the song, slowed the line. Heard Lina fall in beside her, syncing up with her tempo. A split second later, and she felt it from the drummer too. So this Britta can play, if she listens. Good. It's been, what, two months? Twelve?

As she took control, the rave up became a grind. Not the best tempo, Gal had to admit, but at least it was hers again—her song, her band. And she played it for all it was worth, straddling the mic stand, caterwauling the lyrics. "*Gotta make it new.*" That was the line, but she might as well have been talking to her band mates. "*Make it new...*"

The number finished before she really hit her stride. No problem; she had all night, and when this Britta counted off the next tune, Gal caught her eye.

"*One, two, three, four!*" She stomped out the time, even as the drummer clapped her sticks, picking up on Gal's beat, and then they were off. Back to speed, her point made, Gal howled. Riding the waves of sound. Letting the song carry her safely through.

"You okay?" She opened her eyes to see Lina hovering, worry knitting her heavy brows.

"Great." Gal tossed her hair back. "Never better." Okay, so she missed the break on that last go 'round. Fuck it. She always thought the bridge was too fussy for a song called "Outhouse." This was rock and roll. But the question threw her. Knocked her off her stride, a little, and she looked over toward the wings. Gus had to be there. With a shot or a pill. It wouldn't do to snort a line on stage, not at a venue this big. Someone yelled.

"*Wake up, Raver!*"

"Hey, Cleveland!" She turned to face them. "You wanna rock?"

"Gal." She heard Lina behind her. She didn't care.

"Do ya?" Daring them. Leading them on.

"*Fuck you!*" A voice in the back.

"Fuck you, too!" She could give as good as she got, and just then she heard it—*bam, bam, bam*—and they were off. Damn, this Britta was tight. She might even keep her, she mused, laughing, as she whirled around. Grabbed the mic stand to steady herself as Lina plowed into "So Fucking Stupid."

"*Why'd you have to be? Have to be?*" The lines were getting to her for some reason. The song, not the drug, though maybe that, too, the high wearing off and leaving her raw and exposed. "*Why'd you have to be?*" She was wailing by then, her voice breaking with the strain, and she pushed herself through the comedown. This was anger, this song. This was rage. "*Stupid fucking cunt.*" She was shouting over Lina's solo. Reaching for the energy that always carried her through.

205

The heart of the song.

Only it was gone. She heard it, the riff she knew by heart. They'd cut her off. Cut the song short and moved on. "Hold Me Down"—the raging intro. Mimi playing the bass line she knew so well.

"*Hold me...hold me down.*" She was floundering. Damn Gus and his cheap shit. She should be flying at that point. A ray of light cutting through this fog. "*Hold me...*" She sidled up to the mic as if to take it in. Mouthed the head and remembered. Back in the day, she'd taste spit and beer. Puke like sour milk. The club so small and close, the body heat would come up in waves. Everyone packed so tight. A tall figure holding up a slouching girl. "*Hold me...*" The drums behind her, more a feeling than a sound. Aimee's line. Aimee behind her. The room so close.

"*Hold me...*" She remembered Aimee crying. Wiping vomit from her face. Snot, like she was her baby. She was her lover. Both of them crying, drunk.

"*Hold me...*" Aimee had fallen asleep in her arms after a while and she had followed, cradling her friend against her neck. Smelling the soft scent of her hair under the reek of puke and booze.

They'd woken slowly, sometime before dawn, a combination of restlessness and hangover that left them both needy and wanting, and they'd comforted each other the only way they had. Touching each other as others had touched them, only this time with gentleness, with love.

"*Hold me...*" She was crying, hanging onto the mic stand. The words gone. Her friend gone. Damn Gus and his cheap-ass shit. What they had done.

The drummer, though. She kept pounding. A *thud-thud-thud* that woke her. That pushed her down. And then she felt it—the hands. Big mitts wrapped around her upper arm. Pulling her back. Pulling her—

"*Hold me down!*" She pinwheeled back and felt her fist connect with flesh. She had power now. The song—*her* song—the driving beat. The bruises that they'd leave. "*No!*" She kicked out, only to feel the grip on her tighten, twisting like a cat as she grabbed the heavy mic stand and swung it round, desperate to escape. "*No!*" she cried out, screaming against the beat. The *pow- pow-* pounding of it just wouldn't stop. "*Let me go!*"

But they didn't. They never did, and she felt the strength in those hands as they lifted her up and dragged her away, her broken heart left lying there on the floor.

CHAPTER 41

By the time she feels strong enough to stand, the band is playing again. Lina's band, not hers. Their regular monthly set, she figures. Nothing she recognizes from back in the day. Then again, she's not sure what she recognizes anymore.

"I don't understand." She shakes her head and lets Shira help her to her feet. Over to the sink where she can rinse her mouth. Whiskey, vomit. The ammonia taste of semen, but no… She closes her eyes and lets herself tilt forward, head against the mirror, though this time the feel of Shira's hand on her back is welcome. "I'm okay," she manages. Scoops up more water to rinse her face. She's been sweating. She feels clammy and weak.

"I'm so sorry," Shira repeats. "I realized after we talked that maybe I shouldn't have—that maybe I'd brought something up at a bad time. Aimee's death and all."

Gal rights herself, only to slump back against the wall. "Aimee?"

"She told me. I'm sorry." The apologies should be annoying, but Gal is simply confused. She shakes her head. "When we spoke, that last month," Shira explains.

"You spoke about me?" The words an effort.

A shrug and Shira turns, addressing the dispenser while she

pulls out paper towels. "We talked about…a lot of things." She's hedging. Gal knows it, but she doesn't have the energy to push. To dry her face. "I mean, you know that's why I left, right?"

"What did she say?" Her head is bursting. It had burst. It would be better when it did burst. "About me?"

"She'd talked to Lina." Even though the other woman's voice is soft, it hurts. Everything hurts. "She told me what happened, Gal."

"What happened." She closes her eyes, remembering. Everyone knew what happened. A breakdown. Exhaustion. Too much time on the road. Too much drugs and drink and rock and roll. That had been the end of it, that night. She'd caught one of the road crew with the mic stand as they'd dragged her off. Sent him to the ER for stitches and observation. They'd all been surprised, a little thing like she was then. Fighting like a banshee, they told her. Like a wild thing.

Not that the label cared. Of course not. They—Gus—had been the ones feeding her all that shit. Getting her up so she could perform each night, no matter what. But there were liabilities, they said. She hadn't hurt the roadie, not really. What did she weigh then? Maybe a hundred, one ten, tops? And Gus's crews were all beefy dudes, built to haul equipment and chug beer. But that night he'd hired some freelancers. The story comes back in pieces. Locals who worked for the venue, and that one loser had to stay in the hospital overnight. There was talk of dizziness. Lost wages. No, it was easier for them to dump her at Vale Acres. Their way of dealing. Negating the damage. Negating their exposure to her.

"This wasn't…" She swallows. Her mouth is so dry. "I don't drink anymore, Shira. I mean, that one shot…" How can she explain?

"No, I know." That brings her back, and she looks over at the woman standing beside her. Her face so sad it could make you cry. "It was a flashback, wasn't it?" Her voice so soft. "When I asked if you wanted to talk, you weren't ready."

Gal thinks she's going to apologize, but she doesn't.

"Flashback." She repeats the word. It sounds so bright, like the cameras. The truth is different. Darker. The feel of a hand on her upper arm. Fingers digging in. "Yeah, maybe," she says. She licks her lips, as if to wet them. Nerves. Not stage fright this time.

"Wanna blow this popsicle stand?" Shira tips her head, a half smile on her lips. The old line.

"On your heels." She pushes off the wall and stands, steadier than she'd thought. Steady, and ready to talk.

CHAPTER 42

"So fucking stupid." She shakes her head. Stares down at the iced tea. "That was me."

She feels it now, how blind she was. How pigheaded. Clumsy with it, too. A cow lumbering out of the bathroom. Walking through the club, Shira did her best to steer them clear of the audience, but she saw the heads swivel, the curious glances. Gal made herself smile and nod. A momentary illness. Nothing serious. Lina had made her excuses already.

Not that it was that much of an excuse. As Shira led her out to the street, Gal felt the wooziness return and reached out for the wall.

"You okay?" Shira's eyes wide with concern.

"Yeah." She said it automatically. "I think so." The correction, tendered with a self-conscious laugh. "I guess more of that booze went into my system than I thought."

"I don't think it's the alcohol." Shira held out her arm, inviting Gal to take it. She did, but silently, her customary bravado gone.

When Shira suggested the diner down the block, she let herself be led. She listened while her friend ordered eggs and toast for her, and only stopped her when she asked for coffee.

"Tea," she said instead. "Iced, please. Sweet."

Shira's brows went up, and Gal shook her head. "I have no idea," she said, responding to the unasked question. "I just want it. And I'm thirsty, you know?"

"Good." Shira, nodding like Gal had passed some test. Maybe she had, she thought. Suddenly she was not only thirsty but famished, too.

"Here you go, ladies." The waitress set their drinks down and Gal grabbed hers up. But thirsty as she was, she had to pause. The words—she has too much to say.

"So fucking stupid." The words she wrote. Was it really that long ago? She repeats herself. Peeks up from her tea. "Well, I was." A little defensive, as if the woman facing her will argue about that too.

"Young," Shira corrects her, but gently. "Vulnerable."

"Stupid," Gal repeats, only the rancor is gone. "I mean, afterward, I could've taken care of myself. You know? Gotten the pill from someone, from a clinic, and taken two or three. I remember other girls doing that back then, before the morning-after pill became a thing."

She stares out the window, the memories rushing back. Not that night, not yet, but the weeks that followed. The sickness that wasn't tied to drink or drugs. The aching in her breasts. The helplessness, as if she were some stray infested with fleas or ticks.

"Aimee really helped me." She turns back to Shira. Their food has arrived, but now her appetite is gone. She pokes at the eggs. Scrambled, they've congealed like an alien life form on her plate. "She's the one who finally made me go to the clinic—the women's center on Boylston. Shit, I probably would have ignored it until it was too late."

"You didn't think about the alternative? About keeping it?"

Gal looks up, startled. Of course, Shira has kids. A different matter for her. "No," she says, her voice flat. "Never."

For a moment, she's back there. The clinic. A woman doctor, women techs, but such a different energy than the band. No swagger, she thinks now. At the time, she felt so lost, she couldn't see it. Just how foreign everything felt: from the setting to her own body. How much she simply wanted to get her life back.

"It was all about control." The words she would have chosen, if she'd had a moment longer. Only Shira's saying them now. "Manipulation."

She looks up to see her old bandmate is lost in her own reverie. How could she know?

"The drinks, the dares. All that 'come on, it'll help.'" Shira could be talking to herself, and Gal's afraid to follow. "In retrospect, it was all so inappropriate. He was testing us. Trying us out. Grooming us."

Inappropriate. Gal remembers Shira's word. "You were talking about him." She doesn't want to say his name even now.

The woman before her nods. "T.K." Whispers, as if the initials will summon him. Raise his ghost.

A thin line appears between her brows that ought to age her. Instead, it makes her younger in Gal's eyes. Frail or, no, vulnerable. Another Shira word, and it all comes back: the whining. The complaints. Gal laughing at her. Wanting her to shut up. Wanting her gone. "That's why you left." The words need to be said.

A half smile of acknowledgment, a dip of the head. "I know Aimee—you and Aimee—wanted to replace me. I know I wasn't— didn't—hold up my end with the band. It—the pressure—was affecting everything. My playing, none of it was fun anymore. Only, I didn't know how to get out, just that I had to." Shira sucks on her lips as if she could take back words. The lawyerly polish gone. "This last year, when I talked to Aimee, she said she got it. She understood."

Her eyes rise at last to meet Gal's. "She told me what happened to you," she says. "Not the pregnancy. The rape." A lawyer stating a fact.

"He raped me." Gal tries it out, the words like stones in her mouth.

Her old friend nods. "That's what Aimee thought. She said you didn't talk about it, but she had her suspicions. And then when Lina told her what happened when you guys were touring… Well, we'd all heard, and I knew—I thought I knew…"

"You know he wanted to speak to me." Gal hears herself. She sounds bitter. She doesn't care. "Before he died, before whatever. He tried to reach out to me, his widow said. Can you believe he got married? That someone married him?"

"I heard he found religion." Shira's grin is mirthless. "Traded in the booze for God."

"Great." One word, not the one she means. "Well, at least I was spared that particular sermon."

"You think he wanted to proselytize?"

She shakes her head. "Who the fuck knows?" She's feeling like herself again, a little. "You think Lina will ever forgive me?"

"I don't know." Shira smiles full on now. "It all depends what you have planned for the second set."

Gal can only laugh, and with that, her appetite returns. She digs into the eggs, savoring their warmth, the salt she's added. The way they fill her mouth. "Best damned eggs ever," she growls, reaching for the Tabasco, as Shira laughs along. It's like the early days again. She flashes back. The camaraderie. The trust. Only this time Aimee's gone, and it hits her like a punch. Her best friend bawling in her arms. The talk they never had.

She pushes the plate away.

"What is it?" Shira reaches for her but sees something and stops herself. "Gal?"

Aimee. Her friend's name a promise she cannot speak aloud.

She shakes her head and balls her napkin up. Drops it in the eggs. "I'm done," she says.

CHAPTER 43

"Look, I just need to sleep." It's easy enough to make her excuses. She's dog tired. Her body aches, and all she wants to do is crawl into bed, alone, and not deal with the world for a good twelve hours. Shira is hoping she'll talk, she can tell. And God knows, Gal owes her. But not now. "I'm wiped," she says, slumping forward, as if the words alone aren't enough. As if something else isn't on her mind.

She doesn't get an argument, though. That's good. She must look as bad as she feels, because on top of that, Shira offers to go back and get her bass and bag. At that, Gal isn't sure whether to laugh or to cry. Her bass. Shit. She hasn't left her gear behind since, well, since that night in Cleveland. Though in the weeks leading up till then, she'd lost so much, trashing mics and monitors. Gone full out Pete Townshend a few times, as much as a chick singer can.

"Thanks," she mumbles when the lawyer returns to the diner, her bag and the black bass case in hand. Like a roadie, she's about to say, but then the memory of T.K. intrudes and she leaves it at that.

"No problem." Shira has a wistful look. "Lina put your bass aside during the break. But packing up your gear, it brought something back."

"Something good?" This was unexpected.

"Maybe." She's staring down at the battered case. "I haven't played for years. Haven't wanted to. But maybe now..."

"Maybe we could jam." She means it as a joke, but as soon as the words are out, she wonders. Could they? Does she want to? "But not tonight."

"Not tonight." Shira hands the bass over with only a token reluctance. "Lina understands, by the way. I spoke with her as they were breaking down, just briefly."

Gal nods. Everyone knows her business now. Well, part of it, anyway.

The drive back to her motel is excruciating. Not only the fatigue—she can barely keep her eyes open—but the images that keep playing before her. The memories, they must be, flashing like bad TV before her eyes.

Her phone rings as she fishes out the key, and she answers without thinking. Shira, checking to make sure she got home. Lina, maybe. She'll have to talk to her sometime.

"So, how'd it go?" Russ, sounding a million miles away. "The gig," he says when she doesn't immediately respond.

"It was...interesting." She closes the door behind her and flops onto the motel bed. "I'm just getting in now."

"Ah." One syllable drawn out. He thinks she's been out drinking, she realizes. He thinks she's drunk.

"It wasn't that kind of interesting." She closes her eyes.

"Oh?" A fake lightness and it hits her that he cares. At least that he's worried about her drinking.

"We weren't drinking. I'm not drunk." She cuts to the chase. "We went out for eggs, me and Shira. I had iced tea."

"I didn't ask." He's backing off. Offended? Or, no, defensive—he didn't ask, but he was concerned.

"Your voice." She could just drift off, talking to him like this. "I don't know if I ever heard it before, but you were worried. Worried about me."

A noise that could be confirmation. Could simply be him humming along to the radio. It's kind of nice.

"The gig was…it was weird." How to explain? The music. Playing with Lina. Her nerves beforehand and then—what? Did she have a breakdown? Another breakdown? Or was it something else? "It kind of got to me," she says, settling on the most basic version.

That sound again. Flirtatious? She pictures him lying on his bed. Maybe he has his guitar by his side. "Want to tell me about it?"

She opens her mouth. "I don't know where to begin," she says after a moment. With Shira? Lina? The feeling of pure panic? "I think I'm just too tired," she says instead. "I'm sorry, hon. I'll call you tomorrow. I promise."

"Okay, then," he says. His voice sounds warm, almost as if he hadn't suspected her of drinking, of using, again. "Sleep tight."

Only after he hangs up does she realize that she called him "hon," an endearment. Where did that come from, she wonders? And how the hell is she ever going to explain?

Despite her fatigue—her eyes closing even as she rolls to the edge of the bed—she makes herself get up. Those early days in rehab, she prided herself on brushing her teeth. The taste of stale vomit is not something she wants to wake up to ever again.

While she's in the bathroom, she washes her face and takes a moment to look at herself in the mirror. Not bad for almost fifty, she decides, startled by the smile that breaks open at the thought. Not bad, considering the wear and tear. Did those years give her the lines around her mouth? The dark splotches under her eyes, the ones that never go away? Did age? Or was it an asshole former roadie who took advantage of her one night and knocked her up?

The smile is gone, and she looks away. Her teeth are clean at least. Shedding her clothes as she walks, she slips under the covers with a sigh of relief.

Only it's too hot. The room has grown warm and claustrophobic, as if the ventilation has turned off. "That's crazy," she mutters to no one in particular, and flips over, throwing the coverlet off. Warm, cold, she's never had a problem getting to sleep. Even before she started getting shitfaced drunk, she could drop off anywhere at any time, and the pills usually kept her asleep once she was out. The pills. She laughs. She hasn't been taking them, not since coming back to town. Had thought they'd lost their efficacy after all these years.

Only now as she lies there, having flipped on her back, she reconsiders. Her heart is racing. Withdrawal, or the iced tea? As the mirror has only just now reminded her, she's not a child anymore. Maybe her body is rebelling, unable to process caffeine at any hour anymore. Maybe it was the eggs. She'd only had a few bites, but the hot sauce she'd dashed on without thinking was probably a mistake.

She gets up and cranks the AC. Fills a glass of water from the tap and drinks it in the bathroom, making a point not to look in the mirror. Not to look for the plastic bottle in her bag, not after all these nights. By the time she climbs back into bed, the room is frosty, and she pulls the cover back up with a welcome shiver. It's kind of nice to be bundled up so snugly. It's cozy here, she tells herself. Safe. She feels herself sinking, at last, into sleep.

It's a sensation like falling, a tumble back into space. Like she's in deep water or lost in the darkness, no longer aware of the sheet on her body, the texture of the fabric tucked up under her chin. Instead, she feels strangely exposed. Bare. As if the clothes had been stripped from her. Only her arms and legs are so heavy that she can't imagine how she threw them off. So heavy, and her head falls back, her matted hair the only cushion as it hits the hard surface of the floor.

"What? Wait." Did she say those words? She's not sure. Her tongue feels too big for her mouth. *"Wait..."* she tries again. Her belly is heaving, and she's going to be sick. The blanket is back. It weighs her down. It's moving. The motion, the pressure, it's all too much.

"Wait!" She's going to lose it. She can already taste the bile at the back of her throat. Has she been drinking? She must have been. A party. Shots. Someone laughing and urging her on. A face, too close to hers, dark eyes staring. *"Come on!"* A voice like a command. *"Down the hatch."* And she was a good sport. A good girl. Still the hometown sweetheart, the local favorite. No matter what they said. *"PARTY!"*

Someone was yelling then. Laughter. That face again, closer still, redder than that rusty buzzcut. Flushed. Only not staring into her eyes this time. Not urging her to drink. To be a regular. One of the guys. Just like them. This time the eyes are closed, screwed up tight as they pass over her face. A drop of sweat, of spit, drops into her eye, and she turns her face away. Moves to get up.

And that's when it hits her. She's lying on the floor, naked. T.K. on top of her, thrusting away. His friends—her friends?—cheering him on. She's going to be sick. She heaves, her body buckling.

"Whoa!" one of them calls out. "You're getting to her!"

"Get off me!" She manages to form the words. "Stop it!"

But he's too close now, and with his weight on his forearms, pinning her down, it's all she can do to cough and choke, trying not to swallow her own vomit as he pushes himself to orgasm on her nude and inert body, held helpless on the floor.

CHAPTER 44

Her heart is pounding so hard, she thinks he's still on top of her. She throws off the covers in a panic. Gets up and paces around the dark room, the AC chilling her sweaty body until the goose flesh rises on her arms. Until her teeth begin to chatter. Only then does she grab the cover off the bed and wrap it around herself, settling into the one chair. The bed, for now, off limits.

Yes, she knew—she always knew—what had happened that night. That she'd drunk too much. That she'd been fucked by T.K., maybe one of his friends, too, lying on the floor in a drunken stupor until the urge to vomit woke her up. Until the motion—the *assault*, the word comes to her—caused her body to react.

The rest of that night is a blur, but now, shivering in the bedspread, she admits it's not as much of a blank as she'd once wanted it to be. She recalls all too clearly how humiliated she'd felt. How ashamed, even as she hurriedly pulled her jeans back on. Pushed the shirt back down from around her neck. She heard the laughter and knew it was at her expense. She knew she'd been used like a sex toy. Like a thing. That he'd fucked her without a condom, without a care. Just like she knew that she didn't want to know. That she didn't want it to be quite so bad.

So fucking stupid. Yeah, that had been her. But why had she been so angry at herself?

Was it because of the tour? The band had done well. They were making a name for themselves. Girls alone—she flinches as she remembers telling T.K. he wasn't coming. He wasn't needed. God, did she set herself up?

Or was it firing Shira? Was that her sin, the reason she had to be brought down? Fucked with, literally? An uppity chick who thought she was above one of their own?

Only, no, what was it Shira had said? She'd felt the pressure to drink, to party. T.K. had come on to her, too. Had tried to get her drunk. And Shira was nothing back then. Not the leader of a band. Nowhere near breaking out, leaving this shit town behind. She played guitar, sure, but T.K. had liked the band. He'd hung out with them long before any of this started. Started roadying for them back before they could pay him anything at all.

By the time Gal's heartbeat has steadied, she's begun to see. The gray light of morning has outlined the shade on the window. Highlighted the tousled sheets she's half torn off the bed. She almost expects to see sweat stains. Tear stains, cum stains. But she doesn't. Just a bed with messy sheets. Just a room in a motel. She's alone, and the hum of the air conditioner is her only companion. What she does see now is how her shame played her for a fool. How her expectation that somehow, for some reason, she had merited the attack—had brought it on herself—was just so much borrowed nighttime glamor.

She hadn't incited the assault. It probably wasn't even personal to her. T.K. had tried his tricks on Shira first. Pushing the booze. Grooming her. Only Shira had complained and then, ultimately, gotten out. Gal, on the other hand, had felt, what, complicit?

A wave of fatigue washes over her, and she slides down in the chair. Not complicit, simply… She laughs at the words that come to her. Too polite, too well mannered. Too much of a *good girl* to say no to the drinks, to the touches, to the unwanted closeness until the opportunity to choose at all was gone.

So fucking stupid. No, she catches herself, as if listening to another, long-gone girl. Just young. Just a girl, after all. And with that, she bows her head, the hot tears falling onto the cheap coverlet, beading on its polyester surface, as she rocks, her arms wrapped around her knees. She cries until her tears are done, and then she rests her forehead on her knees, cushioned on the wet spread. And there, fetal in a cheap motel chair, she falls at last into a deep and dreamless sleep.

CHAPTER 45

Her head is buzzing when she wakes, later that morning. Full of thoughts and voices. She wants to talk to Shira again. Confirm what she's puzzled out. She wants to talk to Lina, too, she thinks as she luxuriates in a hot shower, feeling fully clean for the first time in a while.

But first, she'll go down to the cop shop again. Talk to that policeman, Bixby. She's not sure how she'll explain blowing him off yesterday. No, she admits to herself even as she dresses. She knows. She'll tell him the truth, because part of that truth involves confessing that she didn't want to know all that she did.

It feels good to be honest. To do—what's the phrase?—a searching moral inventory. Isn't that what the twelve-steppers called it? Well, hell, maybe she's closer to those folks than she knew. At that, an image of T.K. comes to mind. T.K. and his earnest widow, reaching for her hand. No, that's over. The man who assaulted her is gone.

She reaches the station even before she's finished her coffee, traffic and parking lining up as if to support her new resolution. She feels lighter, cleaner, as she marches up to the front desk.

"Gal Raver. Here to see a Detective Bixby."

"Have a seat, ma'am."

Her mouth opens, ready with the risqué retort, but she catches herself in time. The young man at the desk is probably Camille's age. No more than twenty-five.

"Ms. Raver." She looks up to see the detective who interviewed her the week before. His wide mouth looks stern, rather than sensual. The corners turned down between lines that she tells herself are from habit, from the job, rather than her own tardy appearance.

"I wanted to tell you more about T.K.—Thomas, I mean. Thomas Kennedy." She starts talking even as he shows her into a small private room. Even before she takes the red plastic seat across from him. He has questions, sure, but she feels a pressure to tell him all. "I've remembered—well, I've let myself remember more about him."

One eyebrow rises in question, but before she can explain, he begins to speak. "The reason I called you yesterday, Ms. Raver, is that we've received some new information about the deceased."

"I bet." She can't help but smile. God, she was so fucking *young*.

"You previously said that your acquaintance with Mr. Kennedy began in the 1990s? That he worked with your band?"

"Well, that's just it—" She catches herself. She's going to behave. "Yes," she says. "Sort of. He was our roadie. That means he carried our amps and equipment."

"Thank you." A quick glance from under the heavy eyebrows. "I am familiar with the term."

"Sorry." She doesn't mean to flirt. She forces herself to focus. "And, yes, that timing sounds about right."

"At that point, he was also a close friend of Walter Lanell?"

"Close?" She's stalling. She sees where he's going, but he's wrong. "I wouldn't say that. You see, Walter's a good guy. T.K. wasn't."

The scowl deepens, as if he's skeptical.

"Walter was always a nicer guy." Gal scours her memory for an example. In truth, all she can remember is them all drinking. When did Walter stop hanging out with T.K.? It must have been when he married Aimee, if not before. "He's a family man. You know he married Aimee, who played drums in my band, right?"

A nod. "Mr. Kennedy left a wife as well."

A Bible-thumping harridan. "And a daughter. Walter and Aimee, I mean. I don't think T.K. had any kids."

No comment, and even she realizes that her life-value equations don't add up.

"Look," she tries again. "I gather T.K.—Mr. Kennedy," the name bitter in her mouth, "found Jesus in his later years. Maybe he even meant it. I don't know. What I can tell you is that back in the day, when we were all hanging out together, he was not a nice man. Now whether that has anything to do with what happened to him, I don't know."

The detective's head tilts. The question in those heavy-lidded eyes, as well as the words. "He was not a nice man?"

Gal takes a deep breath. Holds it for a second, before letting it out. This is what she'd come for. That doesn't make it easy. "He could be…he was a jerk." That's not enough. As soon as the words are out of her mouth, she knows that. She takes a breath.

"He raped me."

It's getting easier to say. The backlash, though, she can hear all the questions before they're voiced. Are you sure it was rape? Why didn't you tell anyone? Why is there no record? She's so buzzed—caffeine, the truth—she keeps on talking, getting it all out before he can begin the grilling.

"I never went to the authorities because I'd been drinking." She studies his face as she talks. Looking for some recognition, some

226

understanding of the situation. "I had, even then, a problem with alcohol."

Now that she's started, she cannot stop.

"With all kinds of substances, actually. But T.K.—Thomas— played into that. He bought me drinks. Encouraged me to keep drinking, to get drunk. He tried the same thing on another member of my band as well." She'll have to get Shira to come forward. Surely she would, now. "She quit the band, but we talked. She remembers him urging her to drink. Really pressuring her, trying to get her drunk enough so that she couldn't resist. Couldn't consent either." The bitterness is back.

"Trying?" One word, that's enough.

She nods and licks her lips, her mouth suddenly dry. "She was, I don't know, a little smarter than me? Maybe a little less easily pressured."

Both eyebrows rise at that.

"I'm talking about when I was a lot younger, Detective." It sounds hollow, even to her. And yet, her memory says it was true. "I was—it was before we made it," she says at last. "I felt like I had something to prove, I guess. But that's not the point."

She's no longer sure just what her point is. But the honesty feels good. Unburdening—she understands that phrase now. It's like she cannot stop. Then she remembers she has another card to play.

"You know T.K. was trying to get in touch with me, right? When I talked to his widow, she confirmed it. He was in AA. She said he was working the steps. That he was trying to reach out to me. She thought he wanted to get me in the program, but I'm betting that he wanted to apologize. Make amends, or whatever. Ask her. She'll tell you."

"So you're giving me an alternate theory of what happened?"

She sighs. God, it sounds stupid. "Look, I just want you to know that T—that Thomas Kennedy wasn't some upright citizen. Not always, and there might be other people, with other reasons who wanted to do him harm. People he'd hurt, even if it was long ago."

It's out, and she rests. The load is lifted, and then she remembers. "You said you had new information?"

He looks at her, and she sees the question in his eyes. She's gone on too long. She sounds unbalanced. Mad. "You knew some of this. You've been hearing stories about the old days?"

He tilts his head again. It's not a nod, but it's enough. "We know he was reaching out to several people from his past," he says at last. Confirmation. "We've been hoping to fill in some blanks."

"Look, I know Walter has been charged or whatever. And I know that he's not really up to defending himself right now. You do know that his wife just died, right?" She pauses. They were separated, she's pretty sure. Not divorced. "That's why I'm in town, why we all got together. He's grieving. He's probably in shock. At any rate, he's not thinking clearly right now, and I don't want to see him railroaded."

The man seated opposite her nods as if he has finally heard what she's saying, and she exhales, slumping down in the hard plastic chair. And just as quickly bolting upright. He's heard her, all right. Heard her story about what happened and how that bastard T.K. was trying to get together with her. Suddenly, her earlier fears come rushing back, only this time with some reason. This cop would have to be an idiot to not see that he did have another suspect for T.K.'s murder. Someone besides Walter who had motive and, just maybe, opportunity: Gal herself.

Chapter 46

It should have been me. The pall of guilt. That's not what she meant. It can't be.

She tells herself she's being silly. That she's seeing trouble where none exists. She hadn't seen the man in, what, fifteen years? Twenty? Only as the silence after this last outburst begins to grow does she realize how she's screwed up. A wronged woman with a history of erratic behavior. An old acquaintance against whom she has a grudge. The cop had known T.K. wanted to meet with her. Does she have an alibi for the time when he was attacked? There was a party, but she didn't stay that late. And when she left, she left alone.

"You can't think—" she starts, then stops herself. He can. He probably does.

"Excuse me?" A slow blink as if nothing at all had occurred. "You were explaining?"

"I—never mind." Too late, she remembers that he asked her here. "I'm sorry. You probably have more questions for me."

"No, I believe you've answered them." He looks down at the pad before him. She strains to read his scrawl. "Thank you for coming in."

He doesn't detain her, that's something. And so she walks out as quickly as she can without breaking into a run.

Only when she's back at her car does she stop to consider. That feeling of guilt, it's not real, she tells herself. It's a hangover. A remnant from the days when she used to drink and use. Walter is the reason she came in today. He's already been arraigned. He should be her focus. She makes herself go over what just happened, willing that creeping fear to remain at bay. Will what she told the detective make a difference in his case? Is he even still investigating?

Closing her eyes, she leans back on the headrest, exhausted by the effort. Cops. For all her troubles, she's not had much to do with them. Gus and his crew were always there, smoothing the way. At least until they weren't, and she was sent to Vale Acres.

That didn't mean she doesn't have some ideas. Like how slow they could be. How stupid. She remembers one night on the road, smashed and happy. She and Lina? No, it had been Mimi, keeping the party going. Drinking behind the club. She doesn't remember how it started. How did these things ever start? But before she knew it, they were throwing bottles. Aiming for the dumpster, but missing as often as not, the glass shattering on the pavement. On the sidewalk. On the few cars parked around back.

It was probably the owners of one of those cars who'd called the cops on them, she and Mimi and a couple of boys who were hanging out, hoping to get lucky as the night faded. Hoping she and Mimi would fade, too. The boys had known their small-town po-po, hustling them back behind the dumpster as the flashing blue lights approached. But she and Mimi, they were too high to stay quiet. Mimi in particular, with that hyena laugh of hers. It wasn't long before the flashlights were coming their way, big, bold beams blinding them to the boots that crunched on all that broken glass. Right about then, Gus had appeared, ready to share a few words with the officers in blue before ushering his charges inside like wayward children. But Gal had turned to see one of those flashlights coming down like a club on a would-be suitor. Not anyone she knew. She can't even dredge up a name. But his cry, like a frightened animal, has stayed with her.

Hearing it again, in her car, she sits up and opens her eyes. Things are different here. She's not a crazy drunk. The man she just spoke with is a detective, not some small-town thug hating on the local punks. Still, he's human. He's likely to take the easy way out. Why else would they have arrested Walter otherwise?

She makes herself breathe. That dumpster was far away. The boy long gone. And as tempting as it is to blow town, to go home to Russ and her cat, she's got to try something else first. She's got to figure out what really happened to T.K. The stakes have gotten too high.

She pulls her phone out and begins to thumb through the recents. Shira, Lina, then she finds it: T.K.'s widow, the sad woman who said her dead husband had wanted to meet up. Surely she knows more about what Gal's onetime roadie, her rapist husband, was up to in the days and hours leading up to his death. Maybe she has some idea of who else her dear departed had wanted to save.

The number is just a click away. The voice that picks up—chirpy as a mechanical bird—familiar.

"Julia?" Gal remembers the name just in time. "Gal Raver here. I'm sorry I ran out when we last spoke." She pauses, wondering how much to give. "It was a lot to hear," she settles on. "A lot to take in. I was wondering if you'd care to meet again."

She hears the intake of breath. She waits.

"I'm thinking of what you told me about Thomas." She plays her ace. "About how he wanted to help me."

"Of course," says his widow, jumping on the idea like a sparrow on a crumb. "I'd be more than happy to."

It's hard to believe the woman is a professional. Either she's dying to bring Gal to Jesus or her career is simply shit, Gal thinks before the realization hits her—it's Saturday. The weekend to most people, even if she still thinks of it as "amateur night."

Ignoring Gal's low chuckle, the widow gasses on. Suggests lunch again, this time at a diner in Watertown. Gal jots down the address and thanks her before hanging up.

With the rest of the morning looming, Gal considers how to spend her time. She'd like to pack up. Check out. Have everything in the Toyota ready to go. Only she knows she has too many loose ends for that. She'll go over to Aimee's place, maybe for the last time. She's done with the books but maybe there's something there that will help her understand. Maybe she can talk to Walter one more time. Get him to give her more than he has.

The blink of a voicemail reminds her that she has another call to make first. Lina must have called while she was speaking with the detective. Taking a deep breath, she swallows and hits the number to call her old friend back.

"Lina, I'm sorry." She starts in before the other woman can talk. "That was…what I did was unforgivable."

"I was concerned." The guitarist speaks haltingly, as if the wrong word might set Gal off.

"I understand and I'm sorry." Gal winces but forges ahead. "I wasn't drinking, if that's what you're worried about. I mean, I grabbed a shot at the bar, but I made myself throw it up." She winces again. Not a model of sanity, much less sobriety. "I'm—look, I was going through something, Lina. I'm just sorry that it came out when it did. That I lashed out."

"Gal, stop." The voice no longer hesitating. But not angry, Gal realizes with surprise. "I know, okay? I spoke with Shira last night, when she picked up your bass. I'm just—look, I'm sorry too. I didn't know, or, okay, I didn't let myself know, what you were dealing with."

"Shira?" Gal hasn't gotten past this. "She told you?"

"Maybe she shouldn't have, but we were all worried." Her former bandmate sounds so serious. So adult. "I mean, we could all see that you were having a hard time, and then to lash out like that? We simply didn't know what was going on."

Gal hesitates. She wants to know what Shira said. What Lina knows. She wants to get her story straight, she realizes.

"What did she tell you?" It's easier just to ask.

"That you were having a bad time with some memories." Lina sounds like she cares, even if she doesn't understand. "Some PTSD from back in the day. Look, we all knew you had some issues. The touring, the drinking. God, they treated us like canned goods, didn't they? I always knew it was hardest on you."

"Did she tell you about T.K.?" Her voice near to cracking.

"Was that who it was? The man who attacked you? I knew there was someone. I mean, it was pretty obvious from your songs. I guess I just never put it together at the time."

CHAPTER 47

Gal gets to the diner early and orders coffee. She doesn't need it. She can't remember feeling more awake, but she has no appetite for food and she doesn't want to miss a beat. She's turning down a refill when Julia enters, her cheeks pink and her hair in disarray.

"Did I keep you waiting?" She sounds distressed as well. "I'm sorry."

"Don't sweat it." Gal has risen to greet her and waits while the other woman sits, letting her slide into the banquette this time. "You want some coffee?" She turns to beckon the waitress back.

"No, not for me." The widow brushes her hair back from her forehead, revealing white roots in her dark hair. "I'm just—this is just so much."

"Please don't worry," Gal says, anxious to move on. "I appreciate you meeting with me again." She just wants to get to it. Grill this woman, but the plump widow sweating across from her is clearly too flustered to talk. "What's happening?"

"I got a call. We have a court date."

Gal catches her breath: Walter. Has he changed his mind?

"There's going to be a trial?" She speaks softly and with caution, unsure of what the widow knows.

234

"Not exactly, it's a…what do you call it?" She waves her hand, as if the answer were a fly. "After the arrest?"

"I thought Walter—" Gal catches herself, but the widow doesn't stop.

"A hearing. That's it," she says. "I gather that's tomorrow. The woman in the state office told me I might want to be there for that. She told me there probably won't be a trial."

"No trial?"

She shakes her head, confirming, not disagreeing. "The man confessed. He just wants to get it over with, she said. He's going to plead guilty. It's a relief, really. He must have so much weighing on his conscience."

That was the obvious interpretation, especially for a Jesus freak, but Gal isn't buying it. Grief, more likely. That and some lingering guilt over not having been able to save Aimee. Surviving. What this all means is if she's going to help Walter, she has to move fast.

"Have you heard why?"

A blank look, wide eyes blinking in a pale face.

"Why he supposedly did it?" She doesn't even like to form the words.

"He confessed." She seemed to take some strength from this. "Alcohol, I'm sure. The manufacturers are responsible for so many evils in today's world. Of course, one does have a choice." She pulls herself up, her mouth pursing. "One always has a choice, but it's hard to do the right thing. To admit you have a problem and to surrender yourself to the Lord."

Gal takes a deep breath to calm herself. Walter was never an angry drunk, and he doesn't drink like that. Not anymore, though in all fairness the night of Aimee's memorial, he'd had a few. It was an emotional night. For the first time, she begins to wonder—and shakes off her doubt. She's scared, that's all. She doesn't want the cops to consider her a suspect. She needs to get to the bottom of this.

"Like T.K. did?" It's ham-handed, but it works. The widow perks up as if she can see her late husband right there by Jesus's side. "Thomas, I mean?"

"Exactly." She nods like a schoolteacher, grateful that Gal has gotten the right answer. "It isn't easy. It wasn't for my Thomas, but he did it."

Gal nods, gritting her teeth. She's saved by the waitress who has circled back.

"May I take your orders?"

Luckily, Julia is a regular. Not only that, but she sounds excited to order the Denver omelet. No abstemious salad today, and she seems pleased when Gal, not caring, does the same.

"You'll love it." She leans forward as if confiding a secret once the server has gone. "I find I hardly remember to cook now, without Thomas around."

Gal is gearing up to ask her about other contacts. Other enemies of her late husband, when the woman across from her changes her tack. "Are you married?"

"No." That came out too strident. "I'm seeing someone though." Gal wants to keep her sweet. Keep her talking. "But you were talking about T.K.—Thomas." The name like a rock in her mouth. "And I never heard the end of your story." A blank stare. A blink. "You said, last time we got together, that he wanted to meet with me. That he was trying to reach out to me."

"Oh." She looks down, but the server has taken the menu and she's unable to find anything on the table to stare at for more than two seconds. "Yes, yes, I did."

"I'd love to know what it was about." She's causing this woman pain. She can see that, and she gets a perverse pleasure from it. "Was he trying to get in touch with anyone else? Anyone from his past?"

"I believe he was." The sad, wide eyes again as she nods. "Yes."

Gal waits. She has a suspicion. She needs to have it confirmed.

"I told you he had had a lapse recently." The other woman's voice is soft, and she's speaking slowly. Gal only hopes she gets her story out before the eggs arrive. "That he was working the steps again."

She nods to urge her on.

"He started at home, of course. He told me he needed to apologize to me for the hurt he'd done me. The dear man…" She turns toward the window, and Gal fears she is losing her. She reaches across the table and takes her hand.

"And the others?"

"He told me he had not been honest with me. Not been completely honest. That he had skipped some people. That he still needed to make amends." Her voice has faded to a rasping whisper by this point. The blood is pounding in Gal's ears, but she holds her breath, waiting. "He had a list," the widow says. "To make amends, no matter how overdue."

"Amends." The word slips out. "Not apologies?"

"Words alone do not suffice." The widow is quoting some text, but Gal doesn't care. "He told me about his list, about the amends he had to make. About rehab."

"What?" She's missed something. Some vital clue.

"He—we—don't have much money, but we have some. And with no children…" She stops and swallows. "He wanted to spend it making amends. He wanted to reimburse you, pay for your rehab."

"For my rehab?" She can't help it. The words come out loud, and the widow draws back.

"He told me about the drinking." She looks more like a scared rabbit than a grown woman. "How he urged you on. Made you develop the habit."

"The drinking?" It's true enough as far as it goes. It's what she'd told the cop, but that no longer matters. She has both hands on the table. She's standing, the anger taking her. "That's what he wanted to make amends for? My *drinking*?"

Out of the corner of her eye, she sees the waitress. She's carrying two plates. The omelets, bright orange cheese leaking out the sides. But she's stopped in her tracks, staring.

"Your husband raped me." She's loud now, and she doesn't care who hears her. "He poured booze into me and raped me, back when I was just a kid. And now, all these years later, he felt bad about my drinking? Shit."

She sits back and looks around. Everyone in the place is suddenly very busy doing something else.

"T.K. was always full of shit." She can't do it. She rises again. Whatever enlightenment she was hoping for, she's not going to get here. Not now. "I don't need his money," she says, stepping out of the booth. "Never did."

It's not until she's out by her car that she realizes she's done it again. Walked out. Fucked up. What did they say back in group? Repeating yourself and looking for a different response is a sign that you're crazy. Or still a junkie, trying to replicate that first high. Anger, maybe that's her new drug, riding that high when she could have used the widow's discomfort to her advantage. Could have pried out of her what T.K. had been doing his last few days, and with whom. Who else he'd tried to reach. But the thought of going back into the diner, of talking to that sanctimonious bitch again, is as nauseating as the technicolor omelet. No, twice is enough. She takes out her frustration on the car, leaving rubber on the parking lot as she peels off back to town.

CHAPTER 48

She wants to confront Walter. To grab him and shake him. Make him spill what he's doing and why. Today might be her last chance. If she could get him to rally. To understand, he could have a trial, at least. A fighting chance. And even if the police aren't working very hard at finding out what really happened, a trial would give them—give her—more time. Maybe she could hire a better lawyer. A private detective. For the first time in ages, she regrets not having money. If only she hadn't been so reckless when she was younger. So wasted, in every sense.

If only she hadn't been so profligate, she could have a drink now, she adds to the list as she drives back into town. She's conscious of her speed, but her knuckles are white, she grips the wheel so tightly. Anger radiates off her like steam. A nice cold beer to take the edge off. A shot of Jack.

She can't though. She knows that, and she can't face Walter like this, so raw and raging. Walter might be one of the gentlest men she's ever met, but on this he's become mule stubborn. She can't push him. She's tried. She needs to figure out how to cajole.

Almost without thinking, she finds herself detouring downtown, slowly circling the Common, the traffic never letting up. Was it this bad back in the day? A memory of the van. Laughing as they headed out of town that first time. Feeling upbeat. Free. She can't recall coming home—not fully, not yet—and as the light changes from yellow to red, she finds herself thinking about her latest return. The benefit, the night this all started to go bad.

What was Walter thinking that night? All of them—the survivors, the ragtag remnants of the old crowd—all getting together ostensibly to celebrate his late wife, as well as to help him out. He'd been drinking, she remembers, as the light turns green once more. Talked about his hangover like he meant it. Everyone had been drinking, pretty much, though now that she doesn't, she sees most parties like that. He'd seemed out of sorts and out of sync with the general festive atmosphere, she recalls. Grief, she'd figured, aggravated by the liquid depressant. Grief over Aimee's death and just maybe over the breakup of their marriage, the reconciliation that now could never happen. The words he must have left unsaid.

Now she wonders if her initial impression had been correct and anger, rather than sadness, had been what had drawn his mouth down like that. Kept his eyes on the floor, kept him wringing those big, scarred hands. Angry at Aimee. Angry at life. But angry enough to kill? No, that she can't believe.

She turns a corner and edges up the long avenue that runs between the green and the newly revamped theater district. The Common seems cleaner than it used to, at least from her car. She's not seeing the homeless, the junkies nodding out. Waiting for the night. A fancy new cinema on her left, the marquee flashing a fight scene. Battling for the entertainment dollar, but all she can think of are the clubs that once were here. The theater where they had the benefit, back before the water-spotted walls had that new coat of paint. Before the backstage had both light and power.

She's not sure what she's going to do, when a car pulls out in front of her, jolting her out of her reverie. Even as she curses, though, she realizes the benefit: a legal space. Before she can second-guess herself, she backs right in. A walk will cool her down.

But spurred by the questions echoing around her head, she turns from the Common, instead taking the shaded side street that leads around the theater. To the alley where T.K. met his end.

At this time of day, it looks innocuous. An empty lot, used for loading in and out. A dumpster sits at the far end, and from the smell, its pickup is due. The only color, the dull red of the brick walls abutting it on three sides. The pavement appears a dirty gray, dust and grime powdering the asphalt. She steps carefully as she walks in: what look like potholes threaten. Up close, she sees they're gaps in the pavement, a shoddy application of asphalt revealing the cobblestones below. The sight makes her smile. The past is always with us, she thinks. *Right, T.K.?*

But beyond that glimpse of an earlier era, the alley has little to show. Even the shadows look faded, and she walks past the dumpster to an oily patch of pavement where she imagines T.K. lay dying. Closing her eyes, she can visualize the crime scene tape cutting off this corner, but there are no marks on the blind metal door that overlooks it, nothing distinguishing the drab matte surface recessed into the wall or the three steps descending to the asphalt below.

She pauses and lets herself think of him at last. Thrown down, finally, here. Did he retreat from someone, from a fight, hurling himself against that door in a futile attempt to escape? Was he cornered? Pushed back here in the fray, or to keep away from any prying eyes passing by?

She turns back. Yes, the dumpster partially blocks the view of the street, and at night this corner would be obscured. A good place to do a deal. Her old habits kick in, and she wonders: Are the police looking into T.K.'s sobriety? Do they know about the recent lapse the widow cited? She never knew him to do smack, back in the day. Then again, she never knew very much about him at all.

She kicks at the stoop. Twenty years ago, fifteen, she might have found something. A crack vial, a glassine envelope. Some evidence that this was a favored corner for junkies.

Ten years ago, even, or so she imagines. She looks up, looks around. This isn't the club district of those days. It's for tourists and suburbanites. The sober adults who show up for a concert benefiting an old friend. Maybe the widow was right and T.K. was clean. Maybe he was lured out here, to his death.

Or maybe, the thought hits her, he intentionally met someone here. What had the widow said? He was making amends. He was trying to reach her. Could someone have said she'd be back here? That she'd meet him? The old Gal, the drinker, maybe. The dare, the promise—the unwillingness to appear afraid. Yeah, she might have, back in the day. And someone might have told T.K. that. And he would've gone.

But even as she tries it out, another idea suggests itself. Amends, the widow had said. The plural had fooled her. One made amends to one person, but from what that cop had said, the widow too, T.K. had others on his mind. He could have been reaching out to someone else in their crowd, someone there that night. Hadn't she said something about a list? Maybe he came back here with his killer willingly, looking to have a private conversation away from the party's din. A conversation that resulted in his death. She sees— she thinks she sees—a pale shape over by the dumpster. A ghost, or, worse, a memory. The truth come back to haunt her.

CHAPTER 49

After that second tour, the homecoming was different. The band weren't only hometown favorites, they were bona fide rock stars. August and they'd been charting since the previous spring, their music as hot as the after-party at the club that summer night.

"Bring it on." Gal practically growled as Kelly set up the shots on the bar. Nobody had to buy her drinks anymore. She was the one in charge. "Keep 'em coming."

Another round, maybe two, and she stepped outside. The party was going gangbusters. Had been for hours by then, but something—someone—was missing. Kenmore Square was more of the same. Between the lights and a high haze, the city felt like another overheated room, the sky a dirty pearl.

As the door swung shut behind her, it muffled the sound of celebration. They were stars—the only stars in that smoldering night—and any lingering ill will about Shira, about anything, was so much dross to be brushed away.

"What's going on?" She found Aimee huddled by the pay phones out front, a little bleary and the worse for wear. "You looking to score?"

Aimee shook her head. They never bought their own drugs,

not anymore. "I'm waiting for Walter to call me back." She slumped back on the plexiglass and stared down at the ground. "I thought he'd be here."

"Maybe he got the night wrong." Gal felt a nasty little surge of excitement. The boyfriend was a distraction, she told herself. No rocker on the road should waste her precious energy thinking about someone back home.

"No." Aimee didn't hear the glee in Gal's voice. Didn't even look at her as she shook her head. "It's his mother. He went to see her, but…he said he'd call."

"We've got to get you a cell phone." With Aimee to herself, Gal felt magnanimous. "We should all get them. No more hanging out here like you're waiting for a john or something."

It was crass. She heard it herself, but she wanted to shake Aimee out of her mood. And it worked. The drummer looked up, as if the spell was broken. "Come on, kid." Gal wrapped her arm around her, the bare flesh of Aimee's arm felt cool and smooth. "You've got some catching up to do."

It was hot inside. Steamier than she'd remembered, and she licked the sweat from her upper lip as she propelled Aimee to the bar. "Jack," she said. It was salty. She was thirsty. "And a chaser— two."

Aimee was distracted, she could tell, and Gal wanted her friend back. Wanted to share the triumph. "Earth to Aimee," she said while they waited. "Come in, Aimee."

A snort, a smile, and her drummer shook her head. "Sorry. I just…I was looking forward to seeing Walter. We've been talking a lot."

The drinks arrived, which saved Gal from having to comment. They went down easy, too.

"Hey, you two." T.K., his face shining in the lights, the buzz cut glowing red. "Long time no see."

"Get lost." Gal could afford to be imperious. She was a star. They both were. "Get lost or get us drinks, at least. We're dying here."

The grin grew wider. Always eager to please. "Coming right up," he said. And as he turned back toward the bar, Gal slapped him on his skinny ass, hard enough to make him jump.

"You gonna play?" A red-faced boy—a writer, she thought, from one of the local zines—appeared out of nowhere, looming over her like some half-starved crane. Startling her. "Give us a set?"

"Hey, you want to hear us play, you can buy a ticket for next week's show. Same as everyone else." Gal took a step forward. It was hot, too hot, but she'd be damned if some boy critic was going to move into her space. "We played a damn fine set tonight at the Ballroom. This is our downtime." She paused. It sounded too much like an apology. "Private party for our friends."

She'd perfected her glare on the road. Usually, it sent the hangers-on packing. This boy didn't flinch.

"I'm on the list," he continued. "I wrote about one of your first gigs. Don't you remember?"

He said some name that was lost in the roar of the room and held out his hand. She looked down at it. A large hand, reasonably clean. "You writing tonight?"

"Just a scene piece, you know? You got any comments?"

She looked around. Aimee staring off into space. T.K. reaching over the bar to grab another bottle. It was that kind of night. The boy was tall, with big hands. She tilted her head for effect and gave him her best slow grin.

"You want a story, huh?" Even in this light, she could see his face go white, then flush again. "What are you willing to do for it?"

She lost track of Aimee after that. Lost track of herself, really, as she dragged the eager young man into a bathroom stall for a quickie. The sex was forgettable. Rushed and frantic, and she was too drunk to come. But she made enough noise to get everyone's attention. Gal Raver had a reputation to maintain.

She looked for her friend at the bar after, wanting to share the laugh. And, okay, brag a little. When they'd started the band less than two years before, Aimee had been the tough one. Her fearlessness, as much as her ferocity on the set, had drawn Gal in. Aimee would tell her when a song sucked, and Gal had learned to trust her. Take axing Shira, for example, and replacing her with Lina. Not only was that the right call—Gal's new songs were more metal than funk— but Aimee had done the dirty work, taking their longtime guitarist out for the talk.

These days, Gal matched her drummer for both toughness and 'tude. She had almost as many tattoos, the latest celebrating an entire afternoon when they'd slipped out of Gus's clutches to explore Akron on their own. As Gal leaned back on the bar, beer in hand, she thought back on the day. Two months ago? Three? No, it had been cold. Winter then. Well, it was hard to keep track of the days when you lived by night, she told herself, scanning the room. They were together constantly. It wasn't like they were splitting up.

Next month would be different. A beer appeared and she drained it, knowing Kelly would keep them coming now. Especially if this thing with Walter was blowing over. She craned to see above the crowd, looking for Aimee's familiar white-blonde mop. Maybe she'd snuck away with someone, like Gal herself had done. Her friend wasn't quite as cavalier with the boys. Being a drummer, Gal figured, she didn't get as many options. But it would serve her so-called boyfriend right, not showing up. Hell, his old running buddy had.

The thought of T.K. made her turn once more to the bar. "Kelly?"

She wanted something stronger.

"Here you go." With a flick of the wrist, the slight barkeep popped the cap off another PBR, sliding it over.

"Jack, neat." Gal took the bottle and saw Kelly roll her eyes. "What?"

"You want to pace yourself?" She was drawing an ale as she spoke, leaning forward so her bangs fell over her face. It was the tone that got Gal. "It's hot."

"No shit!" Gal felt it, the color coming up her neck. "That's why I'm drinking, Kelly. What the fuck?" She could buy her, she knew. Could buy this whole place. Gal and the band were why the club was packed. Why they all had jobs.

"Never mind." If the barkeep said anything more, Gal didn't hear it. She'd turned to grab the whiskey, filling the heavy-bottomed shot glass and sliding it over in one smooth move.

"Damn right." Gal downed it, slammed the glass back on the bar, and pivoted back to the room. The movement was too much too fast. The room shimmied, but she knew how to cover. Elbows up on the bar, she swallowed the bile that had risen. Waited for the spins to stop. Aimee was here somewhere.

"Hey, Lina!" she called out, having spotted the guitarist at a table with two other women. "You see Aimee?"

Lina shrugged and went back to her friends.

"She can't hear you!" Kelly, behind her, was half up on the bar, shouting in her ear. As Gal swiveled to face her, the couple next to her moved away.

"She's deaf now?" If Lina wouldn't answer, she'd take on the barkeep.

"Go over to her." The woman turned, refusing to engage. "Have a seat. Give the bar a break."

"Fuck you." She pushed off, making her way over to her guitarist.

The crowd parted for her, and a seat appeared. All eyes on her now. "Lina, you see Aimee?"

"She's not with Walter?" The guitarist looked puzzled, to Gal's surprise. She didn't know Aimee's little romance was common knowledge.

"He's not here." Damn, she'd left her beer on the bar and not a waitress in sight.

"Well, I haven't seen her for an hour or so. Not since you two were huddled over at the bar." Gal twisted back. No, no Aimee. "Who were you talking with?"

"Some reporter." Maybe Kelly knew. Then it hit her, and she turned to Lina. "Oh, at the bar? T.K. Why?"

Her guitarist didn't answer. Didn't have to, as the set of her mouth made Gal a little queasy.

"She probably found some boy toy." Gal tossed it off. "Teach Walter a lesson."

"That's more your thing, Gal." There was acid in her tone. "You think we should look for her?"

"Aimee's a big girl." Even as she said it, she was bracing herself on the arms of the chair. It was hot. She was tired. She could make it back to the bar though. In a minute. "She can look after herself."

She had gotten herself back to the bar, when Kelly came over. She wasn't carrying a refill, Gal noted, but by this point she didn't feel like a fight. Still, she made herself straighten up. Put the latest bottle down as the slight woman approached. Something in her face made her brace for a confrontation.

"What?" She'd been closed out, even kicked out of some places. But not here. Not her hometown. Not tonight.

"It's your friend." Kelly craned over the bar, her breath moist in Gal's ear. "She's out back."

"What?" She didn't understand. What was this woman talking about?

"I was taking a break, and I heard something." She looked down at the bar, and Gal let a smile play on her lips. Lots of reasons to step out back. A fix, a fuck. Nice to know Kelly was human too. "She's your buddy." The barkeep snapped at her. "Go take care of her."

Gal was speechless. Nobody talked that way to her, not anymore. Even Gus had learned that much. But as she gathered her slurred wits to respond, Kelly walked away, leaving her off balance. Something like fear turned her guts sour.

"Aimee?" She knew she was staggering. It was late, they all were, everyone left in the party's main room, as she pushed through to the back, swinging out with the door. "You here, girl?"

A pale shape behind the dumpster. Her guitarist, her friend, nude from the waist down, stinking of vomit and booze. The eyes that looked up wide and wet.

"Okay, then." She avoided those eyes as she found Aimee's jeans. An arm around her waist and she helped her into them. Aimee's legs were dirty, she saw, dark streaks on her pale flesh in the dim street light. "Had a party, huh?"

Even as she formed them, the words fell flat. Those eyes, and Aimee's silence.

"Come on." She draped her friend's arm over her shoulders and held her up by her waist. "Let's get out of here. Let me take you home."

Chapter 50

She's thinking of that night as she walks back to her car. Her friend, the mess she'd been. The widow's words come back to her then, too, and she feels a flush rise from her chest. *It should have been me*, she thinks once again. Now, perhaps, she understands. If T.K. had managed to reach her. If he had started to talk to her about his sins, his failings. If he had tried to lecture her about her drinking, when he was the one who pushed her. Always a beer in one hand, a shot in the other. If he had started, she might have struck out at him. She might have…

The sickness rises suddenly, and she has to catch herself, one hand on the Toyota's hood. It all floods over her at once. The drinking. The heat. God, was she so malleable? So—she hates the word with a passion—*soft*? It would certainly be nice to blame T.K. for her problems. Find a big, bad bogeyman who forced her into something damn near addiction, but she knows the truth. She drank too much and too hard for years after the lanky roadie was out of her life. She was a big girl, perfectly capable of bellying up to the bar—or pushing herself away, if she'd wanted to.

No, her problems weren't T.K.'s fault. She drank because she liked to drink, at least after a while. Wanted to feel free and fearless.

To feel strong.

Another wave of nausea, and she feels herself sweating. The flush turns cold and she shivers. She doesn't have time to get sick. Not with Walter's pre-trial hearing tomorrow—his trial's beginning and ending, she thinks, unless he agrees to fight. She gulps in air. That always helped when she was on the road. When she was drinking. God, she was tough then, wasn't she? With an effort, she stands upright. Steadies herself and walks around to the driver's side. She has no time to be useless or weak. To be soft.

To distract herself, she strategizes as she starts to drive. Rush hour has started, and traffic on Boylston is slow. Nobody wants to let her in, and she has to get assertive, advancing just enough to force a choice. That is, unless that Prius wants to hit her. "Pussy," she mutters as the driver gives way. "Fucking Prius." But the words sound strange to her. An older, outdated version of herself. She must be coming down with something for real. A virus, she decides, as the light changes and the traffic surges forward, block by block by block.

"Walter?" She knocks, but when nobody answers, she lets herself in. Finds him in his office—Aimee's office—behind the desk. "Can we talk?"

He glances up, distracted. Maybe he didn't hear her, she tells herself. He's got papers in front of him, a scowl on his face.

"I'm kind of busy." He pulls a sheet of type toward him. The lines on his forehead deepen as he reads, and he signs the page without looking up. Folds it and tucks it into an envelope, adding it to a pile to his left. A few more pages wait, the stack of envelopes threatening to topple. He's finishing up, Gal realizes. His affairs are going to be in order before the hearing.

"Walter." She walks up to him, pulling a chair along the floor. She doesn't need to sit. She isn't sure if she should, really, considering what she has to say. What she needs to tell him. But the noise gets his attention. "Just listen, okay?"

The scowl. When did he start looking so harried? She kicks herself. Probably when Aimee died. His wife—ex-wife, whatever—was the love of his life, and he couldn't save her. He couldn't, but she...

Another wave of nausea. Dizziness coming so hard that she feels herself falling backward. Has to grab at the wall to keep from slipping, to keep from falling down. That night with Aimee, when she held her, crying. She hears the echo of those desperate, choking sobs. Sinks into the office chair and takes a breath. The truth hitting her at last.

She'd tried to fight it. Swallow it down as she drove. Surely Aimee had known about T.K., she told herself. Had seen him for the slime bag he was. Had known how he had attacked her. Humiliated her. Raped her on the floor of a back room at that loft. She wouldn't have been drinking with him—

Except that now, sitting here, the reality engulfs her. Gal had never told Aimee the full story of what happened. Had never told anyone, not for real. Not about the hands on her arms, pinning her down. Her desperate pleas to be let go. For him to stop. She had never said that to herself back then, much less her tough-as-nails bandmate. That she'd gotten shitfaced and fucked someone, yeah. Did Aimee know it was T.K.? Probably. Everyone knew, T.K. made sure of that. But all Gal had ever said was that she'd gotten too drunk and done something stupid. *So fucking stupid.* And maybe, just maybe, left her best friend open to be his next victim.

It's all too much. Oblivious now to the man in front of her, Gal bends nearly double, cradling her head in her hands. No, she wasn't stupid, not in that way. What she has been is blind—willfully so—to T.K. To the extent of his wiles.

All these years of not admitting what had happened. Of wondering, secretly, what she had done to deserve it. To merit the assault. Her rape. Hers alone. But it wasn't. She didn't, and not just because she was young or vulnerable or *so fucking stupid*. She wasn't complicit. She also wasn't special. She wasn't singled out for her strengths or her sins, specially picked to be stripped, humiliated, and abused. She was simply a victim. One, perhaps, of many. The realization is astounding but undeniable. A tall figure in the back of the room, ushering a drunk girl off the floor. Shira, her—and then Aimee.

Oh my God, she thinks, rocking in her chair. This is what has been weighing on her. Not her grief, but her silence. If only they had spoken to each other. No, if only *she* had spoken. If she had confided in Aimee. Had trusted her. If she hadn't felt—she pauses, the word that springs to mind foreign and yet so right—ashamed.

Could she have saved her friend some heartache? Would she have wanted to? The memory of what happened after still so bittersweet. Her first time making love to a woman. The flesh soft and fragrant, so unlike a man's. A different kind of love, Aimee had written, before she left the band. Her song. Their song. Only she decided to bear the child. To marry...

No, it doesn't bear examining. Not now, she promises herself. Not yet. And Aimee went on to so much happiness afterward. Didn't she? As Gal sits back up to take in the grieving man before her, she admits the truth. She seeks absolution—to be washed clean. Can she ask that of Walter? Is it even possible now, so many years later? Can she make amends?

She owes Aimee that much. Hell, she might as well be honest. She owes herself.

CHAPTER 51

"Are you okay?" Walter, still frowning, but drawn out of himself by the woman before him. "Gal?"

Ignoring the question—she doesn't have an answer—Gal dives in. "Walter, I need to confess something." Why is this so hard? She's Gal Raver, tough as nails. "Back when Aimee and I played together I—well, you know I drank too much, right? One night, when I was drunk at a party, I was attacked." Why can't she say it? "Raped." She swallows. "Aimee knew, at least the basic outline, and she took care of me. But I didn't tell her everything."

Another swallow. She is getting sick. The flu. A stomach bug.

"I knew who attacked me. It was T.K. And he attacked Aimee, too." There, she's said it. "I don't know if he was jealous of you and Aimee or-or what." She's trying to think. Trying to put herself back there, as much as she doesn't want to. "Anyway, I wanted to tell you because I feel—I fucked up, Walter. I never really admitted what happened. To myself, to anyone. I know that now. And if I had, maybe I could've saved her. Maybe she would have been on guard. Maybe he wouldn't have been able to rape her too."

"Shut up." Of all the reactions she expected, this was not one of them.

"I'm sorry, Walter. I know it's hard to hear…"

Her voice fails her as he stands. Leaning forward, knuckles on the desk in front of him. "Just let it go. Please."

It's too much. He can't bear to think of Aimee in pain. She's made everything worse, all so she can have her moment of peace.

"Of course." She hurries to him as he falls back into his chair. Reaches an arm around his shoulders. "I'm sorry. I just—this is all kind of new to me, and I was just feeling sorry for myself. And, well, missing Aimee, you know?"

"Yeah." He turns to her, his face a study in sorrow and regret. "Only, she's gone. Please don't let Camille know. She doesn't need this."

"Of course." Squatting there, Gal watches the emotions play across his face. Walter is wrestling to get control of himself. To be strong for his daughter, she thinks. He puts Camille first, as she should have too. She's grateful the girl isn't here.

"Has Camille gone back to school?"

A quick shake of his head, his forehead knotting with anxiety or sorrow. "She won't. She wants to be here tomorrow. For the hearing."

The way he says the word tells her all she needs to know. Reminds her why she came.

"Walter, you need to fight it," she says. "I understand that you're mourning. You're upset, but you need to at least let your lawyer do his job. And if he won't…"

She thinks of Shira. A fundraiser, another benefit, to get someone higher-powered. More expensive.

"And have them drag us through the mud?" Walter is looking at his desk. At the paperwork finished and what still needs to be done. "So they can dig up every little bit of dirt? No," he says once more. "No discovery. No trial, and I'll go willingly. It doesn't matter. Not anymore. I just want the bail back."

"The bail?" The word makes no sense to her. The whole situation makes no sense. "Walter, if you're that hard up for money, I can help—"

"No." He shuts her down before she can continue. "It's fair. It's part of the deal. Camille will get that back."

"Camille." At last, something she can grasp onto. "You think she cares about the money? Come on, Walter. Don't do this to her. Please, you've got to fight it. For Camille."

He doesn't respond. Instead, he reaches for another form. She sees the letterhead of a bank. He signs it without reading and folds it in thirds. She thinks of what she's told him. Of Aimee and the rape. "Is this about protecting Camille?"

She's trying to understand, but she's having problems. She can't imagine a father being so solicitous. Caring so much. She might as well be back in rehab, trying to figure out what normal is. "You can't think that you have to shield her from what happened, Walter." She's feeling her way through the dark once again. "Why, she's as old as Aimee and I were, almost."

She stops. Walter isn't writing. He isn't rustling through papers, as if to block her out. Instead, he's staring at her, with those wide, dark eyes. She looks into those sad eyes, and she knows.

CHAPTER 52

It was a wonder they could get a cab at that hour and in that shape. Gal had to step into the street to get anyone to stop. Even then, she had to hand her last twenty through the window before the hack would unlock the door. "For clean up," the driver said.

She saw his features contract, puckering like an asshole, as the smell filled the cab. Vomit, beer, sweat. Gal didn't want to think what else. But he drove them where she wanted—the Brighton studio that still served as her legal address back then. Unaired and stifling, the pile of mail pushed to the side, the place was a dump. But it was *her* dump, and Gal was half dragging Aimee, her arms too pale and sticky, by that point.

"Let's get you cleaned up." This close, she could see the mess matting her friend's hair. Vomit, like she'd rolled in it. Like she'd fallen or been pushed. Through her own booze haze, Gal registered the placement, the smells. The blood on Aimee's legs. "Man, Aimee," Gal said, "what happened?" She phrased it as a question, but she knew.

"Walter!" Aimee started wailing as soon as the water hit her. Gal had been rough, stripping her down. Pulling her into the bathroom.

257

She told herself she had no choice. That Aimee wasn't in any shape to complain. Not in any shape to clean herself up, either. "Walter!" Softer now, like a child, as she folded herself into a corner of the tub, and for a moment, Gal dared hope. A lover's quarrel. A fight.

As the water pummeled down on Aimee, though, she roused. And her waking words proved Gal's wishful thinking a lie.

"What am I going to tell Walter?" One long cry, barely decipherable as words. "What am I going to say?"

"Don't tell him anything." Instinct. The gut urge to protect oneself, to protect each other. The two of them together. Besides, he hadn't been there. He was the one who had taken off. Left Aimee all alone. "It was nothing. A drunken hookup," she said dismissively, as if she could convince herself. "Shit happens." As rough as she was with Aimee's clothing, before the guilt kicked in.

She was gentler with the towel. Coddling her friend as she helped her out of the tub and dried her. As she tucked her into bed.

"It's no big deal," she said, even in the face of her friend's pain and panic. The memory of her own. "You'll be okay."

The next morning, they found each other. Clung together in a wordless recognition of their shared hurt and need. What Gal couldn't put in words, she made up for the only way she dared. A kiss, a caress. The soft touch of someone who cared.

Afterward, Gal wouldn't even be sure what Aimee remembered. The drummer was sick as a dog later that day, when the afternoon light woke them both. Her groan alerted Gal that she was awake.

"Hang on." Gal was up in a minute, fetching aspirin and a glass of water from the sink. "Drink this."

"I can't." But she managed to get the pills down. Gal busied herself in the bathroom. Gathering up Aimee's soiled clothes. The towels. Tuning out her friend as she talked about going to the doctor "just in case."

"You're not going anywhere." Gal told herself she was being solicitous. Protective, though whether of her friend or herself, she wasn't sure. It didn't really matter. Aimee couldn't keep anything down. She was in no shape go out. Neither of them were. Between feeding her friend sips of apple juice and some ramen noodles she found in the cabinet, Gal had her own hands full. The solace of having Aimee there, that felt too fragile. A cocoon of warmth she wasn't ready yet to break.

"We're going back on the road soon, kiddo." Lying in bed, Aimee's head in the cavity of her shoulder. "We're going to put this little shit town in the rearview mirror, and we're never going to look back."

CHAPTER 53

"Walter, no." The memories flooding back so fast, she feels dizzy. She reaches out as if to stop the man still seated beside her. "You can't."

"I don't know what you're talking about." He's talking to the papers on his desk. Avoiding her eye, and so she steps forward. Staggers, almost, as if she were drunk.

"You can tell them he attacked her." She's making desperate calculations. Looking for an out. "He attacked your late wife. You're mourning, and he—seeing him brought it all up. Your lawyer will know how to phrase it. Temporary insanity or something."

He's closed down, and she's growing desperate. "You have to." Her own memories pricking her. A needle of guilt. Of complicity.

"I won't let you go to jail."

That gets him. "You can't say anything." He's angry, not sad. His voice so hard that she stands up. Steps back. "Do you hear me?"

She nods, the words caught in her throat. She swallows. "But why?" The words come out in a croak. She clears her throat and tries again. "Please, Walter. I don't understand."

"Camille." As if that explains it all.

Maybe it does, Gal thinks, and breaks into a sweat. What if she'd listened to Aimee? Taken her to a doctor that first day. A clinic. Gotten her the morning-after pill. A double dose of Ortho-Novum. Whatever they were using back then, she can't remember. All that comes up is Aimee's pregnancy. Real. Impossible. Her leaving the tour. Leaving the band. At the time, Gal remembers blaming Walter. Raging at Aimee, at the stupid frailty of the female body. At everyone but herself—or the man she now recognizes as a predator. A childless man. His one regret. A serial rapist who played on her vulnerabilities and got away. Who walked free. And yet, if she had…

"Camille." She repeats the name. Aimee's daughter, the light of Walter's life. *A different kind of love.* Aimee working out the chords, that private half smile on her lips. "She wouldn't—she doesn't have to know."

"He wanted to pay her tuition. Her student loans." Walter's face a mask of pain. "Those were his so-called amends. The way he was going to make things 'right.'" Spitting the word out as if it were sour. "He wanted to take a DNA test. Like I would let him anywhere near her. But he wouldn't let up. He kept insisting…"

And then he breaks, turning away with a sob. Gal rushes to him and wraps her arms around him, bending over him and cradling him as if he were a child.

"Oh, Walter." The echo in her mind of another voice calling out for the big, gentle man she's holding. Another time. "I'm so sorry. So sorry." And she is.

CHAPTER 54

The next morning, she goes with him to the courthouse. More for moral support than because she has any plan. The rest of the night has passed in a daze, Walter desperate to make sure all the loose ends are tied up. That everything is in Camille's name, just in case T.K.'s widow stumbles on the truth. Just in case her rapist husband left behind any kind of documentation.

Gal has offered to testify. To perjure herself, updating her own attack and casting Walter as her protector. Never mind what she told that cop. She drinks, everyone knows it. Walter brushed that off.

"It wouldn't work, Gal. They have too much physical evidence. I was drunk and sloppy. Someone might even have heard us. Besides," he takes a breath, leans back in his chair, "that's part of the deal. I can't take the risk of anything coming out, and if I plead guilty, they've agreed to bypass the discovery phase."

"The detectives are still going to want to know what happened." She's clutching at straws, but she remembers Bixby, the way he looked at her. He wasn't one to be easily dismissed. She remembers as well what Shira has told her. "The DA will too. That's why it's taken so long for the hearing, the pre-trial."

His bark of laughter surprises her. "You think this is long? My lawyer said they must have greased this one to get it on the calendar so quickly, the way things are backed up. No, I'm not worried about that. They might be curious, but they've got a ton of other cases to solve. This puts one in the win column for them. I'm not worried."

But he is, she thinks. Else he wouldn't have repeated it.

"And Camille?" she asks instead. "Your daughter will think of you as a murderer."

"Manslaughter," he corrects her. "At least she'll still think of me as her father."

"You are her father." She knows this to be true. "You always have been."

"I couldn't take that chance." His voice soft now, quiet. "And I did kill the man, Gal. Maybe I should have killed him years ago."

She can't stop him. What can she say? The lawyers recite their lines as if they were old hat, and she slumps there, horrified. Only when the judge brings up sentencing does she straighten up. A date is set, a few weeks away. Enough time, she thinks, for something to happen. For her to make her case.

"What if I make it about me?" She's sitting with Shira over coffee. The café is familiar now, like her old friend.

"What do you mean?" The lawyer asking, Gal thinks. The law.

"What if I testify about how T.K. was a serial rapist and that he liked to hurt women?" *You could testify too*, she doesn't say. Better to wait for Shira to offer.

But the other woman only shakes her head. "That doesn't explain why Walter attacked him. Not after all these years."

"What if you got up, too?" Waiting is a luxury, time they don't have. "Talked about him being creepy. We could take the spotlight off Aimee, off Camille."

263

"Is that why you want to do this?" Shira asks quietly, her face intent.

"I don't know," Gal can admit that now. "I want to try, to do something."

"Maligning a dead man." Shira shakes her head. "In front of his widow. It won't play well."

"You think she'll be there?" That gives her pause. So does the way Shira looks at her, eyebrows raised. "Yeah, well, I already said as much to her face."

By the date of the sentencing hearing, Gal has managed to find two other women. Kelly, the bartender, and Lynn, the singer with Delicate Krill. Both had their own stories about T.K., about how he plied them with drink and drugs and then assaulted them. Walter's pissed when she tells him. She sees it on his face, but this isn't about him anymore, she says. This is about Aimee, about Gal, and the rest of them.

Shira explains the process, that their letters are in support of Walter. Mitigating circumstances. Personal testimonies. She also tells them, frankly, that the judge might read them in court, for the record, or in his chambers, or not at all. She recommends that they keep copies for when Walter comes up for parole. It helps to have a friend in the business. Yeah, the thought that Camille might figure it out causes Gal a pang, but she brushes it off. Or tries to, anyway. Nothing's perfect, not even justice. Walter is the girl's father. Camille has enough sense to know that, Gal tells herself. Makes herself believe. No matter what Walter may fear.

Maybe his lawyer has a word with the judge. Maybe she makes her own decision. The letters are never mentioned. Walter has made his deal, but when he only gets five years, Gal likes to think she helped. She's exhausted at the end of it, as if she'd run a marathon.

"You coming home?" Four days later and Russ sounds like a stranger. She has a life in Bearsville, she reminds herself as she walks. A house, a cat. But home? Isn't this home? The place she started? The place where, once again, she's landed?

"Yeah," she says at last, walking a bit faster. Two coffees in her hand, a bag of muffins. "In just a few more days."

She's heading back to Walter's condo—Aimee's once again. Packing up the last of the papers. Camille's putting the place up for sale, and Gal's helping. The girl is exhausted, she can tell. She looks older already. Something around her eyes. Tougher, maybe, but so very, very sad.

When Gal opens the door, it hits her too. Everything's gone, almost. The dinner table, the bookshelves. All the pictures of a happy family. One last box, half full, waits for any odds and ends in the middle of the empty living room, but Gal finds Camille slumped against the office doorframe. She hands her one of the coffees.

"No." Camille shakes her head when Gal offers the opened bag. "Thanks."

"You should eat." She keeps the suggestion gentle. Too many echoes from her own past.

It works, and Camille fishes out a muffin. She even breaks off a piece. Still warm, it releases a homey scent. Sugar, blueberries. Gal watches to see if she'll eat it.

"I just don't get it." She's staring at the space where Walter's desk stood with its piles of paper. Its pictures. "Why Dad…"

She pops the piece of muffin into her mouth, but Gal can see she's covering. The light from the window glints off the unshed tears. She's gotten tougher, but she's still a girl. If only Gal could explain…

"All I can think is that it broke him, Mom dying." Camille isn't looking at her. Isn't looking for an answer, but Gal bites down on her own lip so hard she tastes blood. "He loved her so much, he must've gone a bit crazy."

"He loves you, too. You know that." It's the least she can say. The most, as well. "You're the light of his life."

A weak smile that fades as Camille turns back to that last box. "The piano guys are coming in an hour. I was wondering…" She looks up.

"I can wait, if you want."

Another smile, forcing out a lone tear. "Thanks, Gal."

Gal steps forward. She'd like to take this girl into her arms. Hold her and comfort her, but Camille has turned away again. She's reaching for the tape, to seal the last box, and so Gal walks over to the old upright and sits down at the bench. Folding the cover up, she touches the keys gently and begins to play.

"*A different kind of love.*" Aimee's song. It's almost like the piano remembers.

"That's my mom's song." Camille is behind her, drawn by the music. Gal continues to play softly as the girl sits beside her. "Her big hit—her love song. She wrote it for my dad."

"No." Gal speaks with conviction. "She wrote it for you."

Beside her, Camille starts to sob, quietly, into her hands, and Gal keeps playing, letting the tune run out. Giving the girl her time. A different love, a different life, not hers, she thinks, her fingers meandering over the keys. And just like that, she begins to pick out a tune. Familiar, almost, though she knows it's not. She's playing something different now. Something new.

Acknowledgements

This book would never have been possible without the support, every step of the way, of my wide and varied crew. Ann Porter, whose guidance over the years made this book (and so much else) possible; my dear friend (and law school dean) Susan Keller for connecting me with Professor Elizabeth Jones, who lent her legal (and tattoo) expertise; Gina Scaramella, executive director of the Boston Area Rape Crisis Center, for reading and suggestions; Jason Pinter, who took a chance and brought me to Polis Books; Erin Mitchell, Susan Ryan Vollmer, Karen Schlosberg, Alan Brickman, Ted Drozdowski, Chris Mesarch, Jennifer Ellwood, Tristram Lozaw, Julie Farman, and Brett Milano for reading; Dana Kletter, Lisa Susser, Tanya Donnelly, and Laurie Hoffma for sharing their memories of music and the road. Most of all, for Jon Garelick. This song's for you.

ABOUT THE AUTHOR

Before turning to a life of crime (fiction), Clea Simon was a journalist. Starting as a rock critic, she ended up writing about books and other arts. A native of New York, she came to Massachusetts to attend Harvard University, from which she graduated with high honors, and never left. The author of three nonfiction books and 28 mysteries, she lives with her husband, the writer Jon S. Garelick, and their cat, Thisbe, in Somerville, Massachusetts. She is the author of the Witch Cats of Cambridge mysteries from Polis Books: *A Spell of Murder, An Incantation of Cats,* and *A Cat on the Case.* You can find her online at @Clea_Simon.